The Devil You Know

'Please sit down, Inspector.'

He waited until she had done so before seating himself. 'Now, what is it you want from me?' he asked. And smiled. It changed him completely, lightened a dark Latin face that at first seemed somewhat threatening into something capable of breaching any woman's defences. He was, she noticed, steeple tall, whipcord lean, and possessed of a sensuality that burned like a slow fuse.

Tessa knew all about men like him.

She was married to one.

Vera Cowie has written ten previous novels, including *A Double Life* and *Unsentimental Journey*, which are also available as Mandarin paperbacks. She is a Geordie and lives in Bishop's Stortford in Hertfordshire.

Also by Vera Cowie

The Amazon Summer
Memories
The Rich and the Mighty
The Bad and the Beautiful
Fortunes
Secrets
Face Value
A Double Life*
A Girl's Best Friend*
Unsentimental Journey*

**available in Mandarin*

Vera Cowie

THE DEVIL YOU KNOW

To Mettie

From

Jean Jan 1997

Mandarin

This book is for Deb and my daughter Jane, without whom, etc. etc. (especially the etc.). Thanks to their combined knowledge and expertise I was able to create a 'genuine' policewoman. Many thanks, girls. I owe you one (or two as the case may be).

A Mandarin Paperback
THE DEVIL YOU KNOW

First published in Great Britain 1997
by Mandarin Paperbacks
and William Heinemann
imprints of Reed International Books ltd
Michelin House, 81 Fulham Road, London SW3 6RB
and Auckland, Melbourne, Singapore and Toronto

A CIP catalogue record for this title
is available from the British Library
ISBN 0 7493 1710 8

Typeset in 10.5 on 12.5 point Bembo
by CentraCet Ltd, Cambridge
Printed and bound in Great Britain
by BPC Paperbacks Ltd
A member of the British Printing Company Ltd

1

When the bomb went off, she was so deep into her most intense orgasm yet that when her body lifted them both from the bed, she believed the cause to be the violence of her own inner implosion. Not until she felt the lifting continue, as though they had been picked up by some invisible hand, did she realise that everything was happening outside her body. It was then she began to scream. She was still screaming when in mid-air the hand turned itself palm-down, dropping them on to the Kelim rug, bed positions reversed; she now on top of him. The impact drove the air from her lungs with a breath-expelling *whoosh* which went unheard, for it was drowned by a crack so loud it hurt her ear-drums, followed without a break by a breathy roar which rampaged through the heavy, felt-lined curtains, bringing with it a lethal shower of glass. Fortunately, the bed was a high, canopied tester, so its bulk sheltered them from the deadly shards which buried themselves in the mattress they had been occupying seconds before.

When the room was lit by a lurid red glare and there was

a strong smell of burning, she was sure she was in hell, especially as along with the burning there was another, more acrid smell she could not identify. Burning flesh? She opened her mouth to scream even louder, convinced she was dead and damned for ever, clutching at her lover's powerful shoulders, clawing them in her terror, trying to bury herself in him.

Swiftly reversing their positions once more, he covered her body with his own before pressing her into the skirts of the bed valance where they cowered, waiting for the noise – things breaking, glass tinkling, ceilings groaning, objects falling, to end.

Finally the curtains, which had been torn into tattered strips, fell back limply, and there was nothing but the sound of a fire crackling, accompanied by the occasional clang as metal fell or expanded.

Carefully putting her aside with a terse: 'Stay there and don't move!' the man got cautiously to his knees to peer over the side of the bed. '*Jesus Christ!*' The shock in his voice made her raise her head in alarm. 'I said, stay there!'

She subsided obediently, but as he got to his feet to pick his way with delicate care across the glass-strewn floor towards the windows, she gingerly raised her head above the bed, jaw dropping soundlessly when she saw the wreckage of what had once been a bedroom beautiful enough to be featured in *World of Interiors*.

Reaching the ruined floor-to-ceiling windows, her lover peered out into the square to see the mangled remains of what had been his brand new Bentley Turbo R being consumed by now leisurely flames. He could smell something acrid – cordite? – combined with the taint of burning rubber, scorched metal and petrol.

He stared stone-faced and rigid as the exact meaning of what had occurred hit home, even as his quick brain assessed the situation and what needed – no, *must* – be done.

Whirling on the woman, whose anguished eyes were now dripping silent tears on to the shredded silk sheets, he ordered: 'Get dressed. *Quickly!* They will all be here in a few minutes.'

'Who will?' she asked stupidly, dazed with shock, her anguish centred on the wreckage, causing tears to gout like a broken main. 'Look at my beautiful bedroom . . .'

He glanced briefly at the ruin before saying impatiently: 'Never mind that now! Your bedroom can be restored, but unless you get your clothes on your reputation will be taken apart in tomorrow's tabloids and that will not be so easy to restore.'

His tone made her frown in affront until she comprehended the danger of their situation, then she was running for her dressing room, which opened off the wall against which the bed stood. Apart from the blast flinging open the door nothing else appeared to have been touched. With hands that were shaking badly she snatched up her Rigby and Peller satin-and-lace teddy and began to dress herself. When he joined her and began to do the same, she asked, her voice as jerky as her hands: 'Exactly what has happened?'

'Somebody has just blown up my car.'

Her hands stilled. '*W-h-a-t!*'

'What's left is a heap of smoking scrap-metal. The rest is distributed all over the Square.'

'Oh, my God . . .' Her voice climbed again.

'Sibella!' His tone of voice had her turning to look at him. His face was closed, shuttered, totally unlike that which, not long before, had been intent on her pleasure as he effortlessly pushed her, time after time, up a rising road of mind-bending ecstasy. He had once again gone behind the coolly authoritative mask he used in public. Its effect on her was to firm her spine and calm her panic. She swallowed, took a deep breath, then another, and a third. 'I'm all right,' she said after a minute.

'Good girl.' The brief compliment, accompanied by one of his flashing smiles, increased her confidence. If anybody could handle things, Nico could. He could handle anything.

'Now finish dressing. By the time they all get here we have to have our story straight.'

'What story?' she asked, still stupid with shock.

Patiently: 'For the emergency services. Somebody planted a bomb in my car which means we have to have our story straight when they ask us where we were and what we were doing when it went off.'

'Oh!' Comprehension flooded her voice as she met his eyes, like blue-black ink but with an added iridescence, as if the ink had a mercury base, and read their meaning at once.

'Exactly,' he nodded. 'Now hurry up. We don't have much time.'

'Yes, of course.' She tried for a smile. 'Thank God for your cool head, Nico.'

Somebody thumped on the bedroom door.

'Madam . . . sir . . . are you all right?'

It was the voice of her butler, obviously panic-stricken.

Still tying his black tie, Nicholas Ould went to the bedroom door and opened it. It was not locked but no matter what the emergency the butler knew better than to enter without being bidden to do so.

'We're all right, Baines. How about everyone else?'

There was nothing in his voice, manner or attitude to

indicate that only minutes before he had been fucking the life out of the mistress of the house, who was not his wife but that of another man.

In the face of such commanding assurance, the butler's ruffled surface smoothed out to its usual expressionless urbanity and he once more became the perfect upper servant.

'There are no injuries to the household, sir, but I am afraid your car has been blown up!.'

He sounded apologetic. This was Chester Square, after all.

'We heard,' Nicholas replied sardonically. 'I was just about to come downstairs to check the damage.'

'A considerable amount has been done to the front of the house, sir, I am afraid.'

'Then move everybody into the kitchen. If the front has taken the worst the back should not be too bad. We'll join you in a moment.'

He directed a long, significant look at the elderly butler who met the iridescent eyes and, like his mistress, read the message there. Familiar over many years with the ways (not to mention the means) of this particular household, he knew at once what was called for.

'Very good, sir.'

He stood to one side to allow Nicholas to run lightly down the stairs.

'Do you need any help, madam?' the butler called into the bedroom.

'No – yes. Is Maria there? Send her in if she is.'

The butler turned to the huddle of servants, mostly foreign, herded just beyond the doorway like a mob of frightened sheep. 'Maria!' Obeying her master's voice one of the four women scuttled nervously by him and into the bedroom.

Her mistress was brushing her hair in front of her dressing-room mirrors; those in her bedroom no longer existed and the dressing table itself was lying upturned on the floor.

'Zip me up!' she commanded. 'Quickly!'

As the frightened girl did so the woman turned her head this way and that, examining her appearance for errors and/or omissions, but the glittering embroidery of the Versace masterpiece was untouched. And blusher worked wonders. Picking up her ear-rings, she screwed them into her ears, slid on her rings, finally nodding at her reflection with proud satisfaction. No give-away there. Only she knew about the stickiness between her legs. Ignoring it, as the maid stood aside, she swept out of the room and down the stairs, to find her lover standing in the wrecked dining room, which was directly under her bedroom and thus also in the front of the house. She let out a moan. 'Oh, my God . . .'

Her Waterford chandelier had come loose from the ceiling and fallen on to her beautiful Regency dining table, which fortunately had been cleared of her precious Limoges and the Baccarat crystal, but the satin surface of the centuries-old mahogany was scarred and pitted, and the chandelier was done for. The matching Regency chairs were overturned, though at first glance they appeared unbroken, and all the pictures had fallen from the walls, while the Georgian silver that had stood on the serpentine-fronted sideboard was lying on the floor. On the marble hearth of the fireplace her precious Meissen clowns lay strewn in pieces. As in the bedroom, all the windows had been blown in, and the heavy satin of the curtains hung in shreds, like Cinderella's skirt. As they stood there, a large piece of plaster fell from the ceiling to hit Nicholas.

'What the hell . . .' He dodged aside and put a hand to his

head. His jet-black hair looked as if someone had shaken flour over it and his shoulders were also sprinkled with white, but he let them be. 'Now for the library,' he said, making for it.

It adjoined the dining room, and though the heavy door had been blown open, there was little damage, mostly plaster falling from the ornamental ceiling. The coffee tray was still there on the drum table in front of the fire, now only embers, the brandy glasses had been blown over but the cups were undisturbed, just as they had left them not half an hour before.

'Right', he announced with crisp certainty. 'We were in here, still talking, when the bomb went off. Got that?'

She nodded.

He had been making a comprehensive scan of the room, satisfying himself that the story he was preparing would hold, but on turning to the woman he frowned as he registered her immaculate appearance.

'That won't do! Half the damned ceiling has come down . . . If we had been sitting in here we would both be covered in plaster. Like this . . .' He bent to scoop up two handfuls of powdered plaster, with which he dusted her hair and shoulders, before adding some more to his own.

'Nicholas! My dress! It's Versace . . .'

With casual ruthlessness he overrode her protest. 'And that was a bloody great bomb that just went off. Any minute now the police will be here, so will the fire brigade, not to mention the ambulances. Most important so far as we are concerned, so will the press, along with Uncle Tom Cobleigh and all. The last thing we must look is immaculate. We must also have our story straight. For the purposes of everybody who comes here tonight to investigate this particular incident, I dined with you specifically to discuss your financial affairs, since you are an old and valued client of the bank as well as a personal friend. After dinner we came in here for coffee and more talk. We were still talking when the bomb went off.' He glanced at his wrist to check what time that might have been .

'Shit! My watch . . .'

Turning, he sprinted out of the room and back up the stairs to the bedroom where he snatched his wafer thin Patek-Philippe from the bedside table. The lamp had fallen across it but the second hand was still sweeping round.

Fastening it to his wrist, he scrutinised the bedroom, finally considering the ruined bed. 'That won't do,' he muttered.

Quickly, with the expertise of one used to beds, he rearranged it so that it looked as if it had been turned down by Sibella's maid, putting back in place the pillows which had been thrown on to the floor, swiftly but with careful hands re-strewing the broken glass. Blast followed its own strange logic and they would be searching for pieces of a bomb, not evidence of extra-marital sex.

As he took a last comprehensive look round he heard in the distance the wail of a whole medley of sirens which heralded the arrival of the emergency services. Swiftly he ran downstairs again. Just as he was crossing the hall, the massive bronze lantern which hung above the black and white of the tessellated floor, and which had been swaying drunkenly, now tore loose from its weakened mounting and plunged downwards.

To fall on him.

2

Tessa was in the act of pouring boiling water into the cafetière when she heard the sound of the front door being opened .

'Harry?' she called, for she had not been expecting him home so soon.

'Who else?'

Her husband's voice was cheerful, which led to her releasing a breath of relief. He had come home in a good mood then.

'To what do we owe the pleasure?' she teased, as he came in through the kitchen door, big and bronze and handsome, and bringing with him the fresh briskness of the early-spring morning.

'We?' He bent an enquiring eye on her, as blue as a gas flame.

'Lately I've begun to think I'm married to the other Sarge.'

This was Tessa's large, good-natured, neutered Tom, so-called because he had three white stripes on each black foreleg.

'I've missed you too,' Harry protested. 'Why else do you think I'm here?' Taking off his top-coat, he dropped it carelessly on to the chair by the door, from which it slid to the floor where he left it. 'That double murder made me a fortune in overtime but I'm tired of twelve-hour shifts, not to mention us being reduced to writing notes to each other. It's this business of you being nine to five and me being shifts – '

' – that pass in the night,' quipped Tessa.

Harry grinned. 'Whatever. They nailed the bastard early this morning – caught him hiding under his mother's bed – whereupon it struck me that I hadn't actually laid eyes on you for five days, which led to me fancying a bit of what your father calls "the laying on of hands" . . .'

'Absence actually made your heart grow fonder?'

'Feel how fond if you don't believe me . . .'

'H..a..r..r..y!' Tessa was fitting the plunger into the cafetière so was unable to resist when he slid his arms around her from behind to pull her against his pelvis, which left her in no doubt as to the strength of his fancy. 'You came out of the womb with an erection!' she protested, half-amused, half-irritated, wondering what had brought this on, why he had come straight home after finishing his night-duty shift instead of doing what he usually did at 6 a.m., which was go down to Smithfield Market with a couple of like-minded colleagues to one of the pubs that was always open, officially solely for the bummarees.

'All men are . . . proper men, that is.' He nuzzled her neck. 'And they know how to put it to proper use. Which is what I intend to do right now . . .'

Tessa turned her head to look at him. 'What sort of a night have you had, then?' she enquired dryly.

'A busy one. Nothing but a parade of drunks – every one of them disorderly. Every cell full. Some yuppie do in a marquee in Battersea Park which got out of hand; the lads found them in the bushes contravening just about every clause in the Public Order Act.'

'Drugs *and* drink?'

'Oh, yes. Designer cocaine, uppers, downers, designer everything. Mind you, a couple of the girls lost a fortune when they decided to have a late-night dip in the Thames; some bright spark stole their expensive clothes and we had to supply blankets. The only thing they didn't lose was their cool. I wouldn't have been surprised if half of them turned out to be girls you went to school with.'

Tessa received that barb without flinching. 'Since I no longer live in that world, I doubt I would recognise them. Or, even more probable, if they would still recognise me.' Lithely twisting out of his embrace, she continued: 'So, Sergeant Sansom, what do you want for breakfast?'

'You.' His determination was as firm as his erection and would not be gainsaid. Reaching for her, he drew her into his arms once more. 'I'll eat afterwards. It's always better on an empty stomach. Just so long as you remember it always gives me an appetitite . . . fortunately, you know how to satisfy both mine.'

Harry stirred, then, as if reluctant to do so, slid out of Tessa with a sigh to flop on to his back, drawing in a great satisfied lungful of breath. Beside him, Tessa slowly came back to awareness; of the cooling sweat on her naked body, of the heat emanating from that of her husband, whose long length of leg was still entwined with hers, the rumpled sheet, the daylight streaming in through the voile-covered windows that looked on to the back garden. I'm going to be late, she thought. Which will cause comment, so my excuse had better be good. Fortunately I am a guv'nor and can afford to give one . . .

She stretched, sat up, felt Harry's big hand sweep over her shoulders, down her back, finding each knob of her spine before travelling up again. 'Still as smooth as a length of silk,' he said. 'Inside and out. I've never known a woman as silky as you.'

'Well, you're the expert.'

His hand tightened on the nape of her neck. 'And aren't you glad? I didn't hear any complaints a while back.'

Turning to look down at him, Tessa told him seriously: 'I don't have – never have had – any complaints about sex with you, Harry. You always give total satisfaction.'

His smile was equally satisfied. 'I should hope so.' He dropped a kiss on her shoulder. 'Now, about that other appetite . . .'

She cooked him bacon, eggs, sausages, tomatoes and baked beans – something she loathed but he adored – along with a couple of slices of fried bread just the way he liked it; crisp enough to snap. She also filled the big brown earthenware teapot – Harry hated tea made in anything other than some form of clay – so that he could refill his mug, in the shape of the traditional policeman's helmet, at least three times.

Tessa drank her coffee and ate a slice of wholemeal toast spread with Frank Cooper's Oxford marmalade while Harry hungrily cleared his plate. 'Now that's what I call a breakfast,' he complimented. Cajoling her with voice and smile, he added: 'Get us the paper, there's a good girl. It's in my coat pocket.'

'I know you always give your all when you give me one,'

Tessa mocked, as she pushed her chair back, 'but you will remember that I am your wife and not your slave, won't you?'

When she dropped the *Sun* in front of him, he looked up at her to ask: 'So what's going on at SO13, then?'

'Not much,' Tessa answered truthfully.

'Well, I suppose things must be very slow now that the IRA has declared a cease-fire . . . Still, I'm sure there's a nice little terrorist group somewhere planning some nice big explosion pretty soon . . .'

'Harry! Being in the Anti-Terrorist Squad is not a joke!'

''Course it isn't, but it's not proper policing, is it? Policing is catching criminals. Policing – '

'– is what you do, right?'

'And what you used to do. Why don't you come back to it? Leave that so-called elite squad and get back to what you were trained for.'

Beginning to clear the table, she said: 'Which elite squad is going to mark me as AWOL unless I get a move on.' Tessa did not want another argument. These days, there seemed to be no pause between the highs and the lows, since reaching the heights, as they had done only half an hour before, was invariably followed by a plunge into depths which were already far too familiar. All because Harry could no more help being him any more than she could help being her. And they had both taken far too long to realise it.

'What happened to your posting to a provincial anti-terrorist squad? I thought your name had been put forward,' Harry asked innocently.

Tessa's expression had him laughing and putting up one hand to ward her off. 'Got sent back, did it?'

'Only because the man with the deciding vote invariably decides in favour of a fellow male!'

Harry shrugged as he opened up his *Sun*. 'Well, if you don't know that by now . . .'

'By heart!' China chinked and cutlery rattled as she loaded the dishwasher.

'Is there another cup of tea in the pot?' he asked, as she switched on the machine.

'If you stretched out a hand and lifted it, you'd find out,' Tessa said sweetly, as she went to take her shower.

She was smoothing the re-made bed, crisp with clean sheets, when Harry sauntered in, still damp from his own shower.

'That's my girl. I love a nice fresh bed to sleep in.' He yawned, showing his excellent teeth. 'And I shall sleep well . . . always do after I've given my wife a good seeing to.'

He came up behind her again, began to nuzzle her neck.

'Oh no you don't! I'm already late enough, I am also showered and dressed, and you've a full stomach, haven't you? Sleep it off, and remember – tomorrow is another day.' She wrinkled her nose at him. 'Not that it did Scarlett O'Hara much good . . . If you should wake up before I get back, you could peel some spuds; I thought I'd do lemon chicken for supper.'

'Sounds nice. Did you get my beer?'

'In the cool box of the fridge. A dozen cans.'

'That's my girl.'

'I do my best.'

'Don't I?'

Tessa pretended to consider. 'W-e-l-l . . .'

He seized her hand, guided it under the towel. 'A quickie,'

he said. 'No need to undress. I have to have you again, Tessa . . . *now*!'

And he did, but not until she had taken off her skirt first. He had her up against the wall of the bedroom; fast and wild, and, to Tessa, brutal. Harry was driven by a powerful sexuality and she knew better than to argue when he was in this mood. Something (somebody) had wound his spring, and as she felt him flex and swell and unwind inside her, she was aware that not even her physical self was involved. This kind of pure-unto-passionless sex she found coldly uninvolving and it left her unmoved. It also saddened her, remembering as she tended to do lately those first, fresh days when he used to make love to her as though there had never been another woman in his life. Now, he did it as a means to an end. His own physical release.

Afterwards she went into the bathroom, and when she came out again ten minutes later, crisp as a new five pound note, Harry was already snoring, flat on his back in the bed, his spectacular endowment lying across his thigh, flaccid at last.

Lifting his legs so as to cover him with the duvet, she did not waken him. When Harry slept he sank to the bottom, and after total sexual satisfaction, twice in not much more than an hour and a half, that was a very long way down.

She set the clock-radio to wake him at six – Harry hated to rush – checked that a fresh shirt hung on his dumb-valet, had already brushed his jacket and put his pants in the press. His shoes she left alone. Harry was very particular about the shine on his shoes and always did them himself. Clean underwear, car keys, handkerchief . . . yes, all present and correct. Drawing the heavy curtains, she darkened the bedroom before leaving it, closing the door silently behind her.

In the kitchen she saw that Sarge had cleaned his bowl so she put him down a handful of his cat-biscuits and topped up his bowl of water (he turned up his nose at milk though he would graciously accept cream). The last thing she did before leaving the house was set the washer-dryer going. Everything would be ready to iron when she got home that night. And Harry goes on about me being *over*-organised! she thought.

As usual, he had not put his car in the garage, just abandoned it on the drive. After getting hers out she put his in its place before setting the time lock.

Why is it, she thought, as she put the Golf in gear, that when a husband and wife both work, it's always the wife who ends up doing two jobs?

3

Nicholas Ould was in a foul mood. He was sick and tired of a thundering headache that just would not go away, his skull was tender where they had stitched the four-inch gash inflicted by the massive lantern when it hit his head – 'Just as well you have a good head of very thick hair, Mr Ould,' the doctor had told him cheerfully, 'otherwise you would have had a depressed skull fracture instead of a hairline crack' – and he had a broken shoulder, which meant he was trussed like a chicken. On top of that the hospital bed was anything but comfortable and they kept bringing him food and drink he did not want, not to mention taking his temperature, checking his blood pressure and looking into his eyes with pencil torches.

Like all people who take their excellent health for granted, when his was called into question he took it badly. All he wanted them to do was leave him in peace so that he could struggle to come to terms with the fact that somebody out there had deliberately, and with malice aforethought, tried to blow him to bits.

Nothing in his smooth, unimpeded progress through life – an Ambassador's only son, a doting mother, Eton, Oxford and Harvard Business School – had prepared him for such an eventuality, therefore his first reaction had been one of incredulity. Followed by fury. The Bentley had cost a fortune and he had waited two years for it, only to have it taken out by a bunch of thugs! The trouble was, he had no idea *which* bunch of thugs. He did business with most countries; where a banker is concerned, the bottom line is always the money to be made. If his doing business with one country displeased another then that was just too bad. He had dealt with the Israelis and he had dealt with the Arabs; he had dealt with Ulster and he had dealt with Eire – not to mention most South American countries, including those run by the drug cartels where he had declined, politely but firmly, to assist them in providing laundering services for their tainted billions, profitable though such a service would be. He had seen and learned enough about international wheeling and dealing in the last sixteen years to know that there were certain groups who stopped at nothing. Murder was just another word to them; one they could spell in any language. What really irked was not knowing which of them had decided to assassinate him.

All he knew was that somewhere along the line he had trodden on somebody's sensibilities and this was their way of showing displeasure. *Their* displeasure! he thought darkly. What about mine? If this demonstration is meant to change my mind then they're wasting their time. He had a loathing of being coerced into anything. It had been many years since he had allowed anybody the luxury of any kind of control over him. All the same, once he had been able to think, he'd begun to brood. There was nothing else to do. It hurt his eyes and made his headache worse if he read, and he watched the television only to catch up on the news, satisfied to see that the story he had given had been accepted – by the press anyway. Besides, he was at a fever-pitch of restlessness, of a kind he had not known for years. It was only when he examined it – head on and unblinkingly – that he realised it was because he felt he had lost control of his own life.

They had failed to take it because the bomb had gone off prematurely, but they would regard that merely as an annoyance before trying again.

There had been no warning this time. There would none the next. Which meant his cherished freedom was on the line. From now on he would have to be careful of everything: where he went, what he did, who he did it with, and how; no longer able to take anything for granted because a nameless, faceless group of men were out to kill him, bully-boys of a different kind from those he had encountered at Eton.

Times were now very different. He was no longer thirteen years old: he had not long before celebrated his thirty-ninth birthday, and in all the battles hitherto fought – and won – he had always known who his opponents were. Now, in the frustration of impotence – hitherto not one of his problems – he was fighting a legion of invisible men. The thought of a future under the constant surveillance of a 'minder', someone always watching his every move, knowing where he was and what he was doing at all times, horrified him. It had taken him years to escape his mother's protectively vigilant eye. On the other hand, he wanted to be able to celebrate his fortieth birthday . . .

There was no way he could get away from the prospect. Whichever way he turned it was there, waiting for him.

The compromise he would have to make.

He did not like compromises: they smacked of defeat, and defeat was something else for which he had no use.

He was brooding on this for the umpteenth time when the door to his private room was flung open and a voice proclaimed dramatically: '*Nico!* What is this they tell me – that somebody has tried to blow you up? *Ayie . . . por Dios! Hijo mio!*' The sight of his taut face, bandaged head and strapped arm had Reina Ould surging forward, arms open wide, but her son raised his hand, palm out. 'Mama!'

At once, the fountain ceased to overflow.

'Never mind how it looks, what really ails me is the mother and father of all headaches. No, I am not going to die. No, you do not need to call in specialists from far and wide, and no, there is nothing I want except to be left alone in peace and quiet.'

'Ah, you are your own self again, *gracias a Dios!* Now, tell me why these *terroristas* are after you? I know how dangerous they are. Did they not blow up my very own brother-in-law a few years ago?'

'That was Spain, and ETA, and he was in the Government, a known and protected target. This is England. I run the family bank and have absolutely no political clout.'

'Nevertheless you should heed the warning. Did I not tell you those Colombians were exceedingly dangerous men? I am Spanish; we colonised South America. I have relatives there. Your sister – my own daughter – lives in Mexico City. I warned you – '

'Yes, Mama, you did. Several times,' her son interrupted wearily.

Clicking her tongue reprovingly, Reina Maria de los Angeles de Mora y Castellon Ould flung her sables carelessly on to the nearest chair before leaning forward to embrace her son tenderly, enveloping him in the fragrance of roses.

She was a tiny woman of no more than five feet tall, plump as a pouter pigeon and flatteringly dressed in a soft wool crêpe dress the colour of faded roses that did wonders for her creamy skin and glossy hair, the latter carefully maintained in its original blue-black state. She had pearls at her throat and in her ears, and her nails matched her mouth as well as the flowers in the exquisitely feminine concoction perched on her head.

'When they telephoned me . . . *por Dios, que susto!* But Alejandro arranged a chartered plane and I was on my way within the hour.'

'You had no need to leave Madrid,' her son told her callously. 'I told them to tell you I was in no danger.'

'No danger! They blow your car to smithereens, obviously hoping you would go with it, and you think there is no danger!'

'But I was not inside it, was I?'

'*Afortunadamente no!* But what were you doing in Chester Square anyway? I thought that little episode was over and done with?'

'Sibella Lanyon is a valued client of the bank,' her son returned without so much as a flicker. 'We dined and discussed her financial affairs.'

His mother smiled and lifted one shoulder. '*Si tu dices* – if you say so,' she replied demurely.

Nicholas Ould fixed his shimmering eyes on his mother. '*Si. Lo dice*,' he said softly. 'And so will you, whenever you talk about this little incident. *Comprendes*?'

Her *olòsoro* sherry eyes widened innocently.

'*Naturalmente, hijo mio.* I am well aware that Edward

Lanyon is not a very nice man; between him and the *terroristas*, I do not know which is worse. But if you will persist in paying court to married women . . .' Reina Ould shook her perfectly coiffed head. 'One of these days you will meet one who is not married and want much, much more than an affair. I know of these things. Am I not *Española*? You have sowed many acres of wild oats, Nico. It is time you changed to sowing children. Have you no consideration for my feelings? You know how much I wish to hold your children before I die.'

'You already have Elena's two,' her son reminded, 'with a third on the way. Why look to me to add to an already burgeoning family?'

'Because Elena is now a Santiago; you are an Ould, and the line stretches back two hundred and fifty years. What will happen to the bank if you have no son? You know it can only be run by a member of the family. Your father had two brothers, but the way things came about, the inheritance fell to you. Now it is your turn to see that it passes to your son. If only my last child had lived to be born. The doctors said it was another boy . . .' A dramatic sigh. 'But it was not to be.'

Nicholas had heard that sad story so many times it failed to register. Just then, the door opened again and a squat, bullet-headed man entered. He was wearing a dark suit and chauffeur's cap, and carrying armfuls of hot-house blooms in a massive wicker basket.

'*Muy buenas*,' he said to the room in general, then to the patient, with the familiarity of long and close acquaintance: '*Coḿo estas?*'

'*Bastante bien, gracias,* Mariano.' Eyeing the flowers Nicholas saw that his mother had emptied Moyses Stevens of every bloom on the premises.

She was scrutinising the basket. 'Where is the champagne?' she demanded.

'*Aqui, en la cesta.*' Mariano showed her the bottles hidden under the flowing blooms.

'For God's sake, Mama! Champagne is the last thing they will allow me!' Nicholas protested.

'It is not for you. It is for the doctors and nurses who have saved your life.'

'I have already told you, it was never in danger!'

'Ah . . .' said his mother darkly. 'That is what they always tell you. Mariano, go and get me some vases – *con agua, eh*?'

'*Si, Señora.*'

As he went out, Reina Ould drew a chair to the side of the bed and perched on it. 'Now . . . tell me what happened,' she commanded.

'I lost my brand new car,' her son answered gloomily. 'Then the lantern in Sibella's front hall fell on me.'

'So buy another car! What is a *coche*? You have another three that I know of. It is you I wish to know about – and your poor head.' More tongue clicking was followed by a plangent: '*Pobrecito*! And poor Sibella, of course, but she suffered no injury, I understand.'

'Only to her house. It's a mess, I'm afraid, but I'll see that everything is put right.'

'You realise that *they* obviously know where you are at all times! *Ayie, por Dios, Nico!*' Reina Ould crossed herself. 'What if the car had exploded with you inside it? *Madre mia!*'

Her son echoed her prayer, but said: 'The police will no doubt tell me just exactly what happened when they talk to me, and how to protect myself in future. I understand they want me to make a statement.'

'But of course! They must find out who has done this terrible thing.' Leaning across to brush her son's black hair from his brow, 'Promise me you will take more care in future, *cielito mio*?' she begged.

'Mama, I cannot and will not live in cage! Nor will I be told where and where not to conduct the operations of one of my companies, or how to live my own life! That is not my way and you know it!'

Cold arrogance hung on suddenly frigid air.

'*Si . . . si . . . de acuerdo,*' his mother soothed. 'But all the same you must talk about it with the police and listen to what they advise. They are the experts after all.'

Nicholas said nothing but his mother took note of the stone-carving expression and sighed inwardly. Stubborn. Like all the de Moras.

'How long will you be in this place?' she asked, changing the subject. 'Are the doctors good? Should I call in Sir William Orpington? He is a specialist in brain injuries – '

With tightly controlled patience 'I have a hairline fracture of the skull, not a brain tumour! I see no reason why I should not be out of here by the end of the week. For God's sake, Mama, don't fuss!'

Recognising the signs of a fraying temper she rose to her feet with a relieved: 'Ah, here are the vases . . . over here, Mariano, on the table by the bed, if you please.'

As she deftly arranged the flowers, something for which she was famous, she chatted lightly about this and that, making Nicholas smile and occasionally laugh, lightening his dark, somewhat saturnine countenance.

When the vases – each a Renoir still-life – had been

placed around the room to her satisfaction, he held out a hand to her. 'Sorry to be such a bear, Mama, but I really do have a sore head.'

'*Pobrecito!*' She dropped a featherlight kiss on it. 'Now that I am satisfied you are in no danger I will leave you to rest. But before I go, I wish to speak to your doctors. Now, what are their names?'

Tessa went into the office that morning to find it seething in a way which could only mean An Incident. This was confirmed when she was immediately called to a meeting with her DCI, who gave her a briefing on the bomb that had gone off in Chester Square at 1.08 a.m. that morning. Tessa gave a good impression of one who knew all about it, but Harry's unexpected arrival had done for her regular schedule which had meant her missing the news on Radio 4.

She was told she was assigned to the enquiry, and her first job was to take a statement from the man whose car had been scattered all over the square like autumn leaves. Preliminary forensics indicated terrorists, but no group had claimed responsibility. There was one serious injury. The man in the driving seat – not the car's owner – had lost his legs, since the bomb had been planted so as to go off the moment the seat was depressed.

'He's in Intensive Care in Charing Cross and not expected to live. It looks like it was a special steal-to-order job – the car was a brand new and hideously expensive Bentley Turbo R.

'The owner is in the Wellington Hospital being treated for minor injuries caused by the blast. What is unusual is that the intended victim is wholly apolitical, being a banker – Ould & Sons, bankers to the establishment. Why anybody would want to blow him up is what we have got to find out so pump him for anything he knows . . . And do it in your own inimitable way, Tessa. Evidently this Nicholas Ould carries a lot of clout where it matters. But I don't need to tell *you*, do I? You know how to talk to these people.'

They had allowed Nicholas Ould to leave his sick-bed once he had convinced them he would recover much more quickly if he was on his feet. His persuasive powers, allied to a charm that could kill at a thousand yards, not to mention the power and influence of his name, got him his way. Out of bed (which he considered for sleeping or sex only) he thought more clearly, was able to get things in perspective, because while doing so he could pace, did not feel so helpless as he did lying down. Even if it was only walking back and forth, movement seemed to ease the thundering headache which still held him in its lowering grip, worsening his temper and souring his already irritable disposition.

When he was told by his nurse that a Detective Inspector Sansom was here to see him, he said tersely: 'About time!' He had questions which he wanted answering. But his reaction on seeing this particular Detective Inspector was that of most men when setting eyes on Tessa Sansom's almost stylised slenderness: the instant classification of 'Barbie Doll'. She possessed all the attributes: the endless legs, the guinea-gold hair – though hers was not long and full but short and crisp – and the lapis-luzuli eyes. Handle her and she'd break, he thought dismissively. Probably only does the paperwork.

Tessa patiently met the onslaught of a pair of onyx eyes which assessed every inch of her like a CAT-scan, and though he gave no sign of it, her training made her aware of the moment she was dismissed, though his affable smile did not waver by so much as a millimetre.

Yes, she thought dispassionately. To this man, women would always be associated with evenings at Annabel's, gold and platinum bibelots from Asprey, fittings at Dior, dinner at The Connaught and cocktails at the Rivoli Bar.

In her Marks & Spencer navy suit and sensible heels, carrying a capacious shoulder bag and police briefcase, Tessa was all too aware of the fact that she was at the farthest end of his particular female spectrum. Which did not detract one whit from his well-mannered: 'Please sit down, Inspector.'

He waited until she had done so before seating himself. 'Now, what is it you want from me?' he asked. And smiled. It changed him completely, lightened a dark Latin face that at first seemed somewhat threatening into something capable of breaching any woman's defences. He was, she noticed, steeple tall, whipcord lean, and possessed of a sensuality that burned like a slow fuse.

Tessa knew all about men like him.

She was married to one.

Equally polite – her preliminary research had revealed that Nicholas Ould did indeed have clout where it mattered – she replied: 'We need a statement from you, Mr Ould, detailing what happened when your car exploded in the early hours of Sunday morning, where and when it had been driven that day and the previous ones, and who was driving it during that time. This is to enable us to obtain some idea as to how whoever planted the bomb might have been able to get at your car to do so.'

He said nothing. His attitude plainly implied: It's your ball. You run with it.

'You received no warning of any kind, I believe?' Tessa

went on, ignoring the attitude. With men like him it came with the territory.

'None whatsoever.'

'Do you yourself have any idea who might be responsible?'

A shrug. 'I am a banker. I do business with just about every country in the world, not all of which practise democracy. It is conceivable that I may have – offended – someone, perhaps by refusing a loan.'

His tone was even, but Tessa was aware of anger smouldering like a discarded cigarette stub in a pile of dry brush.

Not trying to ignite it, but knowing it had to be said, she continued: 'I understand the car was not parked outside your own home at the time?'

She made her voice wholly businesslike. What he was doing at 1 a.m. in the house of a noted Society beauty was not police business, even if it was the stuff of canteen gossip.

But he was obviously an old hand. Cool as the submerged seven-eighths of an iceberg, he replied: 'You understand correctly. Inspector. I was in Chester Square, having dined with an old friend and client of my family's bank, a Mrs Edward Lanyon. We were in the library, having had our coffee there, discussing her financial affairs, when the explosion occurred, making rather a mess of the front of her house. What I want to know is – what set it off? I thought this sort of thing was meant to dispose of the driver as well as the car?'

'Somebody *was* about to drive it away,' Tessa enlightened him, not backing down before the hard brilliance of his eyes.

'Who?'

'The thief who was trying to steal it. He was in the driving seat and had turned on the ignition – which was probably what set off the bomb and thus caused the explosion and subsequent fire.'

He was staring at her but did not see her. She knew from experience what he must be thinking and feeling, and while he was coming to grips with it she rapidly wrote down on the statement form what he had told her so far.

'Who was he?' Nicholas Ould asked finally.

'A professional thief already well known to us. One of the kind who steal cars to order; expensive, high-performance cars like yours. He would know exactly how to disable even the most sophisticated alarm circuit and probably had a duplicate key. This was not an opportunist thief. He knew exactly what he was stealing.'

One sleek and silky eyebrow raised itself in a way that had Tessa bracing herself. 'I doubt he would know about the bomb.'

No, poor sod, Tessa thought. Which was why it blew off both his legs. She bent her head over her statement form once more. When she had given him enough time she asked: 'You had driven the car to Chester Square yourself?'

'Yes.'

'And where had it been prior to that?'

'In the garage near my flat in Eaton Square.'

'Has the garage any security?'

There was the faintest chill of sarcasm in his voice when he said: 'I live in what I believe is termed by your colleagues a High Risk Area.'

Tessa maintained her scrupulous politeness: 'And what time did you arrive at Mrs Lanyon's house?'

'At about seven-forty-five.'

'Had anybody else driven the car during the previous forty-eight hours?'

'Only my chauffeur. He drives me to and from my office in the City every day, and did so on the Friday. On the Saturday I did not use the Bentley until the evening. It was brought round to my flat at about seven-forty.'

'Could you give me the name and address of your chauffeur in case we need to talk to him?'

He did so.

When she had completed the statement Tessa rapidly read it through and then held it and her pen out to him. 'Would you read this through, Mr Ould, to verify that it is what you have told me, then sign it where I have indicated?'

He had obviously taken the same speed-reading course as she had because it only took him seconds. 'Tell me,' he asked, as he wrote his beautifully crafted signature, 'what happens now about future protection against more of the same – should there be any, of course?'

'That is not my province. Special Branch will no doubt be advising you.'

'You are not Special Branch?'

'No. I am with the Anti-Terrorist Squad.'

Both eyebrows went up this time, but Tessa stared him down. She had been intimidated by the best in the course of her almost fourteen years with the Metropolitan Police.

'There are female terrorists,' she pointed out helpfully, paying him back for his previous swipes.

She saw his mouth – well-cut and firm – twitch, then he smiled again. It was intended to dazzle, but Tessa had long been used to that kind of male brilliance.

'Point taken,' he said. 'I apologise for my bad manners. I have the most appalling headache and it tends to colour my responses.'

She put her statement block back in her briefcase, picked

up her handbag. 'I am sorry to have had to disturb you, Mr Ould. Thank you for your time and patience. I don't think we will need to bother you any more.'

He rose to his feet as she did, walked to the door to open it for her. As he did so a woman was doing the same from the other side. Dark, vibrantly beautiful, superbly dressed and smelling of something heady and sinful, she was in every way the sort of woman Tessa would expect to be visiting Nicholas Ould.

'Nico! Even in hospital!'

Her laughter was teasing but her sea-green eyes were watchful as they swept Tessa from head to foot, only to warm slightly as they realised there was no competition.

Nico? Tessa thought. No way, lady. This is not a man with whom any woman should use the diminuitive.

Nicholas Ould said smoothly: 'How nice to see you, Sibella. This is Inspector Sansom of the Anti-Terrorist Squad. She has just been taking my statement about the events of Sunday morning.'

'Yes . . . I had a policeman to see me also.' The woman looked at him from under her lashes, and Tessa could have sworn something flashed between them, hot and greedy. It left her in no doubt as to what had been going on between them when the bomb went off. Canteen gossip had it right, as usual.

She stepped out of the room as the woman glided in.

'Goodbye, Inspector,' Nicholas Ould said, Mr Manners to the last, but leaving Tessa in no doubt as to where his interest really lay as he shut the door on her.

As she walked down the corridor in the direction of the lift Tessa was conscious of a feeling she had not experienced for many years; the way she used to feel as a little girl when her big brother Rupert came home from school.

Second best.

Now why should Nicholas Ould make her feel like that? Perhaps because Rupert, had he lived, would now be thirty-eight and thus a contemporary of the man she had just interviewed, although that was all they would have in common. Rupert had always been the Golden Boy, she reflected, as she rode down in the lift. Every bit as attractive as Nicholas Ould – only to both sexes. Men as well as woman had found Rupert desirable. Somehow she doubted if men would feel that way about Nicholas Ould.

Yet the more she thought about it, the more he put her in mind of Rupert; more strongly than anyone else had done these many years. It was no doubt to do with the ultimate in self-confidence both had possessed; that bone-deep, unshakable belief in their superiority – their looks, their place in the world – because both had known, from the first breath they took, that nobody would ever deny them a thing.

When she was young, although she had adored him, hero-worshipped him, Tessa's elder brother had always – by the mere fact of his splendid male beauty and physical presence – made her feel overlooked and overwhelmed. Though she had been a pretty child, Rupert had been beautiful enough to turn heads, metaphorically as well as literally.

That beauty had been his downfall, but it had also been the means of his sister finding a career she had previously never so much as given a thought to. And if it had not been for that, she would never have met her husband.

4

Harry was long gone when Tessa got back to Richmond that evening, having been kept late because of two hoax calls, both made to the Samaritans and thus to be taken seriously, reporting bombs planted in two Burger Kings; one in Hammersmith and one in Putney. It had caused a deal of running around and all for nothing. In the nature of things, they had to be sure, and it was not until some hours after her day officially ended that Tessa came off duty, tired, irritable and angry. If only people understood the hassle they caused by making hoax calls! The time wasted; the checking that had to be done to make absolutely sure that nobody was at risk. They think of it as 'a bit of fun', or so one hoax caller who had been captured in the act had shrugged. I'd show him some fun! she fulminated as she turned into the drive. Only he'd have to go to jail to see it!

It was half-past nine as she turned her key in the door and only Sarge came to meet her, rubbing up against her legs and purring loudly, making it clear he was hungry.

'Yes, I know, I'm late. Didn't he feed you, then? No, of

course he didn't. He never thinks of anyone but himself . . . Poor puss, you must be starving. Come on then, let's see what we can find.'

Tessa stooped to pick him up, feeling him head-butt her jaw, pushing his face into hers. Carrying him into the kitchen, she saw at once that Harry had left the evidence of his earlier activity; he had not done the potatoes, as she had asked, but had cooked himself chicken and chips, leaving the dirty pans, dishes, plates and cutlery where used, which meant that when she went into the bedroom the bed would be unmade, the bathroom likewise a mess. Harry never hung up towels, replaced tops on bottles or caps on tubes of toothpaste. His mother had done all that for him. Naturally he expected his wife to do the same.

Tessa's already shortened temper lost another length. He *knew* she hated untidiness, but Harry had been raised by a rabidly traditionalist mother to believe that tending to men in all things was what being a wife was all about. Tessa had seen her mother-in-law not only sweeten her husband's tea but stir it before placing cup and saucer in front of him. Harry expected his wife to demonstrate the same kind of devoted attention. Husbands were the breadwinners, and in acknowledgement of that, the house was the domain of the wife.

Tessa was of the opinion that Harry acted like a slob deliberately; his way of getting back at her because he thought she had strayed too far from the path all good wives were supposed to follow. And yet, only this morning, he had not gone Out With The Boys, as usual. Instead, he had come home straight off shift and made love to her twice. Well, made love once, had sex once. Sex is Harry's way of demonstrating love, she reminded herself. Giving of his time, his attention, his occasional help to a full-time working wife, is not. Well, two could play at that game. If he could refuse help to her, she could refuse support to him by telling him she was not going with him to Millwall to the celebration in honour of his eldest sister Cissy's Silver Wedding. She did not like Cissy, and her sister-in-law returned that dislike in full measure. All three of his sisters did. Tessa was not what they had wanted for their adored youngest brother.

Feeling better for that bit of tit-for-tat, she fed Sarge, then after changing into a pair of jeans and a T-shirt, began to clear up Harry's mess.

Only when the place was spic and span did she investigate the freezer to decide what to have for her dinner. She had not had time to eat anything since a snatched sandwich at lunchtime. Taking out a packet of frozen king prawns, she decided she would do them with mange tout and saffron rice.

She was frying the rice when the phone shrilled. The answerphone was switched on, but when she heard her mother's voice in its She Who Must Be Obeyed mode, she picked up the receiver. Nowadays, Dorothea only used that voice when it was an emergency.

'Yes, Mother?'

Without preamble, as was her way, 'Your father has had another stroke,' Dorothea announced. 'I think you ought to come down. It's late so I suggest first thing tomorrow morning. The doctor says there is no immediate danger.'

'I'll come tonight,' Tessa said, responding in the old, contrary way, to her mother's high-handed instructions.

'But it is a good two hours' drive and you have been at work all day. Don't they say a policewoman's work is never done?' Even now, Dorothea never lost an opportunity to make known her displeasure at her daughter's choice of career. 'After all,' she had pointed out when Tessa had announced it was her intention to join the Metropolitan Police, 'you will never see a soul you know.'

Now, no longer at her mother's beck and call, Tessa repeated: 'I like driving, Mother. You forget that at one time I drove a Panda car for eight hours a day.'

With unmistakable distaste: 'Very well. I will see you when you arrive. Whenever that might be.'

Always the last word, Tessa thought. Not even God will be allowed to have that when her time comes.

Though Tessa had not for many years now been the malleable, biddable girl whose mother had kept her in cloistered confinement for her first eighteen years, Dorothea still found it necessary to try to reimpose her dominance.

Tessa had warned Harry before he met his prospective mother-in-law for the first time: 'My mother believes in live and let live – so long as you do it her way.'

Harry had grinned. 'She'd get on well with my mum, then, because her motto is: "Everyone is entitled to my opinion".'

Tessa had laughed, squeezed his hand and said lovingly: 'Something we have in common.'

Yes, common, Tessa thought sardonically. As my mother made so very clear at the time . . .

She went back to her rice. It was ten-twenty. If she left around eleven she could be at her parents' home by one in the morning if the traffic was light.

While she was eating she debated whether to call Harry or leave him a note. If she rang Battersea he could well be too busy to take the call. On the other hand, a note would obviate the fit of outrage that would ensue when she told him she would not be going to the party with him. He would, of course, see her father's stroke as an excuse. Any excuse so as not to have to go and see *his* family. They weren't good enough for her, oh no. Too working-class. Harry lacked a top skin where his antecedents were concerned. A note, she decided. Why look for trouble. These days it seems to find me well enough by itself.

She left it taped to the fridge, since his first action on reaching home was always to go for a beer. She did not tell him to ring her, Harry reacted badly to being told by a woman to do anything, but she did ask him to feed Sarge. The big black and white tom was her cat: Harry liked dogs, the bigger the better, but he would not deliberately neglect Sarge. Just ignore him. As a sop she added that she would ring him as soon as she had any news.

By five minutes past eleven she was in the Golf and heading for the M3.

When Harry Sansom came in at seven-thirty the next morning, not in the best of moods after a shift that had been one hassle after another, he knew the flat was empty as soon as he entered it, but as he switched on the lights he realised that his wife had been and gone. The place was neat as a pin. Like her. Never a bloody hair out of bloody place. Unbloody-lived-in! His mother had warned long ago that his wife was far too exacting: 'That flat of yours is so bleedin' perfect it gives me the creeps . . . that's why I don't never visit. What you need is a houseful of kids to give the place a lived-in look.'

Deliberately flinging his coat down anywhere, he saw the note when he went for his beer, read it, crumpled it into a ball and threw it on the floor. Typical! Of all the bloody times for her father to go and have yet another stroke. He'd been dying by inches for years, ever since Harry had known him. For the past six years he'd only been able to communicate by writing, having taught himself to use his left hand when he lost the use both of speech and his right side after his first stroke. He had guts, mind. Harry would say that for him. If ever any man had hung on by the balls . . . Except, of course, the poor bastard had had them cut off years ago by the Arch-Bitch his wife.

Trust him to go and spoil Cissy's party. It had only been in the planning for months. Ma would go spare. Tess could have waited; seen the party through and then gone down to Dorset. It was not as though the old man was dying . . . or was he? Her note said nothing about that. No, she just took the opportunity to get out of going with him to one of *his* family celebrations. Anything to prevent her from spending time with *his* relatives.

He drained half his can of beer. Well, she could bloody well whistle if she expected him to spare so much as a thought for hers. God, but Ma was going to give him an earful! She liked nothing better than a knees up, with all her children, together with their husbands and wives and their children, all gathered round the big table – two sittings because the dining room in the new flat wasn't half the size of the one in the old house, the one where they had all been born and raised.

He could just hear her disparaging sniff, see her pursed lips. 'Can't say as I'm surprised. I wouldn't put it past her to have arranged it all. You know she hates joining in with us. I mean, your dad was only a Millwall docker whereas hers – hers was a bleedin' Bishop! I've asked it before but I have to ask it again, son . . . what in God's name possessed you to marry out of your own kind . . .'

Tell me about it, thought Harry, draining his beer. If his wife called then she called, but she would have to leave her message on the answerphone.

He went to get another can of beer.

It was just on one o'clock when Tessa drove through the gates of the Old Rectory, into which her parents had moved from the Bishop's Palace once it was confirmed that her father would have no choice but to retire after his second stroke. The rolling lawns were silver under the moon, and there were lights on in the hall and the ground-floor room that was her father's.

She left the Golf on the gravel sweep in front of the steps and was hefting her bag when the glass doors opened and a small, nut-brown man came down the steps.

'Good evening, Miss Tessa. Good journey?'

He took the bag from her.

'Yes, thank you. How's everything?'

'This latest stroke has done for your father and no mistake. He's now totally paralysed. All he can do is blink his eyes, and he doesn't always understand what's being said to him.'

Rigg's voice was matter-of-fact but Tessa knew how he felt because she shared his feelings.

'Your mother is with him. You go in and I'll bring you the soup and sandwiches I've got ready.'

'Thank you, Riggsy.' Affectionately, Tessa called him by the name she had used as a child, for he had been with her father all her life. She was not in the least hungry but would not dream of disappointing him by refusing the food he had prepared. Riggs believed that even the shortest journey always ended in a raging appetite.

In what had been the morning room but was now a fully equipped sickroom, Dorothea Paget was sitting in the big chair under the lamp, placidly doing her gros-point. She did not get up, merely tilted one somewhat florid cheek upwards.

'Tessa,' she allowed, with the ineffable graciousness of one who always knew where her duty lay. 'I trust you had a good journey?'

'Yes, thank you.' Tessa bestowed the expected kiss before turning to the bed. Her father was asleep, his long, narrow face quite bloodless, reminding her more than ever of the tombs of the medieval saints in the cathedral that dominated the see of the Bishops of Dorchester. Only the downwards and sideways twist to his mouth betrayed his condition.

'What happened this time?' she asked.

'Riggs found him earlier this evening when he brought in his supper. Dr Gifford says the next stroke will be the last. Only your father's strong heart helped him survive this one. That is what keeps him going, but we can't say for how long. I thought it best for you to come down. One never knows at times like these. How long can you stay?'

'Till Sunday evening.'

'What about your husband?'

Dorothea had never, ever called her daughter's husband by his given name.

'It's his eldest sister's Silver Wedding tomorrow and there's a big party,' Tessa said. 'I shan't be missed but he would.'

'Just as well,' observed her mother. 'He never seems to know what to do with himself down here. No doubt that is why he no longer comes.'

Having dismissed her son-in-law, Dorothea turned her vividly blue eyes, which Tessa had inherited, to her daughter. After the usual invigilating stare, she commented disapprovingly: 'If you get any slimmer you'll be able to go through the eye of the smallest of my needles.'

She herself was very well upholstered, with a bosom like a bolster and hips which could wear only made-to-measure corsetry. But she was still a handsome woman in a yellow-haired, high-coloured, Wagnerian way (as a young girl she had been nicknamed Val, short for Valkyrie), and had the voice to match, along with the highest of self-opinions. When her husband had been Bishop of the Diocese it was understood that while he ran the affairs of the church, his wife ran everything and everybody else. His first stroke had led to a lengthy convalescence and a determined recovery, but five years later a second, more severe one had brought about his early retirement at the age of sixty-five, severely disappointing his wife, whose ambitions were thus cut off in their prime. Fortunately, once having taken the measure of her husband's successor, one of the new, working-class Evangelicals with a redbrick degree in Theology, Dorothea perceived that his wife was likewise totally out of her depth. A second Mrs de Winter to the life, she had put up no opposition to the forceful Dorothea, who had thus managed to keep the Diocesan reins tightly in her own more-than-capable hands. Tessa knew from experience that once her mother took control of anything, no matter how temporary the measure, she never let go of it again without a fight.

'Poor Daddy,' she murmured, wondering yet again how such a gentle, unworldly man had come to marry such an assertive, worldly woman. Tessa had always been closer to her father than her mother – though fully aware that Rupert had been the prime pride and joy of both. It was his death – and the manner of it – which had brought about the disintegration of Hugh Paget.

Tessa brought her mind back to the present. 'It's late. Why don't you go up to bed, Mummy? I'll just sit with Daddy while I have my soup.'

Dorothea pursed her lips. 'No doubt, in the course of your work, you must be used to all sorts of odd hours – not to mention odd people.' Having got that in, she continued in the same, audible-to-the-back-row-of-the-Gods voice: 'Ah, here's Riggs with your soup and sandwiches. Now don't stay up too long. You too, Riggs. I need you around tomorrow. I've got the Diocesan Women at eleven-thirty.'

Riggs and Tessa looked at each other. There was no need to say anything.

Left alone, Tessa pushed the big chair nearer the bed before placing the tray on her knees. Mulligatawny soup to accompany rare roast beef thinly sliced and thickly coated with creamy horseradish on mixed grain bread. Riggs knew what Tessa liked; had always seen to it that if he had anything to do with it, she got it. Whereas Dorothea had operated a publicly proclaimed impartiality where her children were concerned, Riggs had never made any secret of his own preference for Tessa, having – most unusually – marked her brother's card the moment he entered the game. Riggs did not say much, but he always saw everything.

'How come you always knew about Rupert when my father never did until it was too late?' Tessa had confronted him at the funeral.

'Because your father never, ever looked at the everyday reality of anything. Like all idealists he always had an excuse for even the worst offender. In the way of people who take others at their face value, he never saw what was counterfeit about his own son.'

'Well, you have to admit that Rupert's face value was pretty considerable,' Tessa had argued, before realising guiltily that she no longer had any need to envy it.

'Oh, yes. All his life people used to turn to look at him in the street. He was still living proof of that bit in the Bible about the whited sepulchre.'

Except that Rupert had always been warm and full of life. So very full of life . . .

Tessa drank her soup and ate her sandwiches, putting the tray under her chair when she had finished. Checking her father, she saw he had not moved, so fetching the old plaid rug from the bottom drawer of the tallboy, she wrapped herself in it. She did not feel like bed. She knew she would only lie there thinking: for some reason her mind was in overdrive tonight, and not just because her father might die at any time. Once before they had been warned that he was at death's door; once before he had refused to knock. Hugh Paget had passed on to his daughter a core-deep inner strength belied by an outwardly fragile appearance, along with his intensely private personality. His son had inherited both his mother's confidence and her ability to dazzle, for as a girl Dorothea had also been a head-turner. Like her, Rupert had always expected to be the centre of all and any attention, taking it as no more than his due.

Tessa, like her father, had been basically shy, tending to hide when company came, never missed because Rupert invariably gave a performance. Yet when he had gone away to Eton she had been left feeling desolate and at nine years old when taken to her first Fourth of June celebration, she had been overawed by the swell her brother had turned into, long-legged and elegant in his brocade waistcoat.

Then, quite suddenly, one mid-term he had arrived home unexpectedly and there had been Trouble. Nobody had bothered to enlighten her as to what kind; all she knew was that her brother had done something which had led to his being expelled. It had turned her mother from a Valkyrie into a shattered Isolde, while her father had done what he always did in times of trouble: gone to ground in his private chapel to spend his time in prayer. Which was how Tessa had known that whatever it was, it was serious. But this time, not even Riggs would tell her what kind of trouble it was.

'Why won't you tell me why Rupert has been expelled?' she had pestered. 'I know you have to do something dreadful to be sent away from school, so what has he done?'

'He got up to mischief,' was all Riggs would say.

'But Rupert has *always* got up to mischief.'

'Well, now we know exactly what kind of mischief.' Riggs would say no more, leaving Tessa dangling.

It was not until she overheard him talking to Mr Henry, who had been the family gardener for fifteen years, in tones which all but vibrated with 'I told you so' disgust, that she discovered the exact nature not only of Rupert's crime, but of her brother himself. 'Master Rupert is nothing more than a nastly little bugger,' she heard Riggs hiss balefully. Not knowing what that meant because swearing was not something she was used to, she went to look it up in her father's *Complete Oxford Dictionary*, which was still no help because since her mother censored her reading she did not know what unnatural intercourse was either, and knew better than to ask.

Tessa was in her first term at boarding school before she found out just why Rupert had left Eton in disgrace at sixteen before leaving home at eighteen to live a life about which her father never enquired and her mother never spoke. He had been caught in bed being buggered by another boy. Both had been expelled.

Homosexuality had been an open secret at school, because lots of the girls had brothers at Eton and every one of them was worldy-wise enough to be able to deal with it. Not so Tessa, who had been brought up in sexual purdah. She became even more introverted, especially when she was not allowed to go and visit her brother once he had established himself in London. Her mother went up from time to time but Rupert never came home, and Tessa's only contact was the occasional innocuous postcard, enclosed in a letter to his mother, usually from abroad: Morocco, Tangiers, or a place called Fire Island on the East Coast of America. He never forgot her birthday, though, or Christmas, though the knowledge of her presents – handed over by her mother – was kept from her father.

She was eighteen, preparing to be brought out, the scandal long over and done with, when she finally discovered what it was that had kept her brother beyond the pale for so long after his initial transgression. She and her mother were up in town, staying with her mother's younger sister Marianne Willingham, who also had a daughter to bring out. Tessa and Arabella were going to share a joint Coming Out dance.

With great daring Tessa had telephoned Rupert from a call-box, having surreptitiously gone looking for his telephone number in her mother's address book. He had been delightedly surprised to hear from her; at once arranged to meet her in Marks & Spencer at Marble Arch: 'Downstairs in the Food Hall by the sandwiches. Not much danger of our being spotted amongst all the lunchbreakers. If you're off the leash, that is, and Ma has no idea you're breaking one of her rules . . .'

'Don't be silly,' Tessa had chided hollowly, knowing what the consequences would be if she did find out.

He had laughed. 'No, I thought not. Clever girl. You're beginning to learn. Good for you. I was always of the opinion that your waters ran very deep. They were always so still . . . Shall I recognise the new you?'

Tessa had giggled, feeling her doubts evaporate. It was like the old days. Rupert had always teased. 'Of course you will!'

'Let's put it to the test, then, if you're sure it's safe. I don't want to drop you in it, Sprog, much as I'd love to see you.'

'It's because it's quite safe that I rang you. Mummy's gone to the hairdresser's, then she's lunching with Uncle George at the House of Lords. I was supposed to be going shopping with Bella, but she's decided to go to The Sanctuary for a morning's pampering instead.'

'What a helpful girl. She never used to be, as I recall. Marks & Spencer it is then, in thirty minutes.'

She had spotted him before he spotted her. He was being admired by a mesmerised bunch of wide-eyed lunchbreakers, which did not surprise her in the least, since he was even more beautiful than ever. Rupert had a face of classically sculpted features with a chiselled mouth and deep-set, heavy-lidded, extravagantly lashed eyes of the same intense blue as her own. He was also stupendously elegant in a bespoke navy pinstripe three-piece, and she could have applied her lipstick in the shine on his shoes.

Nor had he lost the habit of running his right hand

through his thick, dark blond hair, which still kept falling over his forehead.

She must have changed more than she realised, though, because not until she went right up to him to say 'Hello, Rupert' did he recognise her, eyes widening in surprised appreciation even as his own familiar, teasing smile broke through.

'Sprog? My God, it is you . . . all grown up and, I trust, with somewhere to go. Let me have a good look at you.'

After a fervent embrace he had held her at arm's length for a thorough examination, aware of every stare and whispered conjecture but, like his mother, indifferently accepting it as no more than his due.

'What a ravishingly pretty little thing you have turned out to be – and still capable of blushing, I note. How many eighteen-year-olds in this day and age are capable of *that*, I wonder? Or is it because Ma has you guarded like the Crown Jewels?'

Tessa blushed even more deeply.

'Sweet.' His tone made her squirm with delight. Tucking her arm in his: 'Now let us go to a secluded little place I know where you will not be recognised but I am very much *persona grata*, then we can catch up on each other's life. Are you allowed in public houses?'

'I've never been in one,' Tessa admitted.

'Of course you haven't. Not with Ma as your keeper. Never mind, there's always a first time and I do so like them . . .'

He had taken her to a little pub in a mews off Wigmore Street, and there Tessa had been able to sit and gaze her fill at her adored brother, happy to see he had not changed, only grown even more beautiful and charismatic.

While they waited for their ploughman's she noticed that people still stared at him, men as well as women, some of them covetously, more than one fixedly, and found the old envy swamping her again. But she loved him more than envied him, and Daddy said that a virtue always overcame a sin.

He wanted to know all about her life, so she told him about school, and the 'O' and 'A' levels she had obtained – 'I always knew you were a brain-box,' he praised. She told him about the dance that was being organised and how she had been to the dressmaker's for what was practically a trousseau.

'I've never known Mummy to spend so much money on me.'

'A fly to catch a very fat salmon, my dear sister. And I have to tell you, Sprog, that you make a very attractive fly. Do be careful of all those greedy fish, won't you?'

He put out a hand, brushed her pink cheek with one long finger. 'Sweet,' he murmured again, but in a voice that gave her a pang, it was so regretful. 'I hadn't realised such innocence could still be found.'

'Will you be at any of the dances?' Tessa asked somewhat breathlessly.

His laughter was full-throated. 'Hardly! I never was a debs' delight. Not my scene. All those pink and white virgins lined up for inspection before bidding commences . . . not for me, darling. I never pay for anything if I can help it.'

'What is your scene?' Tessa asked, greatly daring.

She saw the blue, blue eyes flicker and for a moment an expression she could not define darken them, then he was laughing his old, light-hearted laugh and saying, 'Whatever the traffic will bear, sweetie. Now then, what are you going to have? Are you allowed to drink anything other than milk yet? You must be, if you are about to come out. How about a celebratory glass of wine? The cellar here is a decent one.'

'That would be nice,' Tessa said. Then in a rush: 'I have missed you so, Rupert. Do you have a good life? I mean, are you enjoying yourself in London, away from us?'

'I am having the time of my life, young Sprog. And I intend to go on doing so for as long as I can manage it.'

'Why don't you come home? Why does Daddy never mention your name? Why does Mummy come up to London but you never come to Dorset? It was all such a long time ago and other brothers did the same thing . . . I heard the girls at school talking about it. It's rife in boys' schools, they said, so why are you still not forgiven?'

She blurted it all out before she could lose her courage.

Rupert looked at his sister and felt a pang.

The poor little bitch had been kept in a box with the lid down ever since, probably because of his still-regarded-as-heinous sin. Trust his pure-in-heart father to go on his knees for the rest of his life. But he was surprised at his mother. Trenchant common sense had never been lacking there – except, of course, she would need to be circumspect, since she could not afford even the hint of a flaw when it came to Tessa's chances in the marriage mart. Ma was a product of her own upbringing and making a good match was still of paramount importance to her and her ilk.

Rupert remembered the time he'd broached the subject of his sister only to have Dorothea cut him off at once. 'Dearest boy, you have your own lifestyle and far be it from me to condemn what you do; it is no longer against the law of the land, after all. But there are other laws, and if I am to place your sister in the setting *I* visualise for her, then I have to be mindful of them at all times.'

'No hint of scandal?' he had asked derisively, not giving a damn because he had no use for that sort of hypocrisy anyway. Having grown up with religion as part of the air he breathed, once out from under what he thought of as its smog, he had given no thought to it again.

'In our particular *circumstances* she must of necessity be whiter than white,' his mother had said severely. 'Fortunately, I have trained her well and do not foresee any difficulties, provided you keep what I think is known as a lower than low profile during these months of preparation and inspection. Your father would never survive his daughter also falling from grace.'

'Well, if His Grace was not so far out of reach . . .'

'Your father is a spiritual rather than a worldly priest,' Dorothea reminded.

'A Reverend Septimus Harding rather than an Archdeacon Grantly?'

Dorothea had frowned. Not having a sense of humour, she saw none in the apt allusion.

'Poor Mummy,' Rupert said unsympathetically. 'If it had been up to you, you would have been an Archbishop's wife long ago.'

'It would give me even greater scope for my talents,' she had acknowledged complacently.

'What a pity it is *not* up to you then, since Pa is no good at the politics of it all. His trouble is that he is what Christ meant Bishops to be – if he had created any of them, that is, which he never did. A real, honest-to-goodness Christian, obeying God's laws at every turn . . .'

Hearing the cynical edge to her son's voice, Dorothea had

prompted coldly: 'Your father is behaving according the tenets of his religion, which you must know is of the utmost importance to him.'

'More than me, that's for certain. Dear old Dad is so very Old Testament. Not much scope there for forgiveness of the Prodigal Son, which is all so terribly New Testament. Not that I for one minute see myself in his particular light. I have never pretended to be what I am not. Perhaps this is where I went wrong. In not playing the hypocrite.'

'It is your father who finds it impossible to play that role. He deeply disapproves of what you are and what you do, and will never pretend otherwise.'

'Oh, I am aware he will never accept my homosexuality. There will never be any "what has been lost is found" where I am concerned.'

Unlike you, Rupert thought now, gazing across at his pretty-as-a-picture, grown-up sister. What about you? Has any of Pa's religion stuck to you? I suppose my awful example is what the mothers of all the Eligibles see when they look at you. Poor lamb. Being my sister is not going to do you any good at all, I'm afraid, but altruism was never my forte. Hedonism is, and all that goes with it . . . And I haven't the slightest doubt Ma has seen to it that you know absolutely nothing about any of *that*.

'Oh,' he said, shrugging as though her question had been about things that were now old hat, 'I suppose what grieved Pa was that I rejected everything he wished me to embrace. What he wanted for me and what I wanted were – are – poles apart. I'm sorry it caused a rift, but one should not live one's life through another. I live mine my way. Unfortunately it does not happen to be Pa's.'

'But that doesn't sound a good reason for staying away so long.'

'He does not wish to see me,' Rupert said.

'But he adored you! You were always his pride and joy.'

'And his pride certainly did goeth before my fall . . .'

He reached across to squeeze Tessa's hand, aware that he had not wholly satisfied her curiosity. She was no fool, his little sister, which was where their dear mother was making her big mistake. She talked about her daughter as though she had the mental abilities of an eight-year-old.

Not so, he thought. Give her a few years and my little sister will surprise us all.

'Not to worry about it,' he soothed her. 'I don't. Come on now, smile!' he said coaxingly to the grave face, so heartbreakingly pretty beneath its cap of bright gold hair. 'You always were a serious-minded little thing. I am thoroughly enjoying life and have no complaints. I did what I wanted to do and have never regretted it. One should always follow one's star, Sprog. Don't let our dear mama tell you that yours is only a trick of the light. Do what *you* want to do.'

'She won't let me,' Tessa said sadly.

'Do what?'

'Go to university. She says it's not necessary for a girl to get a degree in any subject when she will not have any opportunity to use it.'

'She means to marry you off.'

Another sigh. 'Yes.'

'I'd put in a word for you if I could but I think it best Ma does not know we have met – and will go on meeting?'

'Oh, yes, please!'

'Then I think, as you are now a grown-up eighteen-year-old, that we should celebrate in style. With champagne!'

Tessa met her brother a dozen more times over the next few months, stealing away to do so, the last time to his flat in Ennismore Gardens. She had been there only once before, and briefly. Normally they met at an appointed public (though never fashionable) place, but one lunch-time, when she had been waiting for him at the little pub they frequented, he had telephoned a message to say he was running late and would she hop in a taxi and come to his flat?

Once there, she had been astounded at its sybaritic luxury because, so far as she knew, Rupert did not have a job. Of course he had the money Grandmother Norton had left him – Tessa would also get hers when she was twenty-one – but how far did £50,000 go when it came to gold cigarette cases, Baccarat decanters and glasses, solid silver cutlery, hampers from Fortnum's and luggage from Loewe? Rupert was now twenty-three, and he lived extremely high on the hog, as she had once overheard her Uncle Henry, the MP, say about another MP. Money did not last long the way Rupert spent it, so where did it come from? His flat, for instance, was like nothing she had ever seen; luxurious . . . no, *decadent* was the word which came to mind. Tessa had just finished reading (secretly out of her mother's sight) *The Portrait of Dorian Gray*, and Rupert's flat was as she had envisaged Dorian's apartments; opulent and sybaritic. It had large, high rooms filled with heavy, ornate furniture; the sitting room hung in dark red paisley wallpaper, its windows draped and swagged with matching curtains, so that it was like the inside of a box in which an expensive oriental perfume reposed. There was always the smell of incense – or was it joss sticks? Something exotic anyway.

Most striking of all were the mirrors. Especially in the bedroom. Tessa had never seen such a bedroom in her life. It had a mirrored ceiling and walls; you could see yourself reflected a hundred times.

'I don't think I would like that,' she had said doubtfully, gazing round. 'I think I would get tired of seeing myself.'

'That is where we differ, Sprog, because I don't. I have always taken great pleasure in my own reflection.'

And it was through those mirrors, one sunny afternoon, on her second visit to the flat, that she saw her brother for the last time and learned, in the most catastrophic way, how he went about earning the money he spent so prodigally.

He had said he would take her to tea. Tessa had wanted to go to The Ritz but he had pointed out that there was every chance they would be seen there, which would do her no good at all.

'Me and my dissolute life and you and your pristine perfection out together? It would never do! However, they do afternoon tea at The Waldorf. We won't see a soul we know *there*. Meet me in the lobby at a quarter-past four.'

Tessa had had another fitting during the morning, after which her mother had gone to lunch with friends, having graciously agreed that Tessa could join a group of her own friends at the house of one of them in Cadogan Square.

But after lunch, on the pretext of going to the hairdresser, Tessa had made for her brother's flat, intending to surprise him.

She knew where a key was kept in case of emergencies: in the turban of the eighteenth-century blackamoor which stood on a pedestal outside his front door.

Letting herself in, she breathed in the scent of the flat: that subtly intoxicating blend of she knew not what; only that it made her think of things of which her mother would never approve. She would have to be careful, if she was meeting her afterwards, to obliterate its traces under a judicious spraying of Miss Dior.

Her brother was not in; he lunched out every day. She had noticed that there was never anything in the fridge but champagne, stuffed olives, and a bottle of Tanqueray gin. Quite happy to wait, she plonked herself down on the big, high-backed Knole sofa, upholstered in what had once been a Cardinal's red silk cape, and picked up a pile of glossies – but since she had been to a dance the night before and not got home until three, she found her lids drooping. When she began to yawn, she laid down the magazine and closed her eyes.

She was not sure what had woken her until she heard the noise again. A moan. Long, breathily drawn in, harshly gasped out, it made Tessa feel funny in the pit of her stomach because it had connotations of both pleasure and pain.

Sitting up, she had peered over the high back of the sofa. The room was empty, but through the archway into the hall – there was no door – she saw light flickering from the bedroom.

Checking her watch, she saw it was only three-fifteen. Yet somebody had lit the candles in there. Probably Rupert. Nobody else would do so. Hung over? Was that the reason for the moan? She knew he drank quite a lot. He had been unable to eat lunch with her one day because, he said, he had overdone things the night before. Truth to tell, he had looked hollow-cheeked and sunken eyed.

If it was his intention to renege on tea, she was going to give him a piece of her mind. He had told her several times recently that she had more than enough and to spare, and why didn't she use it against their overbearing mother? So she got up from the sofa and straightened her dress prior to confronting him. Moving quietly in case he really was under the weather, she arrived at the bedroom to find its door not quite closed. Through the gap she could see, by what and who was reflected in the mirrored walls, that Rupert was not alone; the big bed was occupied by him and another man. Both were naked, and Rupert was lying on his stomach, one of the thick cushions which normally strewed the bed placed under his groin, so that his buttocks were raised. His legs were spread to their widest, his ankles tied to two of the four uprights which supported the mirrored tester, his wrists tied to the other two. In the light from the dozens of lit candles she could see his face clearly, turned to one side, eyes wide and raptly fixed on the multitude of candle-lit reflections, fascinatedly, even greedily absorbed in them, especially on the man behind and above him, who was moving back and forth, with the oiled smoothness of a piston, in and out, in and out, of Rupert's body. As she watched, an expression of ecstasy convulsed Rupert's face and he moaned, causing the other man to become quite frenzied in his movements.

Tessa recoiled, stumbling backwards until she met the wall, where for mindless moments she was able neither to move nor to look away from the reflections; not even when she saw what it was that moved in and out of Rupert; rock-hard, enormous, thickly purple and slickly glistening. Only when he uttered a sound that was a cross between a moan, a gasp and a snarl: 'Oh, God yes . . . yes . . . YES!' was she freed from her trance. Feeling nausea rise she clapped both hands over her mouth before backing away down the corridor and into the living room until she came up hard against the back of the Knole sofa where she had been sleeping when her brother and his lover had come in. Instinctively her hand groped for her handbag, found it, gripped it, clutched it to her as though in protection, its familiarity bringing her back to reality and the realisation that she had to escape; that she had made a terrible mistake in coming here unannounced.

She made herself breathe deeply several times, forcing back the nausea produced not so much by shock as realisation, because all of a sudden Rupert's various half-hints and casual allusions coalesced with her own uneasy surmisings to form one huge, hideous reality; the one from which she now knew her father had also recoiled in anguished disbelief. It was some time before she felt able to inch her way stealthily down the corridor to the front door, keeping her eyes averted from the bedroom but unable to avoid hearing the gasps, the now frenzied yelps, until she was able, very slowly and very carefully, to slide back the lock, slipping into the deserted corridor before silently pulling the door to behind her. Taking the key from the blackamoor's turban once more she locked the door from the outside.

Then she ran.

She had no idea she was sobbing, was not conscious of the tears streaming down her cheeks or the passers-by she knocked against in her headlong flight. She only knew she had to get away. When lack of breath and a stitch in her side made her slow down, she found herself by the Serpentine. Looking for an empty bench, she sank down on it, no longer weeping but shaking. Opening her handbag she took out its handmirror. She looked terrible. All blotched and tear-streaked. There was no way she could go home with a face like that. She did her best with her handkerchief, then sat on, staring sightlessly at the children playing by the lake, seeing nothing but the scene in the mirrored bedroom as it played itself over and over again; multiple Ruperts and that thick, purple *thing* plunging in and out of him. Now she knew how, without any visible means of support, he could afford that expensive flat, wear designer-labels, drink only vintage champagne. He entertained clients in that mirrored bedroom. Who but a whore would have a bedroom like that in the first place?

It was not his son's homosexuality which gave her father so much grief, it was how he used it. Her brother was a male whore. Oh, God, she thought, screwing up her face in distaste, closing her eyes as if to block out even the very thought. I can't bear to face him; not now, today. If I do, one look at me and he will know that I know . . . that I saw him .... I can't face him, I can't. Oh, God, what a naive idiot I have been. No wonder Daddy will not have his name mentioned. Oh, dear God, Rupert, what have you become? And what am I to do?

What she did eventually, and with a steady-voiced coolness she had not known she possessed, was find a telephone box and call her brother's flat. He had an answering machine – now she knew why – and rarely picked up incoming calls. She left a message to say that she was absolutely whacked after a late night and an endless fitting, having no difficulty in sounding exhausted. Could they postpone today's outing until the next time Mummy's hold on her leash slackened? Which will not be for as long as I can manage it, she thought.

Her mother took one look at her white face and said: 'You have been burning the candle at both ends for too long, I think. It's just as well we return to the country tomorrow.'

Once safely back home Tessa had taken refuge in her

favourite hiding place; an old Victorian conservatory where Mr Henry still grew grapes. There she sobbed herself into a raging headache and finally an exhausted sleep, returning to the house only when she was sure her mother's sharp eyes would not be the cause of unwelcome questions.

As it was Dorothea had asked dubiously: 'Are you coming down with something?'

'Yes, I think I am,' Tessa answered, grasping at the straw. 'I have the most awful headache. I think the best place for me is bed, with no dinner. I'm not in the least hungry.'

'Too much gadding about?' her father chided, in his gently humorous way. 'Perhaps some peace and quiet are called for.'

It called to Tessa so powerfully that she spent the next week in bed, ostensibly needing to rest, in reality suffering from the after-effects of shock.

'You really have been overdoing it,' her mother scolded, 'but I am as much to blame for giving in to your pleadings and cajolings. No more London for a while for you, my girl. Not until you have recovered your pink cheeks.'

Tessa was thankful to agree. Going up to town where she would have to see her brother was unthinkable. She would not go until she could face him with equanimity. And she had no idea how long that would take.

After spending the week in bed, where she had wept in secret and thought herself into exhaustion, she got up Sunday morning and went to church with her mother as usual, after which she took the dogs for a walk, returning in time for Sunday lunch. For once they had no guests, so only the three of them sat down in the small dining room. They were having coffee in the sitting room when Riggs came to announce: 'The police are here, My Lord, asking to see you.'

'The police! You haven't been breaking the speed limit, have you, Riggs?' asked the Bishop jocularly.

'No, My Lord. I rather think it is more serious than that.'

The Bishop's benign but melancholy face took on an expression of alarm. 'Dear me, then I had better go and see what they want.'

'Probably to complain about your giving those wretched gypsies permission to pitch their camp on Lakey Hill,' his wife said austerely. 'You will remember that I did warn you that no good would come of it. No doubt they have been breaking and entering or some such thing. I trust you did not go walking in that vicinity when you went out with the dogs this morning?' she said to her daughter.

'No, Mother,' Tessa answered.

Dorothea scrutinised her daughter's pale face. 'Are you still unwell? Or is something troubling you? You've been acting of late as though you've lost twenty pounds and found a penny.' She paused. 'You're not – in love?'

Tessa wanted to laugh. Hysterically. 'No, Mother.'

'If you're sulking because we left London early then I would advise you not to do so. And do stop this mooning around as though waiting for something to happen! Girls of your age should not be waiting for things to happen. When they are about to, you may be sure that I will inform you well in advance.'

She returned to her *Sunday Times* and Tessa went back to the treadmill of her thoughts.

Riggs had come back to the sitting room only a few minutes after taking the Bishop through to the waiting police officers, and the look on his face had instantly brought Dorothea to her feet.

'The Bishop needs you, madam,' he had said in a stiff voice.

Tessa had shoved back her chair, preparing to follow, knowing with certain dread that something terrible had happened. Riggs obviously knew so she too ought to know.

'No!' he commanded. 'You stay here, Miss Tessa. You'll know soon enough.'

'Know what?'

Riggs shook his head.

Tessa found herself saying, in a voice such as she had never dared to use, even to him: 'Riggs, I've had enough of being kept in the dark. Now what's going on? Why are the police here – and don't tell me you don't know because you do. It was all over your face when you came back. Why did they want Daddy? What did you hear them tell him? What's so bad that Mummy has to go to him?' Her voice rose as what lay so heavily on her mind and spirit had her asking instinctively: 'Is it about Rupert? Has he been arrested?'

Riggs looked at her narrowly. 'Now why should Mr Rupert be arrested?'

'I know how he makes his living.'

Their eyes met, held for a long, explosive moment, then almost violently Riggs spat: 'London! As a hellfire preacher would say – Soddom & Gomorah. I said to your father it was only a matter of time.'

Tessa felt her heart lurch. Oh, God, that was what this was all about. Rupert had been caught taking money for sex. Oh, God, poor Daddy . . .

As if he could divine her thoughts, 'Your brother has done for your father.' Riggs said viciously. 'Brought a good man down, he has, with his depraved ways. Your mother is a strong woman; what she has to bear the Good Lord gave her the strength to carry. But not your father. This will do for him. And he blames *himself*! Keeps going over and over it all, wondering where he went wrong . . . Where *he* went wrong! I've told him more than once, that Master Rupert was *born* wrong!'

Tessa had sunk down into her chair again. 'At least he went away to London,' she defended weakly.

'Where the family is known and he was sure to be talked about! If they were nobodies it wouldn't have mattered, but your father is a Bishop, and your mother has brothers who sit in both Houses of Parliament. Rupert didn't give a damn about any of that, but he ought to. He ought to have known better.'

Tessa said: 'You never liked him, did you?'

'I'd seen his sort before and had no use for them either. You get all sorts in the Army, and his type was just one of them. Queer as Dick's hatband! I saw what your brother was right from the start. But your father never did. He only ever saw the good in people. It was the same during the war. I was his batman when he was commanding officer and I saw the way he gave the worst type of offender the benefit of the doubt. It didn't surprise me back in 1945, after what we'd seen, when he told me he was going to leave the Army and join the Church.'

He stopped talking, listened, turning his head to pick up every sound. 'I think they're leaving . . .' He went to see, leaving Tessa sitting on tenterhooks. She eventually went in search of her parents when they did not return to the sitting room and found them in the library, seated together on the old leather sofa, clasping each other's hands as if for support.

Sitting facing them was a woman police constable. She stood up as Tessa entered and came towards her.

'What's the matter?' Tessa asked fearfully. 'Why are Mummy and Daddy looking like that?'

The policewoman drew her to one side.

'Why don't you go and make everybody a nice strong cup of tea?' she advised, kindly matter-of-fact.

'Riggs is already doing it. Why are they looking like that? What has happened? It's my brother, isn't it? Something has happened to my brother . . . Has he been arrested? Is that it?'

The Bishop's long, thin face looked like a tomb effigy, while that of his wife resembled nothing so much as the dough Cook pummelled when she made bread.

'It is my brother, isn't it?' Tessa persisted doggedly, knowing that nothing else could possibly make her parents look like that. 'He has been arrested, hasn't he?'

The policewoman eyed the white face, saw no signs of hysteria, only determination, and decided the girl could take it. Besides, somebody had to be there for these two poor people.

'No,' she said gently. 'Your brother has not been arrested, he has been murdered.'

That night, Tessa's father suffered his first stroke.

5

The roar of overhead jets brought Nicholas Ould up to the surface from his deep immersion in the papers he had been reading since he got into his chauffeur-driven Bentley T. He had not got round to replacing the now scrap-metal R, even though the insurance company had already paid up: he had waited two years for the first one, and he was not inclined to do the same again.

Putting the papers away in his Louis Vuitton briefcase, he got out of the car, nodding to his chauffeur with a brisk, 'Thursday evening, Concorde, Matthews.'

'I'll be here, sir. Have a good trip.'

'Thank you.'

As a frequent Concorde traveller he always arrived within minutes of take-off, since he saw no point in hanging around airport lounges, and always had the same seat – at the front near the door. Nor did he ever carry anything but his briefcase. That way he could be off the plane and through immigration without having to wait at a crowded baggage carousel. He had all the clothes he needed in his town house on East 73rd, just off the park.

Once Concorde took off he neither ate nor drank. Well known as he was, the flight attendants left him alone to immerse himself once more in the contents of his briefcase. If he wanted anything he would ask.

He had run Ould & Sons, the family bank, since he was twenty-nine years old, almost eleven years now. A clause in the charter creating it in 1724 stipulated that only a male member of the family could control the bank's affairs, and that no part of it could ever be sold to an outsider. Such shares as there were belonged to family members, now reduced to himself, his mother and sister (women were allowed to hold shares but the charter forbade their playing any part in the day-to-day running of the bank's affairs), his father's youngest brother Francis, a childless widower in his seventieth year, and the widow of the eldest brother, Christopher.

Christopher had run the bank, expecting to pass control on to his own two sons, an heir and a spare, but both were keen sportsmen who were killed by their enthusiasms: the elder in an avalanche while ski-ing off-piste in Gstaad; the other by a horse when, in the midst of a fast and furious polo match, he fell off his own pony right under the hooves of another, which crushed his chest, forcing one of his splintered ribs into his heart. The mantle had therefore passed to the sole surviving male, their cousin Nicholas, who took no part in any dangerous pursuit other than that of chasing women. In the careful manner of the family, which had learned in the course of two hundred and fifty years to leave nothing to chance, his shoulders had been ready to receive it, since he had read Politics, Philosophy and Economics at

Oxford before going on to acquire his MBA at Harvard Business School.

It was through Nicholas's efforts that Ould & Sons had become the kind of global investment bank that former Senior Partners had regarded with grave suspicion, they having been married to the conservative approach for far too long to be seduced by the huge profits the Wall Street firms made. Nicholas was different; he took risks, but not until every one had been studied from every angle and every outcome figured. He had a cool head and the nerve of a born gambler. Because of this, Ould & Sons New York was now big enough to take on the Americans at their own game, especially in the brutal plays of ruthless hiring-and-firing, something the more tender-hearted English winced at and shied away from. The people who worked for him there had thought as he did from the start; in London, the old-school regime, those who said proudly, 'In thirty-five years with this house I have never taken a risk,' were gradually replaced by younger men prepared to do just that, and in the years since Nicholas had taken over, Ould & Sons had become one of the world's great banking houses. His handling of the £6.5 billion bid by Gobal Oil for its deadly rival was still talked about with awe. So was the profit the bank made from it.

He expected hard work and loyalty – long a tradition at Ould & Sons – acquiring it by working every bit as hard as his employees and gaining their respect further by keeping cost bases low and paying bonuses when the bank did well out of a deal.

His great gift, according to both rivals and colleagues, was the ability to communicate. When he was talking to someone he had the rare knack of being able to narrow his focus on them to a high-intensity beam, convincing them that they were the one person in the world who mattered at that particular time. He also commanded a huge network of friends and acquaintances. No matter where he went he knew a great many of the people present at any one gathering.

His father, Nicholas Senior, had flouted tradition and not gone into the bank. At the age of fifty he had been knighted by the Queen for services rendered as one of her Ambassadors. He too had possessed the gift of communication, which was what had made him such a successful diplomat. Nicholas had been born in the British Embassy in Madrid while his father had been representing his country there. His mother was the daughter of Spanish grandees whose title went back to the days of El Cid. Nicholas was an only son, but he had a younger sister, Elena, married to a Spaniard who was at present First Secretary with the Spanish Embassy in Mexico City.

Nicholas's entry in *Who's Who* gave his interests as wine (he had a famous cellar and was as knowledgeable about wine as he was about money), women (he was internationally appreciated as a lover) and song (he was a opera buff as well as having a passion for music in general, along with one for literature, being very widely read in several languages). He was bi-lingual in English and Spanish, having learned both as a child, and had fluent French, Italian and German. He had rowed for his college (Christ Church) at Oxford, but took no interest in any other sport (except the sexual olympics, the wags said). His interests were cultural. He played championship bridge, took on – and usually beat – all comers at Scrabble, and was a fearsome opponent at Trivial Pursuit. He had too much respect for money to gamble except in the business sense.

To the despair of his mother, who had married his father when she was twenty and he thirty, Nicholas was still a bachelor, showing no signs of wishing to change his single status. He loved women, revelled in their beauty, adored their femininity and infinitely preferred their company to that of men. His working hours were mostly spent with men so he devoted his leisure time to women, of whom there were far too many to allow consideration of any single one as a lifetime companion. Variety was the spice of his life, and he liked nothing more than a leisurely investigation of every single bloom in a bed of roses. Besides, he had yet to meet a woman who fixed his interest to such an extent that he was unable to see beyond her; nor was it his intention to marry without the kind of love his parents had shared. His father had adored his mother while she had worshipped the ground her husband walked on. After his death and out of mourning she could have re-married several times, but declined to do so because, as she told her son: 'When you have had what I had, it is out of the question. No one could ever replace your father'.

What Nicholas Ould wanted, but so far had never met, was the irreplaceable woman. He was well aware that if the bank was to continue it was essential that he provide the son to carry it forward into the twenty-first century, and it was something he had been working towards though without a specific date in mind. The attempt on his life, however, had concentrated his mind wonderfully: making it plain it had to be sooner rather than later.

He was first off the plane when it landed, to find his limousine and chauffeur waiting to drive him to that part of the airport where the company helicopter waited, rotors already turning. Within twenty minutes it was landing on the flat roof of the Park Avenue skyscraper which served as company HQ. From there he descended by private elevator to the five floors which held the American operations of Ould & Sons and its various American subsidiaries.

His secretary, middle-aged and unflappable, was waiting by his desk, the mail already opened and marked, a sheaf of messages in her hand.

'Good morning, Mr Ould.' Her smile was the deferential, respectful kind, but she knew him well enough to be able to look at him searchingly. It was not his physical injuries she wondered about, it was the mental ones.

Five years ago, when she and her husband had visited relatives in Israel, they had been caught up in a Palestinian bomb attack which had affected them both deeply, Sam in particular. They had only been back a few weeks when he was involved in the car crash which put him in a wheelchair for the rest of his life. Hannah was convinced that it was because his concentration had been affected since their return from Israel. She had become only too familiar with the long periods of brooding silence, the tossing and turning in bed, the nightmares.

Nicholas Ould, on the other hand, looked the same as ever. His smile was warm, the deep voice pleasant when he said easily: 'Hello, Hannah. How are things?'

'Back on an even keel after the awful shock we all got when we heard about the bomb! Thank the Lord you weren't in the car when it went off! Are you quite recovered from your injuries?'

There was the merest hint of impatience when he answered: 'Everything is back to normal, thank you,' and even though he coated it with one of his honeyed smiles, she took the hint.

Sitting down behind his big but tidy desk he asked briskly: 'So . . . what has been happening in my enforced absence?'

Business as usual, Hannah noted approvingly, and at once became as focused as he was, giving him a brief but succinct run-down on the state of play in both the bank and the market as of 8 a.m. that morning, before going on to cover the happenings of the past five weeks, finally handing him his sheaf of messages and telling him who was anxious to see him.

'All right, wheel them in in order of importance, but not until I've had a cup of your restorative coffee and read this pile of mail.' As she turned to go: 'Hang on a minute.' He picked up his briefcase, opened it and took out a flat package. 'Smoked salmon,' he said. 'Arrived from Scotland not half an hour before I left the house this morning.'

Hannah Behrens flushed with delight. 'Thank you. Sam will be in seventh heaven.' Smoked salmon from the River Tweed was a luxury; so much better than its poor relation lox.

'My pleasure,' said Nicholas, and for the thousandth time Hannah wondered at the contradictions in a man who could, when it was called for, be as ruthlessly competitive as it was possible to be, yet without prompting be as warmly kind.

As she sat down at her own desk she saw the little green light on her telephone console which denoted he was making a call on his private line light up. Back to normal indeed, she thought on a wry sigh of relief. His first call was proof of that . . .

The phone rang in the still-darkened bedroom of the corner apartment overlooking East 79th and Madison

Avenue, and a slender female hand, flawlessly manicured and scarlet-tipped, emerged from the covers to grope for it, bring it to her ear.

'Good morning,' said a familiar voice.

'Nicholas!' The voluptuous red-head sat up in bed, tearing off her black velvet sleep-mask before pressing the button that had the curtains retreating from the big windows to let in the dazzling light of a New York morning. 'Darling, I've been so worried . . . Are you all right? No after effects?'

'I'm fine. I'll prove it to you tonight. Eight o'clock. Your place. Don't dress. We won't be going anywhere.'

He rang off.

Replacing the receiver, Dana Holmes sank back against her pillows with a knowing smile. The instruction not to dress told her exactly what to expect. An hour or so before his arrival a hamper would be delivered from Balducci's filled with all sorts of delicacies, from stuffed quails' eggs to Parma ham destined to go with a ripe canteloupe, through truffle-stuffed pâté down to smoked salmon and cream cheese bagels, followed by ripe California peaches and fat strawberries, all to be washed down with a couple of bottles of Krug.

After one of what she called his 'marathons', they both ate like pigs. Sex of that calibre and duration inevitably took a lot out of you. Besides, near brushes with death such as the one he'd had recently always sent you running for dear life, and what better proof of life than sex? If someone had tried to blow her away she would be in need of the very same sort of reassurance. 'In the midst of death, we are in life' as she had once heard somebody say.

Stretching luxuriously, Dana realised she was as ready as he was. She had not had sex with him for more than five long weeks. Normally she saw him every fourteen days –

when he came to New York. Excitement had her lower belly fluttering already and it was only – she checked her small Cartier Rivoli bedside clock – twenty minutes past ten. Her smile was of the cat-got-the-cream variety. Don't dress, he'd said, which meant that when he rang the pre-arranged signal on her doorbell – the Morse code for the letter N – she was expected to open the door to him naked and ready.

Her tongue crept out to circle her lips. With a sexual appetite like his he must be absolutely ravenous. She went into the bathroom, and when she came out again wearing a poem of a negligee, her maid was just entering the bedroom with her breakfast: half a pink grapefruit into which its own flesh plus that of a chopped melon, prunes, mango and guava had been piled before being covered with low-fat yoghurt, plus a pot of decaffeinated coffee.

Getting back into bed, she said: 'Hand me my engagement diary, will you, Dorita? I think it's on my desk.'

After placing the tray over her mistress's legs and piling the big square pillows into a comfortable backrest, the maid went to get the diary.

Leafing through it, Dana saw she had her manicurist coming at eleven – followed by a lunch at Le Cirque, but that was only with the girls which meant gossip would be dish of the day. They could go. So could tomorrow's appointments. After one of Nicholas's marathons she would need to sleep for a straight twelve to fourteen hours. The thing to do was use the day to get in shape for him . . . She reached for the telephone and dialled the number of her personal trainer.

After dealing with his mail, Nicholas spent the rest of the morning in meetings and discussions, courteously accepting the ever-solicitous enquiries as to the state of his physical well-being. His manner made it plain that the event was now to be regarded as over and done with.

'What do you expect?' they asked each other afterwards. 'You know the British and their stiff upper lips . . .'

He lunched in his private dining room with his CEO and other members of the bank's New York hierarchy, then spent the afternoon in a Planning and Strategy conference. After that, he took a walk through all five floors. He did this on a regular basis, stopping to chat here or have a word there, always open to an approach by anyone with news or suggestions. Pausing by one of the secretarial desks, he handed over a bound sheaf of papers. 'Have Legal put this into understandable English, will you? I have trouble deciphering what they are trying to say so there is no way I can explain it to anyone else.' His tone was pleasant but the reproof was implicit.

'Yes, sir, I'll get on to it right away.'

Turning, he found a young man – one of the trainees, newly equipped with his MBA and come to gain experience – waiting deferentially. 'I thought you'd like to know that we are up four points on all five portfolios of the Genovale trading accounts,' he said proudly. 'Not bad for the first quarter.'

Nicholas smiled encouragingly. 'Good work, Jimmy. Why don't you take a crack at the Nordstrom portfolio? See what you can do with that.'

The boy's face glowed. 'Gee, thanks, Mr Ould. I can really get my teeth into that.'

'Just so long as you don't bite off more than you can chew!'

'I know what I'd like to bite,' one of the secretaries murmured to another, watching Nicholas walk away.

When he got back to his office he buzzed the man who ran the section in which Jimmy Carson worked.

'I've put Jimmy on to the Nordstrom account. Keep an eye on him, see how he does and don't let his enthusiasm run away with him. No over-long positions.'

'Will do. He's a good kid. Got the makings of a first-class trader. I'm bringing him along slowly.'

'I'd noticed. Keep up the good work.'

It was six-thirty when he left the building to wave his car away before walking the fifteen blocks uptown to his apartment, already feeling anticipation for what was to come, his semi hard-on tossing from side to side as he walked, a more than pressing reminder. One of the effects of the attempt on his life had been an increase in the strength of what was already a powerful libido. For some reason he was unable to unwind completely; what had happened in the early hours of that Sunday morning still thrummed inside him. No matter how eruptive the release he felt the need for more. No woman, it seemed, could now drain him.

Perhaps Dana, with her own potent sexuality, could do it. She was always up to going not only all the way but coming back again . . .

Once in his apartment he found his Chinese manservant waiting for him with a freshly made drink. Chang was a student at Columbia, but also ran things at Nicholas's New York home whether he was there nor not, doing everything including the laundry and, on those few occasions when his master ate in, providing excellent food. He lived in two rooms off the kitchen, which he shared now and then with whichever girl was current – Nicholas never enquired. So long as the place functioned efficiently – and at all times it shone with the kind of cleanliness only dedication could produce – Chang's life was his own.

Nicholas took off his clothes, and while he was in the shower Chang took them away; the underclothes to be laundered, the suit to be brushed and pressed, before laying out fresh clothes for the evening, knowing by what was briefly said where his master was going and thus what was needed.

Coming out of his bathroom wrapped in a towelling robe, Nicholas reached for his drink – a perfectly made vodka martini – which he sipped before taking it into the bathroom with him to finish while he shaved.

When he was dressed, Chang came into the bedroom to tidy away. 'I won't be back. The night is yours.'

'Hope also yours.'

The wish was accompanied by a polite bow but there was a gleam in Chang's almond eyes.

Dana lived only a few blocks north and west, but by the time Nicholas got to her apartment building he was aching with pent-up sexuality.

The white-gloved doorman touched his cap as he opened the glass doors, said: 'Good evening, Mr Ould.'

I hope so, Nicholas thought. God knows I'm in need of it!

There was only one apartment on each floor, so there was no one to see Dana's sublime nakedness when she opened the door to him.

She was wearing her bronze hair loose, and it matched to perfection the thicket of curls between her thighs. Her ample breasts – deeply appreciated by her lovers but despaired of by her dressmaker – pointed their large tawny nipples at him, and her flesh gleamed.

Reaching out a hand she pulled him in, pushing the door closed with her foot before moulding her contours to his, standing on tiptoe so as to be able to kiss him with an avidly open mouth. 'Mmmmm . . .' she murmured as she felt what appeared to be an iron bar pressing into her groin. 'You *are* ready.'

'And waiting,' he said harshly.

She drew him into the bedroom, where the big bed stood ready, freshly made with crisp, clean sheets. On a small table at its foot sat an ice bucket containing a bottle of Roederer Cristal, two champagne flutes and a bowlful of glistening, anchovy-stuffed olives.

'Just take the edge off for now. I have a lot in me these days,' he warned, as she unbuckled his belt, 'and we have a long way to go . . .'

Feeling the tension in his long body, understanding that he was in no need of enhancement, she took off his clothes swiftly and efficiently, hissing in a thrilled breath as his erection sprang free from his confining black silk briefs. 'Easy,' he grunted in an impeded voice as she gently took hold of him to draw him towards the bed, where she pushed him down on his back.

Dana had had many lovers, but not one of them had been as beautifully made as Nicholas Ould. Male genitalia had, in her opinion, been designed by a committee, but they had called in an artist where Nicholas was concerned. Everything balanced; the scrotum round and full, the long, thick, circumcised cock the colour of mother-of-pearl, which she knew felt like it looked: soft and silky. Even erect, when the penis could take on a brutality that both alarmed and repelled, his was still a thing of beauty, and she already knew what a joy it could be. Weighing him in her hand, she knew at once from his heaviness that he did indeed have a lot in him.

Quickly she joined him on the bed, legs straddling him as she bent forward, her tawny hair brushing his belly, tickling his rampant cock. He drew in a sharp breath and the muscles of his lower belly rippled. He was on the edge and she would have to go carefully if he was not to erupt before she got the chance to enjoy him. Flexing her fingers like a card sharp, she took firm but delicate hold of him where she could produce the most unendurably pleasurable feelings, then bent her head to take him in her mouth.

He watched her as she began, but as the feeling mounted, closed his eyes and let her take him to where only she knew the way. He had learned early on what a tongue could do, but never known one like Dana's. She knew all the tricks; exactly when to push him over the edge and just how far to let him fall.

As his breathing slowed she lay beside him in tender silence.

'You needed that,' she observed.

'More than somewhat.'

His voice was easier, and when she put a hand on his chest some of the tension had gone. But only some. Which was not really surprising. Nicholas Ould was the only man she knew who was capable of double headers. It was as well she had had her earlier workout, she mused as she poured them both a glass of well-chilled champagne. Both drank thirstily, draining the first glass, sipping more slowly at the second before setting down the empty glasses.

It was his turn. Sitting up, he pushed her down on her

back, lifting her legs to place them over his shoulders. Then he buried his head in her. His tongue, cold from the champagne, met her moist heat and made her shudder and gasp with delight.

Raising her hands, she wrapped her fingers around the ornate brass of her French bedhead and held on tight. Nicholas too had a wicked tongue. He made her buck and writhe, her body becoming as slick and wet as she was, guttural sounds issuing from her throat as she began to jerk uncontrollably, thrusting her hips up against his mouth and tongue, legs twitching, hands releasing the bedhead to grip either side of his head, pressing him in deeper into her until, with one last snarl, she arched herself upwards to bend like a drawn bow for a long moment before collapsing, legs sliding bonelessly from his shoulders to fall heavily to the mattress. Raising himself up, Nicholas ran his mouth slowly up her body until it reached her breasts, the nipples of which were hard nubs of proud flesh. As his teeth nipped at them, he had her moaning as he proceeded to pleasure them with lips and tongue. When his mouth reached hers he kissed her deeply and at length so that she tasted herself, taking her lower lip in his teeth and stroking it with his tongue. Then he ravished her face with kisses as once more he lifted her legs over his shoulders so that she was wide open to him when he slid inside her, stone hard and hot. With him deeply buried inside her, not moving, she nevertheless felt her second orgasm building, welcomed it as one of the many he would bring her to before he would allow himself to partake of his own pleasure. But tonight was different. She had never known him – a man capable of withholding his orgasm until the woman begged for release – go on for so long, by which time she had fallen through so many wrenching orgasms she had lost count. It was as though he was intent on driving her to the brink of endurance; pleasure was becoming tinged with pain. The moan she could not prevent from escaping ended in a wince.

Instantly, as though even in the midst of his own intensity he had recognised the note in her voice, she felt his buttocks clench and the tiny tuft of hair at the base of his spine bristle as he gathered himself before emptying into her in a gigantic orgasm which seemed to go on for ever until he was totally drained, falling out of and away from her to lie heavily inert, his breath harsh in his chest.

When he could speak he said, sounding happily tired: 'That, my sweet, was the one,' before closing his eyes. 'Now I can sleep . . .'

Aware of a pleasurable soreness Dana went into her bathroom and ran a hot bath in which she soaked for a long time, knowing he would not awake. When he slept, he slept deeply. Which was just as well for she doubted if she could take him again.

What had he meant: 'Now I can sleep'? He was not an insomniac, to her knowledge. She was the one who wore the black silk sleep-mask and took the pills. When he stayed over, he invariably disposed himself comfortably before being sound asleep in minutes. Was he still in pain from his injuries? No . . . he could not have disported himself as he had just done if he had not been in shape. More than two hours of unceasing sexual activity. Whatever it was that ailed him, she decided, it was not physical.

But something was not quite right. She could not have said what, or where, she only knew that something had changed. Something in him. He had been as inventive and tireless as ever – no, more than tireless. Like . . . she frowned, searching for the right words . . . he was running from something. The after-effects of the attempt on his life? She had read somewhere about the psychological consequences of that sort of thing.

Trouble was, their relationship precluded her questioning him about it because the only Nicholas she knew with any degree of intimacy was the sexual one. While intimately acquainted with every inch of his body, she knew nothing of his mind; they had never done anything but fuck themselves blind every time they met. She was his New York woman. She knew there was one in Paris, another in Zurich, God knows how many in London . . . He was a man who loved to make love to women. They had mutual friends – which was how they had met – but they themselves were not friends. Only lovers. They had never really *talked*. Talk was not what either wanted from the other.

She left the bath to dry and powder herself, sliding into a thin silk kimono before raiding the basket of goodies, her appetite honed by the marathon she had just completed. She felt no guilt at the thought of the calories she was consuming since she had no doubt she had already expended thousands.

She also finished off the opened bottle of champagne, which had the result of sending her to sleep.

What awoke her was something firm and heated pressing against her buttocks.

'My God!' she exclaimed, pretending shock as she reached behind to feel the silken length of him. 'Is that me or do you need the john?'

Laughingly he turned her to face him. The shimmering eyes were filled with the familiar light they had not held last night. He was back. This was the Nicholas she knew; hair tousled and needing a shave, he was still the most attractive man and *the* most marvellous lover – ever.

Thank God that whatever it was that had held him in its grip last night had disappeared. She had enough problems of her own. Shifting to accommodate him she discovered that her soreness was gone and her energy restored.

What nicer way to begin the day?

6

Tessa turned from the lovely old *bonheur-du-jour* she had inherited from her maternal great-grandmother to regard her husband, stretched out full-length on the huge leather Chesterfield reading the *Mail on Sunday*. He was nights again – that shift came round with monotonous regularity every fourth week – and at 7 p.m. had not long been out of bed, but was shaved, showered and wearing a faded pair of 501s with an old Ralph Lauren shirt she had bought him years ago on their first trip to California. He was still, she thought with the dispassion which had now all but totally replaced her first impassioned regard, a truly beautiful man. Big and splendid of body – Harry kept himself in shape – there was no overhang to his belt or sign of a jowl under his handsome face. Had he not chosen to become a policeman, Harry Sansom could have made a fortune as a male model. His features were as regular as a mathematical equation, his eyes as hotly blue as gas flames, his light brown hair with its overtones of chestnut still thick and shiny, while thanks to the regular and judicious use of a sunbed he had a deeply golden tone to his skin. Yes, Harry took care of himself, which was no doubt why even now, at thirty-seven, women still goggled at him before turning envious eyes Tessa's way.

He had cut the ground from under her feet that very first day when, a brand new probationer fresh from Hendon Training School and reporting for duty at Haringey Police Station, he had been introduced to her as her 'parent constable', known colloquially as her 'puppy walker'. He had the necessary experience (five years) as a beat constable required to walk Tessa over 'the ground', which was what they called the area patrolled by Haringey police.

Tessa had never encountered a man like Harry before; it was only later, off duty and alone in her room in the Section House and therefore capable of rational thought, that she realised he was what David Attenborough had meant when he described a magnificent lion as an 'Alpha Male'. Harry Sansom was Alpha-Plus.

He was also her guardian angel during her first, hesitant, new-girl-on-the-relief weeks, helping, guiding, protecting in a way that bound her to him with hoops of steel. Right from the start Tessa placed his image in the niche marked 'The Ideal Policeman', and the rightness of her decision was confirmed on her very first stretch of night duty. They had just paraded and, sticking close to her idol, Tessa was about to leave the station when there was a 'shout' of 'Suspects on' (premises). The address given meant nothing to her but Harry knew it at once.

'Right – last one there buys the first round!' he shouted as he took off at a run. Still nervously checking she had everything Tessa trotted after him, only to discover she did not have her notebook.

'Oh, God!' Mewing with panic, she fled back to her

locker, snatched it and ran back to find a furious Harry sitting in the only car standing for all the others had gone. He had a face like thunder. 'Come on, girl,' he snarled, 'what the hell are you playing at?'

'Sorry,' Tessa mumbled, deeply ashamed, trying to crawl into the upholstery.

'Well, we've lost the lead, that's for sure. Fasten that bloody seat belt and let's see if we can catch up . . .'

He had been gunning the engine and now took off at speed, taking corners on two wheels, and apart from the sound of the engine he did it silently, no 'blues and twos'. None of the cars had used lights and sirens, but when at last they turned into the square they were all there, already parked, lights off and empty.

'Shit!'

Tessa cringed at the note in Harry's voice. Oh, God, she thought, I've blown it . . . He'll never forgive me for this! She already knew how he hated to lose at anything. He was *very* competitive.

Harry cut the engine and was out of the car before its growl had subsided, leaving her to follow. By the light of the streetlamps she could see they were in a private close of some half a dozen houses, each large, detached, at least six-bedroomed and double-garaged, and centred in a large garden. The house in question was dark, no lights anywhere, but in addition to its ornate iron front gates, its double front door was also wide open. There was nobody to be seen and it was eerily quiet. Harry had disappeared, so in a nervous panic Tessa ran after him, through the gate, up the path, straight through the open front door and into a large, dark hall. Where she at once fell into a large, black hole.

The burglars had thoughtfully lifted the carpet in order to

remove the first four or five floorboards, something she was to learn was common practice, so she went into the gap up to her knees, ruining her tights, painfully scraping her shins, and letting out a yelp of shock and agony. At the same time as she fell through the hole, her flailing arms struck the neat pile of extracted floorboards leaning against the newel post of the staircase, causing them to fall with a clatter.

'What the hell . . .' someone bellowed, and a mortified Tessa was exposed in the light of two accurately aimed torches, scarlet with embarrassed shame at having made such a prat of herself.

'Jesus Sweet! Will you look at that . . .' The two policemen fell about laughing until the sound of running feet and the shout: 'Look out! The bastards are doing a runner!' had them whirling to see the shapes of three men all but falling down the stairs two at a time, leaping over Tessa, who ducked instinctively, before having it away down the close, hotly pursued by the owners of the torches.

As the noise faded, somebody upstairs asked loudly, in disgusted tones: 'What stupid prat announced our presence, then?'

Tessa was so mortified she burst into tears.

'Are you all right?' She could see him only as a bulky shape in the darkness but she recognised the voice.

'Oh, Harry . . .' she wailed. 'I'm sorry . . . I didn't realise there was a hole . . . nobody told me . . .'

He shone his torch at her, exposing her shamed and tear-streaked face, her dusty uniform, the floorboards all around. 'No, love, I can see that,' he said, without so much as a hint of reproof. Bending down, he held out both hands. 'Here, let me help you out of there.'

He clicked his tongue sympathetically when he saw her

shredded tights and bleeding shins. 'Let's get you back to the station for some first aid,' he soothed. 'You've made a right mess of those lovely legs.'

Tessa sniffed. 'I didn't know about the hole,' she apologised again.

'No, well, that's something you learn as you go along. Tricks of the trade, you might say. I know them and you don't. I should have waited for you to come in with me. My fault, sorry.'

Tessa sniffed again. 'No, it's not. It's mine. If I hadn't had to go back for my notebook we wouldn't have been last. Now you'll have to stand the first round.'

'Then learn from it and don't do it again. When you go on parade, you go on ready for action, right?'

Tessa nodded meekly. Whatever Harry said was gospel to her.

'Right. Let's get you seen to, then.'

But he drove around for fifteen minutes to enable her to compose her shattered nerves and restore some of her battered self-esteem before taking her back to the station. Nor did he ever tell anyone why they were so late back.

From then on, he could do no wrong in her eyes. Nor in the eyes of any other woman who met his flame blues. This was confirmed to Tessa some weeks later when, by now feeling more confident of herself and brave enough to ask, she had enquired of the other WPC on her relief, a girl with fourteen months' service behind her and an obviously close relationship with Harry, why he was known as 'H'.

The WPC had grinned. The new plonk's naïvety was the talk of the station.

'Because he's hung like a horse, of course!'

Tessa had gone scarlet. But the new knowledge became the cause of some disturbingly erotic dreams.

Naturally, the WPC had gleefully told the story in the canteen, which was how Tessa came to acquire her own nickname: Grassy Bank, otherwise Verge, short for Virgin. Bets were placed as to who would be the first man to mow it.

Harry was favourite, since apart from his looks and reputation, he was in prime position as her puppy walker, working closely with her, introducing the new probationer to the people who mattered, teaching her the ins and outs of the streets until she was familiar with them and confident enough to go out on her own.

Everybody knew Harry and everybody liked him. Especially the women. When he went into the baker's for a couple of ham rolls to go with their coffee his were always extra thick, and came with a couple of unasked for jam doughnuts. And on the stalls in the market it was always: 'Nah, 'arry boy, 'ave it on me.'

Tessa was no different. Within days she was hopelessly in thrall, and never having experienced such powerful feelings before, was totally at a loss as to how to handle them. Normally very self-contained, around Harry she found it hard to control these new and disturbing emotions. A chance meeting of eyes made her nipples harden and her stomach drop, while if their hands should touch she went up in flames. When he smiled at her she felt it down to her toenails. That very first time, as their eyes had met – his so blue they burned – something had hooked a finger around her heart and lifted it right out of her body. So overwhelmed was she by him that often she did not hear what he said, had to say stupidly, flushing bright red, 'Sorry?' so that he would repeat it. In her first almost-nineteen years Tessa had had very little to do with men who were not of the cloth. Harry therefore had the effect of a direct hit. That he should find her worthy of his consideration was something she had actually gone to church and fervently prayed for, even though past experience had taught her that while God was inexorable in demanding that you give up everything for Him, He was not so forthcoming with the *quid pro quo*. It never occurred to her inexperienced mind that her impact on him was as startling as his on her. Harry went to church only for family christenings, marriages and funerals; a Bishop's daughter was a totally unknown quantity.

With his simplistic approach to religion he had expected to find her boringly pure, prim and proper, and about as sexually interesting as a drink of water. He had not expected to find that her lovely voice with its crisp, upper-class accent, her slender body and endless, elegant legs in their black nylons, were a decided come-on. Harry had not had much use for virgins since ceasing to be one at the age of fourteen, but something about Tessa Paget's lambent innocence had lasered through the rusty shell of his attitude to women, which had become corroded by his unfailing success with them. She was so wide-eyed and legless with admiration for the great Harry Sansom that he had no choice but to let out his ego as he gave her the benefit of his experience, which she proceeded to absorb like a sponge.

But it did not take him long to discover that the Barbie Doll had brains. When he also discovered that thanks to her umpteen 'O' and 'A' Levels she had not had to sit the entrance exam as he had – twice – he was truly impressed. He had always been of the opinion that acquiring knowledge for its own sake was a waste of time. Until he saw how useful hers could be to him when she offered to help him study for the Sergeant's exam he was supposedly swotting for.

Harry found studying hard. He had left school at fifteen and marked time until at seventeen he could join the Royal Marines, so he had few educational qualifications and making headway with his studies was hard. Tessa, on the other hand, had no difficulty explaining things which, as printed words, he found it hard to untangle. More important, she had boundless faith in him, which spurred him on to prove her right. A further – equally important – consideration was that it gave him the opportunity to get her into his room at the Section House.

When he ploughed the exam she was even more devastated than he was. *He* had to comfort *her*, and he did it the only way he knew how. He put his arms around her, saying soothingly: 'It's not your fault, love. I was the one who failed.'

'But I don't understand why.' Tessa was distressed, feeling it to be her fault, not his. 'You knew everything when we had that question and answer session the night before the exam. Did you miss something out? Mix something up?'

'God only knows. But most people take the exam at least twice. Only the geniuses pass first time. I know somebody who took three tries to get it, so don't upset yourself.'

'But I so wanted you to pass. You are such a good policeman, Harry. I was awfully lucky to be put on your relief. You'll make a marvellous Sergeant so you must try again.'

'Oh, I will . . . so long as you help me?'

She had looked up at him, her big blue eyes so wide with

adoration he just had to kiss her, having to run his tongue over her lips to get her to open her mouth.

He had gone more slowly and carefully with Tessa Paget than he had ever done with any woman before because he had recognised at once that she was different; not one of the station slags, such as Poppy, known as Martini since with her it was a case of 'any place, any time, anywhere', or Turtle, who had acquired her name because once she was on her back she was fucked. Nobody had 'had' Tessa. She was not the kind of girl you 'had'. She could make any man uncomfortable by just looking at him with that cool, clear-water gaze of hers. But under Harry's delicate coaxing that night she had opened up more than her mouth; let him unbutton her shirt, put his mouth to those pale pink rosebuds, tongue and nip at them with his teeth, making her quiver and catch her breath as he made her acutely aware of a body she had hitherto taken for granted. And not only hers but his.

Having established his beach-head, each time after that he had advanced a little further, but still slowly overall. One wrong move and she would make a run for it. A fast one, for he had discovered that Tessa was as fleet of foot as she was of mind. As it was, the first time she'd felt his own personal truncheon straining through his trousers her eyes had dilated and she had leaped from his lap like a scalded cat. It had taken him a long time and a lot of patience to recover *that* lost ground; still longer to get her to the stage where she would not only look at it but actually touch it. She seemed to regard a man's pride and joy with both fear and revulsion.

He had bragged to the locker-room, nevertheless. 'I've got her just where I want her.'

'It took you long enough to get this far,' an envious voice

sniped sourly. 'You'll have done your twenty-five by the time you finally get to do her.'

'That's because this one is no push-over. Which is what makes the fact that I've got this far that much more of a triumph. From now on, lads, it's downhill all the way.'

But by the time she had been at Haringey a year it was Flash Harry who had fallen, so deeply in love he could not see the sky any more. Having her – and all to himself at that – had become an obsession. Every time he saw the way other men looked at her, molten bolts of jealousy fused his already scrambled brains. He wanted her badly, and not just that delectable body. He wanted Tessa to feel for him what he felt for her – and for the first time in his life he was prepared to do for her what he had not been prepared to do for any other woman.

Marry her.

After all, when he totted up her pros and cons, the total was eminently and satisfyingly pro. She was as virginal as he could have wished, but he knew by her reaction to what she had allowed so far that when she did finally take to full, penetrative sex it would be with all the ardour he could wish, since you only ever had to tell or show her once. She was young enough and adoringly malleable enough to mould to the shape he wanted; she was capable of bearing the children he intended to have – eventually – and whatever else he wanted her to be he was confident he could make her into it.

The con was the difference in class.

Tessa was the kind of woman who would normally have been out of his league. Had she not joined the job he would never in a million years have got to meet her. But he *had* met her, more incredibly he had bowled her over, which only proved that when it came down to the bedrock of sex and physical attraction, class had nothing to do with it.

So he asked her to marry him.

And she accepted.

Afterwards they went out to celebrate, and by the time they came back to the Section House Tessa had been plied with enough alcohol to loosen every single inhibition. When they got to her room and he followed her in she did not object, nor was there any protest when he began first to kiss and caress her as a preliminary to undressing her; instead, she eagerly began to do the same to him.

They were engaged now, she explained owlishly, so it was all right. Centuries ago a betrothal was as binding as marriage; she herself had been brought up to believe that. They were promised to each other. That was what made the difference.

She got no argument from Harry.

When they were both naked she prowled round him, the liquor making her bold enough to do her own touching and caressing.

'But you are beautiful, Harry,' she whispered, overcome by her first proper sight of male nudity. 'I've only ever known one other beautiful man in my life and he was my brother.'

'I never knew you had a brother?'

'He's dead.'

She was staring at his equipment so fixedly her eyes went out of focus. 'I always thought – this – ' she gestured to his male member, standing to attention so stiffly it was all but touching his belly button – 'was ugly and horrible, but yours doesn't frighten me at all.'

At six feet two inches, Harry weighed thirteen stones ten pounds. His shoulders were broad, his waist narrow, his hips lean. Nor was he hairy. Tessa had regarded hirsute men with loathing since she had seen the one in her brother's bed. Long afterwards, before she was finally able to rid herself of the image, she had remembered what she had not consciously taken in at the time: the thickly matted chest and hairy arms of Rupert's lover. Harry's chest was smooth and shaped like a centurion's breastplate.

'Beautiful,' she repeated, stepping close – to run a suddenly needful hand over it.

'Not as beautiful as you are. But we do go together. Look . . .' Harry turned her to face the mirror which was inside the wardrobe door of every room in the Section House. 'See.'

She had examined both their bodies: hers almost stylised in its feminine curves and slender lines, her waist narrow, her breasts small, but full and high; his typifying broad-shouldered, well-muscled masculinity.

'Yes,' she agreed, with the awed realisation of one who finally sees that the wood is made up of individual trees. 'We do, don't we?'

'We fit,' he murmured, having noted the intake of breath which had marked her first sight of his tumescence in all its much-admired glory. 'Let me show you how well we fit . . .'

He began by using his mouth and his hands, and as the demonstration progressed, Tessa's body began to tremble and her breath to catch, her blood to roar and her juices to flow. An almost screaming tension built in her because of the exquisite friction of skin on skin, and because of what he was doing to her. He set her ablaze with a *need* she either had to satisfy or die.

'Love me, Harry,' she moaned against his mouth, pressing

herself against his questing tongue but wanting more than that inside her. 'Please . . . love me *now*.'

With his first thrust he felt her tense for a microsecond and then as he broke the slight barrier and penetrated deep, deeper, deepest, she inhaled a long, drawn-out 'Aaaaahhhh . . .' as her hot, virginal tightness contracted, gripping him, massaging him, making him gasp: 'No! Stay still or I'll come!'

Brought up to be obedient, Tessa instantly obeyed the voice of authority and they lay unmoving while he fought for control because for the first time ever he was having trouble withholding. Only when he knew he could, did he begin to move. Slowly, deeply, plunging in and withdrawing almost completely before plunging in again. Tessa began to moan and her hips lifted as she instinctively began to thrust back.

'Oh, God . . . oh, God . . . oh, God . . .' Each small spurt of words accompanied a cock-thrust, deliriously slow at first, bringing unendurable pleasure as the friction created sexual melt-down. The spurts increased speed even as Harry did, faster and faster, until they were both mindless bodies concentrating on squeezing the last, ultimate pleasure from each other before their little deaths occurred. When they did, Tessa's reaction was to open her mouth to scream, which Harry blocked by covering it with his own: this was the Section House after all, and he did not want knowing looks where his future wife was concerned. But the cords of Tessa's throat stood out when she made animal sounds deep in her throat as she felt Harry tense and all but snap his teeth as he ejaculated copiously and, it seemed, endlessly, Tessa's vaginal muscles milking him until he fell forward, drained and spent, gasping for breath.

When he could, he raised himself slightly to kiss her own, open, deep-breathing mouth. 'You are a natural,' he panted, sounding pleased with himself. Could he pick 'em or could he pick 'em? He hadn't had anything so good for ages, and he'd had them all. 'I haven't come like that in years . . . you too . . . you're soaked.' Then he smiled. Smugly. 'Told you we'd fit.'

They were married six months later in spite of parental opposition. His mother and hers. United for the one and only time in the mutual conviction that their children were absolutely wrong for each other.

His because Tessa was: 'not for the likes of us, Harry. She don't know our ways and we don't know 'ers.'

Hers because Harry was plainly: 'Simply not one of us, darling.'

But Tessa was stubborn. Having discovered the joys of independence, and knowing that she did not need her mother's permission for anything any more since she was of age, nothing Dorothea could say had any effect. Tessa was mad for Harry Sansom and she was going to have him.

Harry likewise was deaf to his own mother's forebodings. Yes, he was well aware that Tessa was different. That fact did not stop him wanting to marry her; in fact it was what had attracted him in the first place. He hadn't wanted to marry any of the others, had he? This was the one he did want to marry and marry her he would – in a register office if need be.

Which was when his mother knew he was serious, since Sansoms always had big church weddings.

Both mothers eventually met at the wedding, recognised themselves immediately and as quickly loathed each other.

'They'll come round,' Harry had said to Tessa confidently. Everybody liked his mother.

Not to our house they won't, Tessa had sensed but forborne to tell him. Not when we are both in anyway. You are the only Sansom with any time for me, my love.

And so it had been. Dorothea came to visit her daughter only when she knew her son-in-law was working. Mrs Sansom and Harry's sisters came once only, and obviously hated every minute of it. But Harry never let a week go by without visiting his mother.

Alone.

Now, eleven years later, Tessa could look at her husband in all his male splendour and feel nothing.

Her mother had been right. It had been a matter of hero-worship, hormonal urges and the frantic desire to procreate – except that Harry had ordained: 'No children for at least five years,' and like the obedient little wife she was then, she had a coil fitted – the pill produced unpleasant side effects. Now, she was shudderingly grateful that she had been so tractable, for she had realised some time ago that it had not been love she'd felt for Harry. It had been infatuation.

He noisily turned a page of his paper. 'How long to dinner?' he enquired.

'Seven-thirty.'

'Good. I'm starved. I hope you did plenty of roast potatoes?'

'Yes. Lots.'

'Good.'

Tessa had taken a Cordon Bleu course because it was the sort of thing girls of her class were expected to do, but she enjoyed cooking for its own sake and because she regarded good food as one of life's pleasures. As a new bride she had been eager to show off her skills to her husband in her very own kitchen, but to her disappointment she discovered he did not like what he called 'messes', which meant anything with a sauce, or 'bits' (by which he meant herbs) in it. He loathed mushrooms, was doubtful about salad dressings, very suspicious of garlic and shuddered at kidneys, at the same time refusing to eat any vegetable not represented on his father's allotment. Harry's taste ran to the meat and two veg, deep dish pies and tarts – with custard, never cream – the mince and dumplings, the pies and mash, of his childhood, and he expected his wife to continue the tradition. It had taken Tessa years to get him to try redcurrant jelly instead of mint sauce with his lamb, and to eat it roasted with rosemary.

'Look, love,' he had said, seeing her crestfallen face one Sunday early into the marriage when she had slaved all morning over the preparation of boned, garlic-stuffed poussin, 'I wasn't brought up fancy like you. I like good, plain food and lots of it. You're learning a treat, but if you want Mum to give you a few pointers then all you have to do is ask. She taught my sisters and they all came up trumps.'

He had gently closed the *Larousse Art of Cooking*. 'Don't think I don't appreciate you doing all this for me. I do . . . the trying, I mean. It's just that I prefer more down-to-earth dishes than – what do you call these things?'

'Poussin. It means small chicken.'

'Yeah. Well, I love chicken, but roasted plain, no garlic, with new potatoes, a nice cauliflower, peas picked fresh from the allotment and a lovely bit of stuffing.'

He had tipped her chin, smiled down at her, blue eyes tender.

'We're newly married and I can't expect you to know

everything about me yet. I don't know everything about you, do I? But I'm having a great time finding out.'

And he had turned off the oven and drawn her into the bedroom and rendered her mindless with pleasure and dewy with moisture which he lapped up with his tongue. Then he had taken her out to a place he knew where they served exactly the kind of Sunday dinner he liked. Tessa sighed at the recollection. Things had been good then. They had been happy. *That* had been love. Hadn't it?

This particular Sunday Tessa had caught up on household chores – the washing and ironing in particular – and after putting the lamb in the oven had decided, as there were quite a few bills in the clip, to do the household accounts, which meant balancing Harry's cheque book. He had the infuriating habit of filling in cheque stubs but never subtracting them from the total, thus never knowing how much he had in his account. Until Tessa balanced it.

For their first few years, while his wife was still under his spell, Harry had taken it upon himself – as he appropriated everything he saw as part and parcel of his 'rights' as the Senior Partner – to handle their finances, until it became apparent to Tessa that he was the originator of the old saw: 'A fool and his money are soon parted'.

'But, darling, we have two salaries going into the bank every month,' she had protested in horror when she saw the state of their account. 'What on earth are you doing with it all? Why aren't these bills paid? Why is there a red one from the Electricity Board and a pay-up-or-we-cut-you-off from British Telecom? And have you seen the size of your credit card account? Just look at this bank statement! We have only the one joint account yet seventy-five per cent of the cheques and charges are yours!'

'This flat costs a lot to run so don't think I'm spending it *all* on myself!' Harry had bridled, in a way which made it all too plain that he was. Harry had 'enthusiasms'. They had gone through photography – a hideously expensive Pentax plus all the gear and the spare bedroom set up as a darkroom: picture framing – that had lasted through one set of pictures taken with the Pentax during a holiday in the Greek islands; his Harley-Davidson, until he came off it at Chiswick roundabout; and the final one – a horse (one of his friends from Hendon had been in the Mounted Branch and Harry had been seized with envy when he saw him on television, dealing with a mob in Trafalgar Square). That had also gone by the board when Brigadier – which was what the horse was called – threw Harry over his head one morning, bruising the latter's pride more than his body. Brigadier had been sold within the week, but all the tack, including the expensive hand-made English saddle which had been Tessa's Christmas present to her husband, had hung in the garage for months until she put an ad in *Horse and Hound* and sold the lot for a good price.

After she had taken over the finances the joint account had become three; one each plus a third 'household' account into which each transferred an equal share every month. What Harry did with his own money was his business, and she never asked, but she was damned if she was going to allow him to squander hers.

That had caused their first rift, because while Harry was willing for his wife to handle the household finances, he had not expected her to be so adamant about handling her own. His mother had been given her housekeeping by his father and that arrangement had worked a treat.

'Ah, but your mother never had a job outside the home,

did she?' Tessa had pointed out when he argued his case. 'I do. This money is what *I* earn, Harry, not you.'

He had not liked that but was unable to refute it. Let her make a hash of it, he rationalised in his own favour. It was a well-known fact that people who were born to money did not know how to handle it, since they had accountants and lawyers and such to look after it for them. It thus confounded him utterly when Tessa proved to be the kind who could make one pound do the work of five, and always knew where every single one had gone. For the first time in his life he had money in the bank – Tessa had cajoled him into saving a regular amount – and no debts, not even a mortgage, because the house they now lived in in Richmond had been left to Tessa by her maternal great-grandmother, Clarissa Norton.

When they were first married, Harry had wanted to live near his family. Their first home had therefore been a police flat in Bow, which Harry wangled by sweet-talking the Super's clerk into allocating it to him, telling him there was a bottle in it. When, five years later, the chance came not only to get away from Bow but the giant octopus of Harry's family, Tessa had seized it, and after discussions with her family solicitor had used money already in her possession to convert her grandmother's mansion into five large flats.

Harry had not been so easy convince. When she had taken him to see the house on the bluff above the river, he had been aghast.

'Live here! In this huge place? What for? Richmond is the back of beyond . . . and I never did like West London.'

'You wait until the conversion is done; it will all look entirely different. Plus we will have a secure income from the other four flats. And no rent or mortgage. We've been talking for ages about buying our own house. Now we can have one and it won't cost us a penny!'

Having grown used to more money than he had ever had, the promise of more was the clincher for Harry, as Tessa had known it would be, and when he finally saw the finished result he approved of the fact that she had chosen for them the best set of rooms, the one called the 'garden' flat. It had five large rooms as well as kitchen and bath, all with high ceilings and big windows. The enormous living room opened out on to a glorious garden which overlooked the river from Richmond heights and there was a vast garage in what had once been stables. No mortgage meant rates only, which in turn meant Harry could have the new XR3i he had set his heart on. When he finally made Sergeant he had automatically been transferred to Battersea. From Richmond, driving to work would be a doddle.

He had not been too happy, though, about Tessa's taking over a lot of her grandmother's furniture. It had been bad enough when her mother had given them a lot of stuff that had been in storage since she and the Bishop had moved from the Palace into the new, smaller house. Dorothea had pronounced it nonsense to waste money buying furniture when there was so much waiting to be used but Harry was not best pleased. Inherited furniture looked as though you could not afford to buy your own. It was a matter of pride that when you set up as a newly married couple you did so with everything brand, spanking new to match. It had to last the rest of your life, after all. His mother still had the three-piece utility suite that had been bought on the never-never, way back in 1947.

But his doubts were smoothed away when Tessa explained how not having to buy furniture would mean so much more to spend on holidays. Harry had become addicted to holidaying abroad, and was only too happy to have once a year become twice a year. He became the very first Sansom to visit the United States, not to mention Hong Kong, and the Caribbean. His siblings had never got further than Benidorm or Tenerife.

But when his family came *en masse* to take a look at the new house, it was at once obvious to Tessa that none of them liked it. For some reason they spoke in voices only just above a whisper, and sat on the edges of their chairs, and when Tessa had used her grandmother's Rockingham china at tea, they had handled the cups and saucers uneasily.

'Far too fancy,' she had heard one of Harry's sisters mutter to another. 'Like living in a bleedin' museum . . .'

Tessa had looked round the lovely rooms, filled with sunlight and polished, lovingly tended, eighteenth-century furniture, and realised that what to her was beautiful was neither comfortable nor beautiful to her husband or his family. Just old-fashioned.

Which was when she finally began to accept what she had been struggling with for some time: in the throes of her physical passion for her husband, she had totally misjudged his basic character. While she had developed, matured from a girl into a woman, one who was capable of continuing development, Harry was cemented into attitudes that had been engraved on to a mind which did not approve of anything it neither knew nor understood. He was incapable of seeing any point of view but his own. Worse, his innate selfishness and lack of imagination made it impossible for him to understand either his wife's emotions or state of mind. Harry was rich in physical skills, sexual and otherwise, but he was emotionally impoverished and did not like, because he did not understand, the changes in his wife. To his way of thinking she was stepping beyond the boundaries he had defined.

When she had joined the job, she had been the novice, he the experienced copper generously prepared to allow her the benefit of that experience. It was when she began to learn from her own, to rely less on him and more on herself, that the rot set in. When she passed her Sergeant's exam first go, his reaction had rocked her on her heels.

He furiously resented it. He felt it 'showed him up'. He was willing to acknowledge that his wife had brains, but it was her duty as his wife to keep them hidden except when he told her to put them on show. The least she could have done was fail her first try . . . Sailing through it with a high pass mark first time was markedly lacking in respect. He had his first fit of the sulks. Tessa was disbelieving until she realised he meant every word he said. He really did think she should have failed out of consideration for him. But they got over it, mainly thanks to her efforts at cajoling him down from his high horse.

But when she told him she had been selected for the Accelerated Promotion Course, he had looked at her with that flat, cold stare which turned his blue eyes to marbles.

'What do you want with Bramshill and its bunch of wankers?'

'I've had six years in uniform. I thought I'd try for the CID, do something different.'

'Different! You mean selfish! I never heard of anything so bloody self-centred in all my life!'

Oh yes you did, Tessa had thought. I could give you chapter and verse of a dozen or more instances when, if I had objected to something you wanted to do, all hell would have broken loose. But she knew that if she reminded him of them now he would turn even more ugly. So she reined in her tongue and stuck to the matter in hand. No matter how he blustered, she was adamant. 'What difference does it make which branch I am in? We've never worked together since Haringey. How long have you been at Battersea now? While I've been at West End Central *and* Paddington Green. I don't dictate to you what you should do or where you should go in the Job.'

'I should bloody well hope not!'

'What gives you the right to dictate to me then?'

'Because I'm your bloody husband, that's why!'

'Yes, husband. Which is not spelled o-w-n-e-r.'

He had glared at her, face red, fists clenched, before flinging out of the house in a fury. She knew that had he not, he would have hit her.

Six months later she was posted to City Road as Detective Sergeant, where she worked first on an Enquiry Team, then on the Crime Desk, and eventually on a Murder Squad. Harry, meanwhile, spurred on by his wife's onward and upward trend and his mother's tight-lipped and gimlet-eye disapproval of his evident inability to control her, had been studying for his Inspector's exam, coached as best she could by his wife.

And failed.

Unfortunately, at the same time, Tessa got her course at Bramshill, and three months later left the police college as an Inspector. Harry neither wrote nor telephoned all the time she was there, and the first time she suggested coming home for the weekend told her brusquely he was spending it at his mother's. The second time he said he would be going away with his brother for a weekend's fishing. The third time he was, he said, working. Tessa did not bother again. When she had told him she was to be promoted the marriage suffered real, lasting damage. 'An Inspector! You! Male Inspectors are bad enough but a female one is taking things too bloody far. I don't want you to become an Inspector. We're all right as we are.' Tessa had looked into the hot blue eyes and become aware of an added ingredient: jealousy. But he had hidden it behind his usual blustering contempt. 'I don't know why the hell you wanted to go to Bramshill in the first place. It's full of people who think they're too good for the rest of us.'

'I was told I was Bramshill material.'

He rounded on her. '*Told!* What do you mean, *told?*'

'By Ian Mackay.' He had been 'A' relief's Inspector at Haringey, and was now a Chief Inspector at Barnes.

'*McKay!*' Harry had flushed. Dangerously. 'What do you mean, McKay told you? When did you see him?'

'He was at the station to see the Superintendent and I met him on the stairs. He said he had been hearing good things about me and had come to the conclusion that I filled all the necessary requirements for a Bramshill course.'

'How the hell would he know?'

'He was my very first Inspector for three long years – remember?'

'All that bastard wants is to get into your knickers. He always fancied you. A man in that state will tell you anything,' Harry dismissed scornfully.

'Ian McKay is infinitely superior to Jim Napier. That small-minded, petty excuse for a senior officer made my life a misery precisely because I would not "let him into my knickers" as you so graphically put it! He blocked every application I made for transfer and ran a personal vendetta against me because I had the effrontery to turn him down.

Ian McKay never so much as tried! He always treated me as policewoman first and a woman second! I'd like to have seen Napier recommend me for *anything* that could lead to advancement! If Ian is of the opinion I have what it takes, then I am going to go for it! Every step of the way.'

'Oh, Ian, is it? Since when have you been on bloody first-name terms with *Chief Inspector* McKay?'

'Since he asked me to call him Ian.'

'And in just what kind of circumstances would he want you to do that, I wonder?'

'Oh, for God's sake, Harry. Can't you *ever* visualise a situation between a man and a woman that does *not* involve sex?'

But Harry had mounted his favourite high horse and once on it, used it as an excuse to ride off into the sunset with a WPC from the Family Unit. For the first time he deliberately went 'over-the-side', something that from then on became a regular occurrence whenever Tessa did something that displeased him or which he regarded as demeaning to his standing. It was his way of reasserting his authority. His wife was breaking the vows she had made to love, honour and *obey*, so why should he bother to keep the ones he had made about forsaking all others? It also meant that Tessa had to do without while he got it elsewhere; his way of punishing her.

Which was another mistake, for Tessa had discovered, after the first, greedy rapture, that she did not need sex on a daily basis. It was Harry who had to have his daily fix. She enjoyed it, having become – thanks to him – adept in the giving as well as receiving of pleasure, but it was not the absolute necessity to her that it was to him. Naturally, canteen gossip soon made her aware of just what was going on, and with whom, because Harry made sure of it.

In time, as he always did, he came round, for though he liked to throw his sexual weight around, when he missed his target and got nothing for his pains but bruises from his own fall, there was not much point. Her indifference also scared him, for he sensed that he was losing his last hold on her: the sexual one.

But the crack became a rift which was still widening.

Having done the accounts, Tessa turned to the correspondence, and picking up the beautifully engraved invitation from her desk, said: 'I can't delay replying to this invitation any longer, Harry. Have you made up your mind? Are you coming with me to Caroline's wedding or not?

He spoke from behind the paper. 'Why should I? You never came to Cissy's Silver Wedding.'

'How could I? My mother sent for me the night before the party because it was not known if Daddy would live through it.'

'That was all of eight weeks ago, and like always he's still hanging on. You *could* have – *should have* – come with me to that party, you knew how important it was to Mum that all the family be there, but no . . . You used the excuse that your father – who has been a death's door ever since I've known you – was ringing its bell again and you seized on it with relief. Any excuse not to have to sit down at the same table with *my* family. Well, I'll be damned if I'll come with you to the hoity-toity wedding of some second or third cousin or whatever. Nor am I tarting myself up in top hat and tails just to drink champagne in some fancy marquee on somebody's ancient lawn. You're so bloody used to going places and doing things on your own, why change now?'

Obviously Harry had been diligently storing grievances. Come to think of it, all the signs had been there had she but bothered to notice. Trouble was, where Harry was concerned she was noticing less and less. With hindsight she saw that there had been frequent absences, long silences, short temper and no sex. Which meant he was over the side again.

Now what had she done to wound his macho sensibilities? She couldn't think of anything. It had to be that damned Silver Wedding . . .

So when she said pointedly: 'The invitation is addressed to Mr and Mrs Sansom,' he snapped: 'I don't give a damn what it says. I was probably only asked as a sop anyway. I always am.'

'Don't be ridiculous,' Tessa snapped back, aware that the rattle of the paper as he folded it made it clear how close he was to the edge, but past caring. 'They want us both. We are invited as a couple, Harry.' She was in no mood for yet another brangle, and as her mother would also be at the wedding, wanted to give her no cause for conjecture. The less Dorothea knew the better – for the time being, anyway. So she added as a flattering sop: 'You know you always look good in a morning suit.'

'Rented from Moss Bros?'

'Lots of people rent from Moss Bros.'

'Not the people *you* know. Their suits all have the right label sewn in the jacket.'

It was obvious he was spoiling for a fight. Whenever he sulked, the explosion always simmered slowly before coming to the boil. Now, as he finished folding the paper, she saw that his colour was up and the blue eyes had been switched to High Beam.

I can't take much more of this, she thought tightly, feeling her own, desperately worn patience tear as it struggled to break free from the control she had imposed on it. Why the hell should I? And when it comes right down to it, I can't take much more of you either. For years now I have struggled to accommodate you and your macho stupidities, but enough is enough.

Icily, she said: 'I don't notice you saying that when we go to police functions.'

'That's different. I have a lot of *friends* in the job.'

Tessa closed her eyes. It was no use. He was bent and determined. The hell with it! she thought. Enough is enough. I am sick and tired of backing off. For what? What is there to preserve any more?

She struck first. Getting to her feet, she said in a no-nonsense voice: 'Harry, we have got to get to the bottom of this inferiority complex of yours. You knew who and what I was when you asked me to marry you. Why has it started to matter so much to you now?'

He flung the paper to the floor. 'Because you are no longer the girl I married.'

He was starting off from it today. Hitherto they had always gone round the roundabout until they reached the turn off which led to the point where it was his right to complain about the unwelcome changes in his wife, which in turn led to the dead-end where she was supposed humbly to apologise for upsetting not only him but the status quo.

The trouble was, Tessa no longer saw it that way. Nobody should rule. Marriage was a partnership. Moreover, an *equal* partnership. If women had been able to accept a subordinate position for centuries, why couldn't men make the necessary adjustment to level pegging?

'I should hope not!' she replied tartly. 'I was only twenty-one when I married you. Neither of us is the person we were then. It's called growing up.'

'How about growing away?'

'All right, so we don't get to spend as much time together as couples do; we're police officers. It's par for the course in our job.'

'It's not bloody par for the course to have a wife who is superior in rank to her husband!'

At last. The thorn in Harry's macho pride.

'Since we don't work together, you never have occasion to have to address me as Ma'am,' Tessa pointed out logically.

'That doesn't alter the fact that a husband shouldn't have to say it to a wife in the first place.'

Tessa finally lost her patience. 'In other words, you were happy for me to be a skipper, like you, but being an Inspector is getting above myself, as your mother would say?'

'Leave my mother out of it.'

'Would that I could! She has your strings tight in her hands at all times. By her lights, I should never have taken that Accelerated Promotion Course, not after you had failed the Inspector's exam. I should have held back, put your pride before my ambition and toed the line which you, of course, had drawn. That's what a good wife is supposed to do, isn't it? Because that's what your mother has always done – exactly as she was told to do by your father.'

Harry's blue eyes blazed as his head jerked up. She had said the unsayable.

His voice made her flinch when he snarled: 'My mother has been a *real* wife to my father for the past forty-five years.'

'Oh, yes? And you'd like me to live the same "reality" wouldn't you? Hobbled by children, chained to the house, but always with your boots cleaned and your shirts ironed and a hot meal ready and waiting, just the way you want it.

Never mind what *I* want. Your wishes would take precedence every time.'

'If I was the one who was providing the roof over your head and putting the food in your mouth, they bloody well ought to!'

'Which is what you resent, isn't it? That I earn my own living – worse – I actually have the temerity to earn more than you do!'

'I didn't marry a smart-arse career woman – or so I thought. I wanted a wife, a home and children.'

'I was willing to have children back at the beginning, if you remember. There was nothing I wanted more than to have your children. You were the one who said: "Let's wait."'

'That was before you got the bloody bit between your teeth. You took all I had to teach and then put me back on the shelf! How the hell was I supposed to stand for that?'

'You encouraged me to take the Sergeant's exam!

'But I wasn't expecting you to go into the bloody CID, or swan off to Bramshill for that matter!'

'So when they offered it to me I should have said, "Thank you, but no thank you – my husband wouldn't like it"?'

'You should have asked me first.'

'*Asked!* For what, your permission? And there was I thinking you would actually be pleased for me!' It never occurred to me you would be jealous, she thought.

That he still was came through loud and clear when he said bitterly: 'You've never been the same since then. That Accelerated Promotion Course doubled the size of your ambitions – not to mention your head!'

They glared at each other. Then Tessa said: 'I am not

going to argue any more. I am sick and tired of arguing. Perhaps – '

For the umpteenth time she found herself biting it back; only this time she thought even as she did so: but it can't harm Daddy any more. Daddy is beyond being hurt by anything I do ever again . . .

All during his career Bishop Paget had been known for his unfashionably outspoken views on divorce, which were that what God had made, man had absolutely no right to put asunder. In that respect he had always been at one with the church from which his own had been torn by Henry VIII and it was why, while he had been capable of understanding what was going on about him, Tessa had resolutely gritted her teeth and done whatever she could to shore up her collapsing marriage. After what the scandal of Rupert's violent death had done to her father, no one was going to be able to say she had completed his destruction by flying in the face of his deeply held beliefs. But this latest stroke had removed him to the point where nothing could hurt him any more.

So when Harry rasped: 'Perhaps what?' Tessa faced him with an expression that had his own changing for the worse.

'Perhaps we should call it a day. If I'm not what you want in a wife then why keep up the pretence? Let's end it. That way you can ask your mother to find you one who meets the Sansom Specification. God knows, she made it plain from the start that I never did.'

'I don't want a divorce!' It came out doing the three minute mile. Face congested with anger – and something else, she could not tell whether it was shock or pride – Harry left the sofa to move towards his wife. Tessa forced herself not to retreat. 'There's never been a divorce in the Sansom family and I'm not going to be the one to break the record. All I am asking is that you put your husband first for a change; move your ambitions to the back burner and go back to being the girl I married.' The blue eyes deepened in colour. 'I want you to get rid of that thing inside you. It's time we started a family . . . more than time.'

Tessa closed her eyes in despair. Oh, God, Harry, she thought despairingly. You think *that* will tie me down? It won't, because I don't want your children. Not any more. I don't want *you*. With chilling clarity she faced the fact that Harry Sansom was no longer the centre of her life. These days she got her satisfaction and fulfilment from her job.

She stared at him, no longer really *seeing* him. The handsome face, the big, splendid body, the rigidly prejudiced mind. All surface glitter and no depth. Harry saw only what he wanted to see, accepted only what it suited him to accept. She had never managed to convince him, for instance, that there were more important questions at stake than his own security and well-being.

'Tessa? Tess! Why are you looking at me like that? Look at me as if you know me, for God's sake! You're the one who has changed, not me!'

Of course, she thought, he would naturally never expect that I could fall *out* of love with him, but she had. Except it never *had* been love. Finally, irrevocably she accepted that fact. It was a long time now since she had felt her pulse do a racing change, or her stomach drop to the basement to either his look or his touch. Even the orgasms to which he brought her every single time – he would have regarded himself as a failure had he not – had become programmed, long lacking their first ecstatic newness. Nowadays, even his repeated adulteries could not breach her indifference.

Her eyes lost their fixed inward gaze as he came into view again. He was staring at her in a way that she recognized. Deep inside, where he was careful to keep (hidden, he thought) all his doubts and insecurities, Harry was worried.

And when Harry was worried he tended to lash out. Careful, Tessa thought, feeling her skin prickle. He had never hit her before. Raised his fist, yes, but though it had hung, clenched and poised, it had never landed. That first time, dominating her fear, she had told him flatly: 'You will only get to hit me once, Harry. I shall not be around for you to do it again.'

Now she sensed dangerous frustration. He was no good with words. Where he came from arguments were physical rather than verbal. Just then, the kitchen timer began to ping.

'Lunch is ready,' she said, turning away, but not too hastily.

He followed her into the kitchen. 'You haven't answered me – about getting rid of your IUD,' he persisted. 'Will you?'

Tessa drew on her padded gloves, opened the oven door and took out the lamb. A shoulder roasted to perfection with rosemary and garlic, the potatoes around it crisp and golden. Carefully, she put it down on the worktop.

'Harry,' she said, controlling her impatience, 'my getting pregnant will solve nothing. If we do get a divorce, it will only make one more thing to fight about.'

'I've told you: I'm NOT having that! I don't WANT a divorce!' His face had congested again, his voice high with outrage.

'But you complain I've changed. You don't like the new me. I keep telling you that I can't go back to what I was when you married me. Life and people move on. We are that much further down the road, too far to go back. If you're not happy with me, why not find someone else, someone prepared to be no more than you want them to be?'

She did not say: I don't *need* you Harry. Not since I found myself . . .

He had been watching her, saw the way her face – her whole being – closed, shutting him out. Which alarmed him because it lessened his hold, prised away his *rights*. What was not right was that she should go off into her own private world where he was not allowed to follow.

But: Go carefully, he admonished himself throttling back his rage. Don't force her into a corner; she'll only kick you in the balls. She has changed in that respect; become much less vulnerable, much more independent. Too fucking independent.

With what he considered great magnanimity, he said: 'Let's call a truce for now. No more fighting. I don't like it either. We never used to fight . . . All I want is those early days back again, before you got sidetracked. All right, all right . . .' He held up a calming hand as he saw her mouth open. 'Let's have our Sunday dinner in peace. But please, Tess, think about us. I don't want a divorce. I love you and I want us to stay together. All I'm asking is, could you maybe think a little less about your job and a lot more about us?'

Unmoved, Tessa thought: with you, 'us' means 'me'.

'All it needs is a little give and take,' he went in persuasively.

Yes. Me to give and you to take, like always. Oh, Harry, you are so transparent.

He took her resigned sigh for capitulation and relief

blossomed in response, though he took care to hide it as he went towards her, pulling her into his arms. 'I hate fighting with you,' he said, nuzzling her, 'but lately it seems we never do anything else. We never used to have so much as a cross word back at the beginning.'

'I'm sorry, Harry,' Tessa said plangently, grieving for his loss, understanding how bewildered he must feel at the *volte-face* which had taken place in his compliant, shy little wife, knowing there was no going back, yet feeling uneasily guilty at her own desire to go forward – alone.

'So am I,' he soothed, thinking she meant for the quarrel. 'Let's leave it at that for now, shall we? Talk about it later, when tempers have cooled and we can look at things calmly and reasonably.'

With the sweet reason all on my part, Tessa knew, her grief turning to contempt as she spotted his clumsy attempt at manipulation. No way can you persuade me to give up what makes *me* happy, just to make *you* happy. And that, as the Police Captain from Chicago said when he lectured us at Branshill, is the bottom line.

But she said: 'All right, pax for now. Let's both think about what we want for the future – and I mean really think, Harry, so that when we do sit down and talk about it, we know exactly what we're discussing.'

'Fine, fine . . . I'll set the table, shall I?'

Tessa turned to dish up the vegetables. One small gesture from Harry Sansom, she thought, preceding one large gesture from me. . . .

7

Looking around the small, twelfth-century church, Tessa was glad she had chosen to wear deep, creamy yellow since most of the female wedding guests had opted for various shades of pink. What was it about June and pink? And why was it always worn by women who were far too old for it? The bride's mother, for instance. Julia Fairfax had chosen cyclamen, a difficult colour to wear unless you were a vivid brunettte. Julia was blonde, like her cousin Dorothea. But then, Tessa reflected, Julia's taste always had been in her mouth.

The groom's mother, on the other hand – clever lady – stood out like a beautifully manicured thumb in that she had chosen to wear crisp French navy, which suited her silver hair (under an absolutely *stupendous* hat) perfectly. It was obvious from where her handsome son got his looks.

The bride, as she had progressed up the aisle on her father's arm twenty minutes before, had looked like a helping of *crème Chantilly*; somebody ought to have told her to lose twenty pounds before she wore a dress with so much exterior trimming. Still, for a girl who had never had much going for her in the way of looks, she was absolutely radiant today. Not that it mattered: if the gossip had it right the groom was marrying her for her money. Well, thought Tessa sardonically, I married for sex, so who am I to throw stones?

Harry had flatly refused to accompany her to Wiltshire once she had made plain her own refusal to become pregnant merely because he wanted her to. That had led to their worst row yet, after which he had stormed out and gone straight over the side. If his wife did not appreciate him then he was damned well going to find a woman who did.

As his normal way of dealing with problems was to ignore them, Tessa had not been surprised when, the day after the row, he did not return from work. But there was a message on the answering machine from his triumphant mother, announcing that Harry would be staying 'at home' until such time as his wilful wife was willing to do right by him. What about *my* rights? Tessa had demanded of the machine in a voice that caused Sarge, sitting watching and waiting placidly for his supper, to make a bee-line for his cat-door.

I hope you're not following my example, she now silently told the triumphant bride, about to disappear into the vestry for the signing of the register. When you marry in haste you have years in which to repent at leisure . . .

As they all sat down to wait and the organist launched into 'Sheep May Safely Graze', Tessa allowed her eyes to wander around the lovely old church. She knew a lot of the guests, either family or friends of the family, but many were strangers, especially those seated on the groom's side. Suddenly her roving gaze was arrested, went into reverse and came to a halt in the middle of the third row from the front on the groom's side of the church. She was right; no mistaking that midnight hair or striking profile. Of all people, Nicholas Ould! Sitting next to a dark and still beautiful if no longer young lady wearing dark red and a hat composed entirely of coq feathers. His mother? There was a definite similarity in their profiles. What on earth was he doing at this particular wedding? Then she remembered that the bridegroom's mother was Spanish. Nicholas Ould's mother, as she had discovered since her encounter with him three months ago, was also Spanish. Enough said.

The bride and groom, followed by their respective parents and witnesses, finally came forth from the vestry, and the organist opened all the stops to give a bravura performance of Mendelssohn's 'Wedding March', which to Tessa had always been the musical equivalent of the champion boxer's winning salute.

Down, girl, she told herself dryly. Just because they didn't play it at your wedding . . .

She and Harry had been married in somewhat subdued fashion by her father, once he had recovered not only from the worst effects of his first stroke but sufficient command of his tongue to be able to pronounce the words and thus perform the ceremony. It had always been his dearest wish to officiate at his daughter's wedding, which was why Tessa had asked Harry to wait until the doctors pronounced the Bishop well enough to do so.

The low-key ceremony had been performed not before the great altar of the Cathedral and in the face of a large congregation, but in one of the smaller side chapels. The Bishop's wife had been implacable on that issue. There was no way she was going to expose her brain-damaged husband to ridicule or herself to the agony of waiting for him to come to an abrupt stop during the ceremony because his tongue would not obey his brain. But Tessa had been equally adamant in that she had promised her father that when she married he would officiate, and she had been brought up to regard a promise as sacred. When Dorothea realised there was nothing her own irresistible force could do to prevent her immovable daughter making a shocking *mésalliance* she regrouped her forces and took command of the wedding instead, making it as small and quiet as she could.

Because her father expected it, Tessa had worn the traditional white wedding dress, but there was not a single bridesmaid, never mind the half a dozen the Sansoms naturally expected, along with the flower girl and the velvet suited boy carrying the rings on a satin cushion. Dorothea had put a stop to that. She was the bride's mother, the Bishop was paying for everything, so things would be done her way. As quietly as possible. Her husband's frail state of health provided the perfect excuse. Sparks had flown as two titans clashed but Dolly Sansom met her match in the woman who had once routed a whole Diocesan conference, including an Archbishop.

Tessa had not looked at her wedding photographs for years. She had no need to. She remembered every minute of that day. Only she and Harry looked happy, and that was because they were blinded by their passion for each other. Except for Dorothea, her two brothers and their wives, and her sister and her husband, their children, and ninety-year-old Clarissa Norton who had insisted on being present at the wedding of her favourite great-grandchild, there had been no other Nortons present, and no Pagets either, because her father's parents were long dead and he had been an only child. Riggs had been the only other guest on Tessa's side.

Nor had the Sansoms turned up *en masse* as was usual with their family weddings. Only Harry's parents, his brothers and sisters and their respective spouses, all *sans* children and friends, were there. Harry's best man was his nearest-in-age brother.

It was a disaster for everyone but us, Tessa remembered now. All we wanted was to have it over and done with so that we could fly off to Morocco and fall into bed. But the water was suspect and Harry got gyppy tummy, added to which the food was lousy and when he finally did recover he got badly sunburned because he overdid it on the beach . . .

Omens? she thought now. Or was it doomed from the start, the result of causality, about which they lectured us at Bramshill? If Rupert had not been murdered she would never have joined the police force, which had in turn led to her meeting and marrying her husband. A plain case of mistaken identity. Tessa smiled sardonically to herself. And don't I know from experience how difficult witnesses find it to identify the right man in a line-up?

She changed her smile as the glowing bride and her new husband passed her pew in their triumphal progress back down the aisle. Yes, she mused, still on the subject of cause and effect, Rupert's murder threw a mighty big rock into the tranquil pool of my life and though the ripples rocked a great many boats, it was we, his immediate family, who almost drowned. Under the tidal wave of publicity for a start. Because of who and what the victim was, of who and what his father happened to be, and of how and why he had been murdered in the first place.

The tabloids had done the occasion and the shattered family anything but proud, the press camping outside the gates day and night, while inside the police were asking endless questions.

After the murder, when the Bishop suffered his first stroke, his wife had flatly refused to leave his side in case he died in her absence. When the police asked her to go up to town and identify her son's body, she declined.

'Riggs shall do it. He knew Rupert from the day he was born. My husband needs me to help him survive, both his stroke and this terrible thing. I must do my best for him. There is nothing more I can do for my son.'

On hearing this from Riggs, Tessa went to her mother. She needed to confront her, driven by grief and anger to demand the truth of something which had deliberately been kept hidden from her. 'You knew what Rupert was – what he did – didn't you?'

Her mother had obviously decided there was no use in locking the stable doors now that the horse was miles away for she answered with her usual measured calm: 'He was my son. I knew everything about him.'

'Then why didn't you tell me? He was my brother. I had as much right to know! Why wasn't I told?'

Dorothea overlooked both her daughter's unexpected forthrightness and her daring in broaching the subject so bluntly. Exceptional circumstances called for exceptional behaviour. 'Your father was most insistent that it be kept from you for as long as possible. He thought you too young to be acquainted with the darker side of human nature. You must always remember that for your father there is only one light, and it shines from his God. Rupert occasioned great hurt and deep disappointment, his father having hoped for so much from him.'

'And you didn't?'

'I am able to accept things more . . . easily. Your father sees everything in the light of his faith and thus tends to be somewhat absolute in his judgments.'

Tessa had wanted to laugh but did not dare go *that* far. Her mother accusing her father of being absolute! But she took advantage of the new rules to announce rather than confess: 'I had been seeing Rupert, you know.'

'Yes, I do know.'

Tessa's astonished eyes had met those of her mother. 'You were seen,' Dorothea said on a thin smile, 'and commented on, of course. The world is full of people who hasten for their long spoon the moment they become aware of a noxious brew to stir.'

'I'm not sorry,' Tessa said, chin up, tone defiant.

'I was not aware I had expressed disapproval. I am glad that you saw your brother again, even if you had to disobey me to do so. In the light of recent events I can only think that you must have been inspired by that same hand of Providence to which your father always used to refer. I am aware of just how much your brother meant to you. You were always very close as children.'

For one brief moment Dorothea's voice thinned, allowing Tessa to read the pain behind the rigid façade of a mother who could not permit her inner desolation to show. That was when she understood about Riggs. Her strong, unflappable, unshakeable mother was not up to doing what she had been asked to do: identify her son's dead body. It was also when Tessa knew what she had to do. Taking a deep breath, she announced: 'That is why I have decided to go with Riggs to identify his body.'

Her mother looked at her. Tessa looked back. And in that

long look the balance of their relationship shifted as Tessa took another step away from her overprotected girlhood.

'Yes.' Dorothea nodded finally, adding uncharacteristically: 'Thank you, Tessa.'

The momentary breach was closed, never to be glimpsed again. But both knew there had been an alteration in the *status quo*.

A kind and understanding policewoman, privately aghast that a teenager should be doing such a thing and with only a family servant for support, had accompanied them to the mortuary. Tessa was grateful, since Riggs made his disapproval plain by speaking to her only when necessary, addressing her with scrupulous politeness as 'Miss Tessa' instead of his normal 'Tessa'.

She was sorry to have upset him but saw no reason why it should change her conviction that she was the right one do this last service for her brother. His shocking death had forced her to come to terms with his lifestyle. Besides, she knew that had the positions been reversed he would have done the same for her.

And when it came to it, he looked no different. The blows which had killed him had been to the back of his skull so that his beautiful face was unmarked. Had it not been for his – literally – deathly paleness, Tessa would have thought him to be sleeping. But his flesh had that marbled whiteness she was to see so many more times as a police officer, so markedly different from the warm pink of living flesh.

'Yes,' she had said, finding she did not feel faint, or want to throw up, although the smell – something else she was to become familiar with – was not very pleasant. 'That is my brother Rupert.'

Then she had bent to kiss the cold lips.

Riggs had been the one to be shaken.

Questions had followed. When had she last seen her brother? What did she know about his lifestyle? Had she ever visited him at the flat? When was that? Had she ever seen any of his friends there? Did she know any of their names?

And so on, and on, but unlike her mother, who found it all unbearably distasteful, Tessa had found herself handling it with – if not aplomb – then confidence, telling the police all she could because she wanted them – with a fierceness that came across like a flame – to find her brother's murderer. The one thing she kept from them was her last unexpected visit to his flat. She could not have given the police a description of the man enjoying her brother's beautiful body – her eyes had never reached his face – and there was no way she was going to give them a description of what she had seen; still did sometimes in her dreams. All she wanted was for them to catch the man who had beaten Rupert to death; wanted it with a passion she also had not realised she possessed. She even went into the Cathedral to pray for his capture and conviction. Had there still been a death penalty she would have looped the rope around his neck herself.

But it was how the police went about finding him she found fascinating, holding long, avidly curious question and answer sessions with the kindly policewoman, who was a veritable fount of information.

Three days later the case was solved. Another male body was found, this time dead of a lethal dose of self-administered drugs. Propped up against one of the empty bottles was a confessional note saying that since he had stupidly and jealously killed the only thing he had ever loved, life without it was pointless.

Once again the tabloids had exploited the facts to the full: QUEER KILLER OF BISHOP'S MALE PROSTITUTE SON TAKES OWN LIFE one of them shrieked, above pictures of all three; one of the Bishop in procession at his Cathedral, wearing his robe and mitre, the other of Rupert and his dead lover, both reclining on a beach somewhere, wearing identical, almost indecent bathing slips, of which Rupert's in particular made no secret of just what it was he had sold.

And sold high. Which was no doubt how he had managed to make so much money in so short a time.

Which he left to his sister.

'*How much?*' Tessa had asked when she was told.

'A quarter of a million pounds after all duties and debts have been paid, mostly invested in a first-class stock portfolio. It seems your brother had the best possible advice from his bankers, but then, even though it is only a very small part of their business, Ould & Sons' private accounts are very efficiently run.'

Tessa had left the money where it was. Although she had accepted what Rupert was, she regarded the money as tainted.

Once the case was over and the body released for burial, she had consulted her mother about the funeral arrangements.

Dorothea had pronounced: 'Rupert will be cremated, but your father must not be told. You know his views on the disposal of the dead by burning. It is as well he will not be able to attend, or indeed be cognisant of the funeral itself. For me, I know that for Rupert it is the only way. Not for my beautiful son the worms and the slow decay. Better the clean, bright flame.'

And that was how it had been. A private, unannounced-in-the-press cremation, which Tessa had expected to be desolately unattended but which drew a churchful of Rupert's friends, predominantly men but with a goodly sprinkling of women. She had made it her business to shake the hand of every one of them, following that up with a personal letter thanking them for their presence and their flowers, a profusion of which had completely covered the coffin.

Only when it was all over did she realise that during it she had arrived at a firm decision, one which had been forming ever since the Detective Sergeant who took her statement had said to her: 'You have a sharp eye and a good memory. You would make a good policewoman.'

Why not? Tessa had thought, seized by excitement. What she had seen of the way the police worked during the handling of her brother's case had held her interest and captured her imagination.

Whatever else it was, police work would never be dull or boring. Why not indeed? she thought, feeling the idea take hold of her. What else is there for me to do? I am not trained for anything, except the Cordon Bleu cookery course I did, and what Mummy had planned for me. Before is no longer practicable After – well, not for a long time after – until the scandal has died down, if it ever does. Thank God, because it is was never what I wanted anyway.

As soon as he was capable of understanding what was said to him, she carefully broached the idea to her father, now struggling to recover both movement and speech, the steely determination he had bequeathed to Tessa spurring him on. She had expected him to demur in his sweet yet firm way, to point out that she had been gently raised and would find the work uncongenial, even distasteful: 'Though fortunately,' he wrote on the writing pad he used to communicate, having taught himself to write with his left hand, 'I have seen *you* absorb what I tried to teach you both; that hard work, self-discipline and consideration for others at all times are invaluable allies in the constant struggle against the temptation that is daily life. I have watched with pride as *you* learned to balance desire with duty.' Then, surprising her utterly, he continued, writing slowly and shakily: 'These are things which would be very helpful to you as a serving policewoman. Perhaps it is God who is pointing you His way, and who am I to challenge His authority? I shall pray, and ask for guidance.'

After several days Tessa's father summoned her to his bedside to give her his blessing, ending by congratulating her on deciding to do something worthwhile with her life. It was only afterwards, coming to terms with her surprise, that she realised that her father saw her decision in the light of atonement for her brother's sins. She left him his illusions. He had little else.

Dorothea's response had been glacial. 'A policewoman! My dear Tessa, I have never heard anything so inapposite in all my life. There is no way you could possibly do the kind of work that the police are called upon to do. As yet you have very limited experience of life. I shudder to think of the kind of experience you would acquire as a member of the Metropolitan Police.'

'I identified my brother's body,' Tessa pointed out doggedly, 'and I neither fainted nor threw up.'

'That,' her mother squelched, 'was an unfortunate, once-in-a-lifetime experience, which brings me to another salient point. Have you thought of the reaction of possible colleagues when they hear your name? They, of all people, are bound to connect it with all-too-recent events!'

'Yes, I have thought. I shall not send in my application as Tessa Norton-Paget but as Tessa Paget.'

Her double-barrelled name had come about when Dorothea Norton, a considerable heiress, had married Hugh Paget. The marriage settlement had specified that any children of the marriage should bear both names and be known as Norton-Paget. It was because Tessa did not want to be known by this now notorious name that she sent in her application to the Metropolitan Police as Tessa Paget.

After which she had waited. Eventually she had received a summons to go before a Selection Board, after which she waited again until she was informed that as she already had nine 'O' and four 'A' levels, including the obligatory English and Maths, there was no need for her to take the entrance examination. She was to report for training at Hendon Police College in two weeks' time.

That first morning she had to attend at Paddington Police Station, from where the new intake was taken in green buses to Scotland Yard. There, in a vast lecture hall with tiered rows of seats, they were sworn in *en masse*, raising their hands as they would do many times more in their future career when they took the oath before giving evidence in court.

That done they were bussed to Hendon, where the boys had their hair cut by the barber on campus while the girls had either to put their hair up in a bun or back in a pony tail. Either way it had to be off the collar. Then they were measured for their tailored uniforms by a little old lady from Lambeth Clothing Store. After that, they were given their room number: X Block, Room No. Y. After six years at boarding school institutionalised living came as no shock to

Tessa, unlike most of her fellow intake, who had for the most part spent their lives in the bosom of their families. For a start she did not share a dorm; she had a whole room to herself: bed, wardrobe, fitted sink unit, desk-cum-bureau where she could study, a comfortable chair and plugs for her music centre and portable TV. The view from her sixth-floor window was of the Northern Line, which passed her block on its way to Colindale.

Until uniforms were ready – about a week – the boys wore dark suits, the girls a dark skirt, white blouse with V-necked dark sweater over it, black tights and black lace-ups.

That first day, Tessa also made her first friend: a girl who had become a police cadet at seventeen, and thus had two years' previous experience. Vanessa Sewell was a mine of information. She it was who showed Tessa how to 'bull' the toecaps of her job-issue shoes once the uniforms had arrived and they were fully kitted out: a cotton wool bud and a tiny bit of water in the lid of the shoe polish tin. One of the other cadets cheated by using Johnson's Kleer, but at his first parade, as soon as he stamped to attention, his high gloss crazed. So did his drill sergeant.

The weeks were filled with study, lectures and practical demonstrations, with stooges pretending to be members of the public in various stages of difficulty or distress. They learned first aid, how to deal with a drunk, how to cope with an accident, how to case a pub for licensing offences. Every six weeks they were tested; if you failed to reach the required pass mark at each stage of training – 60% – you had to go back and do that part of the course again. If you failed twice you were out. The classes were dominated by men; 85% of the intake was male, and Tessa made her first enemy in class. A very bright, incredibly ambitious twenty-two-year-old who saw her – and her high pass marks – as somebody he had to better. Especially as she was a girl. Conscious of his enmity, Tessa applied herself. Her graduating mark was 90%. His was 88%. Years later, it came as no surprise to her to learn, when she decided to take her Sergeant's exam, that he had just become the youngest Inspector ever. So young they called him The Cornflake Kid.

By the end of that year she had celebrated her nineteenth birthday, passed out at the top of her intake – which only Riggs turned up to see – and been posted to Haringey as a probationer.

And the cause of it all was my brother's murder, she mused now as she prepared to leave her pew. Cause and effect with a vengeance.

Outside the church, Tessa and her mother mingled with the large crowd watching from the sidelines as the wedding photographs were taken. The photography over, everybody but the bride and groom, who rode in an open carriage, walked across the churchyard to the lovely old Queen Anne house in whose gardens a huge, pink-lined marquee had been erected on the lawn, and while more wedding photographs were being taken – indoors in the lovely drawing room and outdoors in the glorious gardens – Tessa and her mother helped themselves to champagne, which they sipped while they chatted with fellow guests. On hearing the gong that announced luncheon, Tessa went to check the seating plan, pinned up on a blackboard by the entrance to the marquee, to see where their table was.

Finding it, she turned to leave and walked straight into Nicholas Ould, obviously intent on the same thing.

'I beg your pardon,' he apologised promptly, moving out

of the way at once. There was absolutely no recognition in the mercurial eyes, but there was a distinct gleam of appreciation. Oh, yes, Tessa thought smugly to herself as she went in search of her mother, there is one hell of a difference between a Marks & Spencer navy skirt and jacket and a Caroline Charles silk-tussore suit. She was also wearing a very smart hat of wide-brimmed silk straw, its turned-back brim lined with yellow roses. Gotcha! she thought on a grin as she walked away.

She did not see him turn to stare after her.

She found her mother enjoying a comfortable prose with friends, saw her seated at her table with family members of her own age and connection, then went to find her own table. As she did so, a woman already seated on the other side of its circular expanse exclaimed: 'Tessa! My God it *is* you . . . I wasn't sure in the church and I lost you in the crowd afterwards . . . they seem to have invited the world and his wife. Darling, it's been an absolute age. How are you?'

Tessa's pleasure withered on its vine. Of all people she was seated at the same table as London's most notorious – and vicious – gossip. Davina Bruce-Alleyn had never been a friend, only someone she had gone to school with. They had not seen each other for years; once done with school they had gone their separate ways. On those later occasions when Tessa had seen her coming she had taken the kind of evasive action that was not possible now.

'I must say that is an absolutely divine suit! Clotted cream always was your colour. You are bride's side, aren't you? I'm groom's. His father and mine are step-brothers, would you believe? Look, let's get together after lunch and have a nice long chat. I've got tons to tell and even more to ask . . .'

Not if I can help it, Tessa decided, as she tucked in to orange, lemon and dill grilled salmon served with watercress, fresh asparagus and tiny new potatoes, followed by raspberry mousse-filled peaches, all washed down with copious champagne, talking first to the fellow guest on her left, then the right, leaving Davina to her neighbours.

But as coffee was poured and the elderly man seated next to Tessa got up to go across to talk to people at another table, Davina at once pounced on his empty chair. 'Good, now we can have a lovely chat while we drink our coffee . . . Mmmm, will you look at those *petit fours* . . .' Greedily popping one into her mouth, she caught Tessa's eyes and said: 'I never could resist sweet things . . . unlike you. You always had an incredibly strong will, yet you still look as if one could snap you like a wafer.' A sigh. 'I'm afraid I still have to watch everything I put into my mouth.'

What a pity you don't watch what comes out of it then, Tessa felt like saying, knowing better than to do so. Davina made a vengeful enemy.

'Now, tell me, what you have been doing with yourself? Is it true that you are an actual police Inspector? Married to a Sergeant?'

Her frankly incredulous tone covered the obvious implication that it was just one more example of the peculiarity of the Norton-Pagets. First the queer brother getting himself bashed to death then his sister becoming a common or garden policewoman.

'Absolutely true,' Tessa confirmed calmly.

Davina's grass-snake eyes glittered. 'I suppose you got a taste for the work through all that ghastly business with your brother?'

Tessa said nothing, but the way she did it had Davina

rushing on in her babbling brook way. 'Such a tragedy, but thankfully all a long time ago.' She essayed a delicate shudder. 'Let's not dwell on just how long but do let us catch up. I'll tell you what I've been doing . . .'

Tessa let the voice pass over her like a jet at thirty-five thousand feet; vapour trail seen, but too far away to be heard. She drank her coffee and enjoyed the warmth of the mid-June sun streaming in through the open side of the marquee. Suddenly, a name penetrated her abstraction.

'. . . Nicholas Ould, but of course his mother and the mother of the bride are cousins, you know. Both Spanish . . . that's Lady Ould over there, the one in that incredible feather hat and the dark red dress. Saint-Laurent or I don't know my couturiers. You know who Nicholas Ould is, of course?'

'He manages the family bank, I believe,' Tessa said neutrally.

'That's not all he manages. They don't call him Old Nick for nothing. He's supposed to be some kind of financial whizz-kid – except he's pushing forty.' With spiteful glee: 'I wasn't thinking of the bank, I was referring to his other reputation, the one that really got him his nickname.'

'He has two?'

Davina frowned. Mockery was not the usual response she got from women to the name 'Nicholas Ould'. Not until she was through trashing him anyway.

'Surely you've heard of Old Nick?'

'It's a colloquial name for the Devil.'

Davina's laugh sounded like glass breaking. 'Of course, I'm forgetting, you now live in an entirely different world . . . so how would you know anything of your former one?' The stiletto slid home with delicate precision. 'Nicholas

Ould not only has the devil's own luck, he is a heartless devil where women are concerned. Always has several on the go at the same time and changes them with the sheets. They say the IRA or some other terrorist organisation tried to blow him up a few months ago but in my opinion it was one of the many men he has cuckolded. His devil's own luck still held because all they got was his car. Typical! He was injured, but again not seriously. It was poor Sibella Lanyon's house which got the worst of it. He was in bed with her when the bomb went off, you know. It was the talk of the town . . .'

Her cold eyes glittered as she struck again. 'But you don't live in town any more, do you? Where *do* you live nowadays? I think somebody once mentioned Richmond.' Davina made it sound like the back of beyond. 'No wonder you don't hear the gossip. That particular tit-bit spread like wildfire.'

Thanks to your matches, Tessa thought.

'. . . of course, when the police and the ambulance and the bomb squad got there they were both dressed and as cool as two Pimms. You've got to hand it to him.' Davina's voice made it plain what she would love to hand him. 'I mean, he's had half the women here this afternoon – the ones under forty, that is – and no doubt has plans for the other half.'

Davina brought herself up sharply as she saw the way Tessa was looking at her and let go a laugh as false as her eyelashes. 'No, darling, not me . . . I know better. Besides, we're almost related now and one has to draw a line somewhere.'

Not through the name Nicholas Ould, I'll bet, scorned Tessa. Davina had taken a First in insincerity.

'Mind you, I've been told – at first hand – that he's absolutely fantastic in bed, capable of going at it for hours.

Not since Aly Khan – not to mention Porfirio Rubirosa of sainted memory – has there been, so they say, such a sexual virtuoso. Which means, of course, that he has to have a fabulous set of equipment . . .'

You haven't met my husband, Tessa thought. And smiled.

There was no disguising it's meaning. As Davina interpreted it and the gleam in the cobalt blue eyes, a bolt of jealousy all but fused her to her seat. So it was true, then. Tessa Paget *was* married to a stud. A while back, Susie Darlington had seen them together at a police charity do – Charlie Darlington was on some Parliamentary police committee – and had reported back disbelievingly that butter-wouldn't-melt Tessa Norton-Paget's *gorgeous* husband had to be seen to be believed.

So why wasn't he sitting next to her? Did she keep him under lock and key? He must be something if her reaction to Nicholas Ould was any guide. Davina had encountered all sorts and kinds of reactions to that name but this was a first for indifference.

'Is your husband with you?' she queried. 'I'd love to meet him.' She looked as apologetic as she was ever likely to get. 'I'm sorry, but I don't know your married name?'

'Sansom,' Tessa told her, 'and Harry is working'. He would be quick changeover today; that worst of all shift changes from nights to late turn, when you came off duty at 6 a.m. and went back on at 2 p.m. after practically no sleep.

'Oh, what a pity . . . I would *so* like to have met him. Perhaps I will manage it one day, but if you will persist in hiding yourself away in Richmond, of all places . . . Now, do tell me, what is it like to be a police Inspector?' Davina giggled, pretending to look apologetic. 'Sorry, but I just can't seem to believe it. I mean, you of all people consorting with criminals. You were always Little Miss Prim-and-Proper. How on earth do you cope? You must meet some very peculiar people . . .'

'One does not have to be in the police force to do that.'

Davina was not to be thrown. 'But what do you *do* exactly – as a female police officer, I mean. Do you actually arrest men?'

'When it's necessary.'

Davina leaned forward eagerly. 'Heavens! How absolutely extraordinary! Do tell . . .'

Tessa decided to do just that.

'The very first arrest I ever made,' she said, with a reminiscent smile, 'was a well-known merchant banker, for being drunk and disorderly.' Her blue eyes twinkled. 'No, not Nicholas Ould.'

Davina frowned. That was not what she'd expected to hear.

'This particular specimen was haranguing a traffic warden who'd had the temerity to give his BMW a parking ticket, threatening all sorts of retribution. When I cautioned him he took a swing at me, and since he was too big to handle on my own, I radioed for assistance. When we got him to the station he refused to get out of the van; two PCs had to haul him out. He seemed to calm down when we got him into the charge room but the moment they loosened their hold he made a lunge at me, calling me an interfering bitch who needed to be taught a lesson; it seemed I had not only forgotten my place I had forgotten who he was . . . I should be devoting my time to catching real criminals, not persecuting my betters. He grabbed my jacket, and buttons started flying all over the place.'

Davina's eyes were hard and she was tight-lipped. Tessa was speaking treason.

'From my jacket he went for my throat and began to throttle me, hurling invective – and it was very choice, especially in an Old Etonian accent. Fortunately, the skipper on duty was six feet four and built to match and he just picked the drunk off me, but the idiot had a tight hold on my shirt and he took half of it with him. I had already lost every button on my jacket and my cravat was heaven knows where, so my shirt was ruined too. I was down to my bra, and he'd torn one of the straps of that, so it was plain to see where he had scratched and bruised me.'

Davina drew in a sharp breath. 'But didn't the men do anything?'

Tessa's smile was a slow burn. 'Oh, yes, to a man they offered to "rub me better".'

Davina's miser's mouth drew its purse-strings tight. 'How unbelievably unpleasant.'

'He was indeed – then. Next day he had to go to court, and sober he was a very charming man who apologised profusely. He got a sixty-day sentence for the assault on me, suspended because it was a first offence, plus a hefty fine. A couple of days later he sent me the most marvellous Janet Reger bra and briefs in ecru satin and lace along with a dozen roses and another apology.'

Davina smiled thinly. 'It would seem that television does not exaggerate after all.'

'No two days alike,' Tessa agreed sunnily. 'That is what I love about my job. One never knows who one is going to have to arrest – a lord or a lout. I've nicked both.'

Davina rose to her feet. 'Fascinating,' she said in her best insincere. 'It's been lovely talking to you, darling. We must do it again some time.'

Not if I see you first, Tessa told her retreating back.

Nicholas Ould had been seated at a table on the other side of the marquee, but it was placed so that he had an unobstructed view of a ravishingly lovely face which for the life of him he could not place. He had met it somewhere, and fairly recently, but where? All he knew was that it was the face he remembered, not the body, though the yellow suit hinted at equally memorable delights. He never forgot either as a rule, but for some reason this one defied definitive identification. One of his few strike-outs, as they used to say when he was at Harvard Business School. His ego's way of coping? He had not had a failure for as long as he could remember. These days, thanks to people like Duplicitous Davina, whom he had been careful to avoid since spotting her in the church, his reputation preceded him like an advance man.

Still, the little mystery had livened up the wedding no end. He had expected to encounter the same old collection of women, most of whom he had mounted and framed at one time or another, so he was bored until a new one began to tantalise his memory.

It was, he decided, studying the face from across the marquee, the better for being subtly enhanced by make-up, for something told him it had been unadorned when he had seen it first. But where the hell had that been?

He had to find out. He would not rest until he did, but as he began to move purposefully in its direction he saw Drear Davina get there first. A thousand pounds to a penny she was doing another demolition job. It had been reported to him by more than one 'good friend' that Davina never lost an opportunity to pull a few more threads from what she hoped was his rapidly fraying character. All because he had turned her down.

He fell back on Plan B, searching the tables until he found the face he was looking for: that of a portly man with the red cheeks and purple nose of the toper. He was sitting with four very pretty young women, all seemingly hanging on his every word. Making his way across the marquee – not without being buttonholed every few yards by one woman or another – Nicholas eventually reached his target. 'Hello, Bertie.'

The florid face looked up, beamed, and in a whisky-coarsened voice burbled, 'Nicholas, dear boy, do sit down . . . . I was hoping to run into you. Now do go away, my poppets. I have some serious talking to do with Nicholas here . . .'

They went, but not until each had directed a hopeful 'I'm available' smile in Nicholas's direction.

'Sit down, dear boy . . . try to be inconspicuous if you can. Every female eye is on you, as always. Whatever it is you use, I wish you'd give some to me. Here, have a chair and a glass of champagne while you tell me what on earth you have been doing to incur the wrath of the terrorists. Whose wife did you tup in one exotic location or another to make them so displeased with you?'

'None that I know of. The police are unable to point the finger at any one group and as I do business with most countries and a lot of them operate organised terrorism, you pays your money and you takes your choice.'

Bertie pursed his lips and shook his head. 'You always did believe in living dangerously.'

Like Davina, Bertie Somerset collected gossip, not out of spite but for his column in a fashionable glossy. He knew absolutely everybody, and such was his status he was invited everywhere in the hope that the function would receive a mention. If anyone would know the identity of The Face, it would be Bertie.

'I am not living dangerously right now,' Nicholas said. 'On the contrary, I am avoiding Drear Davina.'

'Of tainted memory,' agreed Bertie. 'Where is she?'

'Over there, bending the ear of the blonde in the delectable yellow hat.'

Bertie looked. Frowned. 'Don't know her. Lovely face, though. Can't think how I've missed it until now . . . Ah, but there is a face from the past . . . my past. Still a fine figure of a woman, but forty years ago . . .' Bertie sighed reminiscently. 'A true Valkyrie.'

'Who?'

'The lady in lilac who has just joined the lovely blonde. Dorothea Norton as was. We once had a thing, years ago before she married Hugh Paget.' Bertie could click his tongue like castanets. 'Terrible tragedy, terrible.'

Nicholas turned to see that an imposingly large and handsome lady had paused by Davina and the Unknown.

'Tragedy?' he prompted.

'About – oh, it must be ten years at least – Dorothea's queer son was bashed to death by one of his lovers. Terrible scandal . . . wrecked poor Hugh Paget's health and ended his Bishopric. But Dorothea is pure titanium. She held firm. The blonde must be the daughter . . . what's her name, now? Tessa, yes, that's it. Haven't seen her since she was a teenager – nobody does any more. Lives in Richmond. Married to a police officer. Not only that but she's one too. Looks far too feminine for such a tough job but don't they say you know you are growing older because all the policemen seem so much younger? Probably gets her backbone from her dear mama, who is as tough as old boots. Mind you, to do her justice I heard that Dorothea was not best pleased, either by her daughter joining the police force or marrying a fellow officer. They told me she was fit to be tied, but then, she always was ambitious. That's why she turned her nose up at me. Said I had no goal in life. When I told her it was to have as good a time as possible she said that was an own goal and left me flat. Next I heard she'd married Hugh Paget . . .'

Triumphant that his fabled memory had not let him down, Bertie buried his nose in his champagne flute.

'Well, well, and well again,' Nicholas Ould said softly, staring at Detective Inspector Sansom. 'Thank you, Bertie. You are as infallible as ever.'

'I do my best, dear boy, I do my best.'

'Whenever you are ready to leave, Mummy, just say the word,' Tessa hinted hopefully.

'Oh, but I haven't seen half the people I wish to see,' Dorothea returned, looking round for them. 'That is what I came to tell you. Go and amuse yourself; I believe there is to be dancing eventually.'

Having issued instructions she sailed majestically off across the marquee. Tessa shrugged, and getting up from the table, went out on to the lawns, only to run slap into Nicholas Ould.

'Good afternoon, Inspector.'

Tessa turned to meet the unforgettable shimmering eyes, now making a leisurely but pleasurable survey of the yellow suit, the stunning hat, the lovely face enhanced by both.

'You had me fooled for a while but I knew it was only a matter of time. What threw me was your Miss Penny Plain disguise when you came to take my statement. Had you been Miss Tuppence Coloured, as you are today, I would have made every effort to make it that much more interesting.'

Tessa's smile broke into laughter, his insouciance reminding her of the young Harry who had dazzled her, even though her eyes had long since become used to that kind of glare. Catching the conversational ball she tossed it back at him. 'You live up to your reputation.'

'I would return the compliment except I am not familiar with your particular area of expertise.'

'Detection,' Tessa offered helpfully.

'Ah. Is that why you hide your light under a plain, navy blue bushel?'

Poor Davina, Tessa thought, as she felt something inside her sit up and stretch itself: exhilaration. With Harry the attraction had always been purely physical, thus it had been a long time since she had engaged in the verbal sparring which presages a bout in the battle between the sexes. Tessa appreciated verbal foreplay, having developed the skill during her time at Hendon. Her quick wit had also served her well in her early days in the job, where it helped her survive as a woman in a predominantly male culture. Canteen banter, as she soon discovered, was capable of a sexual savagery which had reduced many a girl to tears.

Her own baptism of fire had come only weeks into her first posting, via a constable on another relief who was fiercely jealous of Harry. At change-over time, with one relief coming off and another coming on duty, there had always been a bit of horseplay, and the two rivals had contrived a game played in the locker room and known as Cock-up. Each man would stand at ease facing the other, wearing their helmets and with truncheons held firmly at the ready, sticking up like erections. When another member of the relief shouted 'Draw!' the one first to lunge forward and knock the other's helmet off with his truncheon was the winner.

But the basis of the game was sexual.

Totally unaware of this at the time, Tessa's innocent curiosity had been aroused by the truncheon belonging to Phil Stavely, Harry's rival. Made of lignum vitae, as were all truncheons, it was frankly sexual in shape, resembling nothing more than a God-like phallus, black but with an unusual streak of paler wood running down one side.

'What's that?' she had enquired naively, indicating the creamy yellow variation, never having seen anything like it before.

He had looked up at her and smiled and in that split second before he spoke she had instinctively braced herself. 'It's a vein,' he had answered sibilantly.

Tessa's face had turned so red it had hurt, but she had made herself face down the knowing, malignant smile and from somewhere deep inside she had dredged up the right words. 'Oh, you mean your yellow streak.'

From then on he had been known as Streak.

It had been, she thought now, almost the exact colour of the suit she was wearing today. She smiled to herself and Nicholas Ould felt it dig his libido like a spur.

'So where do you stand in relation to the hopefully happy couple?' he asked, lifting two glasses from the tray of a passing waiter and proffering one to her before skilfully separating her from the herd.

'The bride's mother is first cousin to my mother.'

'Snap! Only with me it's the groom.'

They began to stroll across the lawns. 'Are you fully recovered now?' Tessa asked, remembering her manners.

'From my injuries, yes. From the blow to my independence, no. I am finding it very hard to come to terms with having not only to look but search before I leap.'

'Have there been any more threats?'

He smiled down at her. 'You would know about them if there had been, surely?'

'There are one hundred of us in the Squad,' Tessa pointed out blandly. 'I just happened to be Duty Officer the day your incident landed on my desk.'

'Ouch! And there was I thinking it was my reputation which had drawn you.'

'At that time I was not aware you had one.'

'At *that* time?' His look told her he had been watching her. So he knew about Davina.

'Let's just say that since then it has been divulged to me.'

'By someone who takes a rather – shall we say? – *jaundiced* view of my lifestyle.'

Tessa laughed. Yellow again . . . Causality was running rife this afternoon, setting pointers whirling madly. 'We used to call her Devious Davina at school; she never left a stone unturned, always putting them back in such a way you weren't supposed to realise she had lifted them.'

'In my case, after she has turned them she picks them up and throws them at me.'

Tessa let her eyes rove over the dark face – not handsome in the way Harry was handsome, but compellingly, no, disturbingly attractive – before countering teasingly: 'Obviously you have quick reflexes since I see no scars.'

'I have Spanish blood. Our pride will not allow us to admit to suffering.'

Tessa burst out laughing. She was enjoying this as she had not enjoyed anything for ages.

'Tell that to all those suffering El Grecos.'

'I prefer Goya.'

Her face lit up. 'Do you? So do I.'

She had had to do the Prado on her own when she and Harry had done Madrid during their first tour of Spain. Art galleries were not his scene. He had gone to a bullfight instead.

'I happen to own one.'

Eyes widening: 'You do!'

'A portrait of my I-forget-how-many-times-great-grandfather. At present it hangs in the hall of my mother's house, although it belongs to me. It always passes down the male line.' With a straight-face, he added: 'Very Spanish.'

'Yes, you look it,' Tessa said.

'The other half of me is very English.'

Tessa eyed him innocently. 'Mmmm, I have been told that you're a heady combination of both,' she murmured.

His teeth were very white in his dark face as he laughed, catching her drift at once but not being swept away by it.

Tessa felt her own spirits sparkling – but that could have been the champagne.

'Tell me,' asked Nicholas Ould, 'what led you to swop divinity for detecting?'

'My father is the Bishop, not me, and he fully supported my choice of career.'

'And your husband – does he support it too?'

Tessa easily blocked that one. 'It was from him I learned

the basics of policework. He was my "parent" constable when I was a probationer.'

'Is he also in the Anti-Terrorist Squad?'

'No. He's station sergeant at Battersea. He's working today,' she found herself adding. 'That's why he's not here.'

Now why should I want to explain that to you? she wondered, vexed.

'You work different shifts then?' Nicholas Ould pursued.

Well aware of where he was leading, Tessa followed with deceptive naïvety, 'I am afraid so, not that it's unusual in the Met. Married couples have to accept not seeing each other – sometimes for days – it is an occupational hazard.'

'That must be frightfully frustrating.'

Not to me, Tessa thought, answering demurely: 'My husband hates it.'

'I can understand that.'

I should imagine you understand a great deal, she thought, but I am not interested in allowing you to reach an understanding with me. I've already got one like you, thanks very much.

They had reached the end of the lawns, which ended in a flight of stone steps down to the parterre. Turning to look back over the grass, Tessa saw that they had become an object of intense, almost avid scrutiny. She could read their joint surmise. 'Nicholas Ould's about-to-be latest?'

Time to nip this in the bud, she decided, and spotting a familiar face in the crowd, seized her chance. If t'were done well, t'were best done publicly . . .

'Oh, there's my very favourite uncle . . . I must go and say hello.'

Offering her hand, and bestowing on him a smile of which her mother would have been proud, she said dismissively:

'It's been nice talking to you, Mr Ould. I'm so glad you are over the worst of things,' before heading in the direction of the octogenarian sitting in an old-style wicker basket chair.

'Uncle Hector.' She bent to kiss his wizened cheek. 'How nice to see you again.'

8

Tessa pushed open the door of the coffee bar and looking around, spotted Ian – Superintendent Ian McKay – sitting at a table in the far corner by the window, reading his *Independent* and sipping capuccino. Heaving a sigh of relief at the sight of him, she wound her way through the tables towards his.

'Sorry I'm late,' she apologised somewhat breathlessly, subsiding into a chair. 'I got waylaid just as I was leaving the office . . . nothing urgent, just a query about a witness statement, but the enquirer wanted to nit-pick.'

He put aside his paper at once to smile warmly across at her. A short, dark, pleasant looking man of forty-four, only a year away from completing his twenty-five years in the Met, he was now Tessa's oldest and closest friend in the job, having been Inspector on her Relief at Haringey. He knew more about her than anyone, and inter-police relationships being what they were – as intense as war-time ones in that you daily lived a shared, ever-present danger – they had become the closest of friends, sharing an entirely asexual relationship. In the early days Harry had only shrugged and smiled dismissively at the mention of Ian McKay. His nickname at Haringey had been 'Mother' McKay because he was regarded as a pedantic fusspot. It was only when he became active in promoting Tessa's career that he was put on Harry's Shit List – as they said in the Met. But Tessa trusted him absolutely. When you were laying your life on the line every time you went on duty, the knowledge that you had such a friend as back-up was vital to your well-being.

She had lost her first real friend in the job halfway through their second year. Only eighteen months out of Hendon, Vanessa Sewell, beside whom Tessa had sat on the bus that took them from Paddington to Scotland Yard that very first morning, had been knifed by a bag snatcher she tackled in Kilburn High Road. She was twenty-one years old. Tessa had been devastated, for they had become firm friends as well as colleagues. Vanessa had been an out-going, cheerful, confident girl, the antithesis of the shy, introverted Tessa, and had kindly taken the unsure probationer under her wing. For her to be knifed to death while doing no more than her job had shocked Tessa almost speechless, providing an unpleasant reminder of just how dangerous it was out there. Known as Loch Ness, from her diminutive Nessa, and sometimes as Monster, she had been five feet ten and built to match, as well as far and away the best of their class at judo. That was why she had not hesitated to tackle the thief, who had slashed her throat with a Stanley knife when she attempted to arrest him. She had bled to death before the ambulance could get there.

Ian McKay had been Tessa's tower of strength during that traumatic time, because she had turned to him in the face of

Harry's callous: 'She should have known better. But then, she always did think she was as good as any man. Now she knows different.'

As well as being infinitely more sensitive than Harry, who could have given a rhinoceros a run for its money in the hide stakes, Ian was the kind of friend with whom Tessa could – and did – talk to more intimately than her mother. He had also, for the past year or so, been her 'mentor' – the senior officer appointed to be 'there' for Bramshill fliers – which meant providing monthly chats as to how things were going; offering help, advice, and if need be a shoulder to cry on. Tessa had availed herself of all three more than once.

'Not to worry,' he said cheerfully now, as he beckoned to the waitress. 'I haven't been here long myself. How are things?'

'Not so good.'

Which in Tessa-speak meant bloody awful.

So his 'In what way?' was non-committal. If she wanted to tell him she would.

'I think I'm in need of a change. I've had almost three years on the Squad; I could do with some more action in my daily routine.'

Which meant, Ian surmised shrewdly, that there was a dearth of action elsewhere. 'You mean go back to the CID?'

'It's one option.'

Lightly, testing for strength of conviction: 'I think you've got itchy feet. It's well known that Bramshill people don't stay; they suffer from the Butterfly Syndrome.' His smile took away the sting. 'What appeals to you, or aren't you particular so long as it is a change?'

'I don't know,' Tessa admitted. 'I only know that I am not as content in my job as I used to be. There was a time when I looked forward to the day; the enjoyment and challenges it would bring. Not any more. I don't think I'm cut out for office work, and as a woman in SO13 that is what I am doing more often than not. The men do the interesting stuff, but not until some terrorist group has planted a bomb. Even then I don't even get to do anything worthwhile . . . *I* get to interview the informants and witnesses or take the inevitable statement from a victim – if he's able to give one.'

'That's what being on the Appeals Team means. Its job is to handle general information.'

'I'd rather be in the Bomb Data Centre – that way I could at least learn a lot about explosives, but my request for transfer was sidelined. Oh, now and again, if something gets blown up when I am Duty Officer I get to go to the scene to assemble the witnesses and question them, but most of the time nowadays I'm stuck in the office moving piles of paper around.'

'Somebody has to do it.'

'Yes, normally the token woman! And it's not as though I don't know my Police and Criminal Evidence Act. I can all but recite it verbatim, so I know all the procedures about tape recordings at interviews. And another thing. In three years I have yet to be seconded to a provincial force to share my so-called expertise, yet I could name you four men who have.'

'I thought Dave Hawkins was pro-women?'

'He is. But he's boss of my section only; there are certain more senior officers who don't share his enthusiasm.' Tessa met Ian's quizzical expression. 'I know, I know . . . women in the job these days get to do a hell of a sight more than they did when you joined. But how do you get past senior officers who think as Harry does?' She shook her head dispiritedly. 'In the end it all comes down to the individual, and dealing with them is what I like and what I am good at: being "out there". What is it the jargon calls it these days – "interfacing"? That has always been more my line; it calls for the kind of involvement I prefer.'

Which also tends to keep you out of the house? wondered Ian, before he said mildly: 'Constantly changing shifts will give you that.'

Tessa winced.

'Forget about early turn, did you?' Laughter lit his rather ordinary face. 'It's a long time since you did shifts. Besides which it's all changed now that the old Relief system has gone.'

'I know. Harry doesn't like it at all.'

Just then the waitress came over and Tessa ordered an ordinary coffee.

'How is Harry?' Ian asked, able to now that she had introduced the name. Though no one could be warmer or more friendly – once she had decided to admit you to her life – Tessa had never lost that aloof air of self-containment which held you at both arms' length when she wanted to. Now, as she answered briefly: 'He's fine,' Ian's well-attuned ear read the nuances, which meant he could ask: 'But?'

'Things between us have been going from bad to worse for ages, but in the past few weeks it has become a case of Worst Scenario.'

'In what respect?'

Tessa told him about Harry's sudden desire to become a father.

'He still can't handle your being a Ma'am, can he?' Ian knew Harry as well as Tessa did.

Shaking her head in agreement: 'And never will, that's his cross. Mine is that no matter how I rationalise it, I can't rid myself of the feeling that I am being equally selfish in insisting on remaining one; doing what *I* want without giving due regard to his feelings.'

'You mean prejudices. You being an Inspector goes against everything Harry believes in. A baby is his way of putting you back where he thinks you – all women, come to that – belong. I know you set great store by fairness, Tessa, but there are times when unfair decisions are called for and this is obviously one of them. If your marriage was the most important thing in your life we would not be having this conversation. You would be planning a nursery and deciding on names, maybe asking me to be godfather.' He paused, before going on, uncompromisingly. 'It's either your marriage or your career. That's how it was with me, only my wife made the choice for me.' Ian's marriage had come to grief six years earlier when his wife, tired of being second best to his job, had left him for a bank manager.

'However,' he continued, 'I happen to have some information which may force Harry's hand.'

'Oh?' It was only one short word but in it Ian heard all the hope of a desperate woman.

'It's in Police Orders today that they are forming a Selection Board to consider candidates for promotion to Chief Inspector. Applications have to be in by the end of the month. I think yours should be among them.'

'Do you really think I'd be in with a chance?'

'Would I suggest it otherwise? A mere two per cent of CIs are women. If the police force is to become what the powers that be keep saying they want it to be, then women must be given more responsibility within it.'

'That's how Dave Hawkins thinks. We get on well, he's a good guv'nor and he's given me excellent AQRs. He judges by performance, not sex. He'd give me a good reference, I know.'

'Then you have to decide which way you go. Onward and upwards in the job or to the ante-natal clinic.'

There was a silence as Tessa mulled that over. Eventually, in troubled tones, she asked: 'But how do I reconcile my ambitions with the fact that I married for better or for worse? I can't help feeling it's monstrously selfish of me to dump Harry just because he no longer suits my purposes.'

'Well, seeing your father is a Bishop. Scruples are something only someone with a Christian upbringing ever bothers about.'

Tessa's absent smile covered, Ian thought, a rash of red marks where the injections of her father's indoctrination had been administered, most of them failing to take, yet now and then surfacing from the depths.

'Have you asked Harry for a divorce?'

'Even the mention made him go spare. You know how he sees himself. Never in a million years would he be able to accept that any woman could possibly reject him – the original *homme fatale*.'

'There is one absolutely foolproof way you could divorce him – adultery.'

'But he knows that I know – along with everybody else – that even though he has been over the side times out of number, I've always allowed him back on board. In the eyes of the law that's collusion.'

'Even so, surely it's worth a try on the grounds of the last straw. The one that finally broke the camel's – your – back.'

'Which in no way lessens my debt to him. When I was

finding my feet he was the one who supported me if I tripped. He also saved my life. That time when I was cornered in the alley by the rapist with the jack handle? It was Harry who took him on and held him off until assistance arrived. And that other time, when I was brand new to the Panda cars and that prat Tony Lambert went joy-riding in Panda Five at the end of his shift, damaging the suspension, which he then tried to pin on me because I was the one who took the car out after him – it was Harry who did the snooping that put me in the clear. I owe him, Ian, it is as simple as that.'

Her torment only served to fuel Ian's contempt and dislike for a man he also resented: Flash-Harry Sansom, who had swaggered his way into Tessa Paget's life without so much as a by-your-leave and filched her from under Ian McKay's longingly envious nose. Which was why he said caustically: 'Perhaps he sees your capitulation as the only full and complete discharge of that debt? It also does not suit him that you don't need protecting any more, and playing Macho Man is what Harry does best. It is precisely because you have become your own woman that your marriage is in difficulties. Marriage is a contract between two people, so why should an obviously broken one – and Harry has broken yours so many times it's a wonder there are still pieces left to pick up – be regarded as sacrosanct?

'All right, so he helped you at the start – for how long, one year, two? – but all you have achieved since then has been obtained through *your* efforts, not his. And what about your enormous help to him? Had it not been for you he would never in a million years have got his Sergeant's stripes. Harry is a good copper and a brilliant thief taker but he is not and never will be senior officer material. You are.'

Having delivered himself of his opinion, Ian drank his cooling coffee, sure that Tessa would find no flaws in an argument which, he assured himself, was in no way coloured by his jealousy of her husband.

'The trouble is', she said finally, and with calm reason, 'that while I know logically in my mind that what you say is the truth, my conscience keeps telling me it is a selfish truth. I was brought up always to look at both sides of any question before making a decision.'

'While Harry is not looking at any side but his own. What happens if you pass the Selection Board? He can't accept you as an Inspector. God knows what he will do if and when you become a Chief Inspector.'

'*He* will divorce *me*!'

Ian sat back. 'There is your answer then, except . . .'

'What?'

Ian grinned. It took years off him. 'Can you sue for divorce citing your wife's job as co-respondent?'

Tessa laughed, and for a moment the dark clouds rolled away; she was once more the woman he had known and loved since she first reported for duty on 'A' relief all those years ago.

Having sown the seed, he was content to let it grow. Casually moving along he said: 'Oh, by the way, while I think of it, I've been advised of a network reconvention coming up at Bramshill. The usual course of lectures and seminars on current policing; people from just about every force in the country. They want someone to talk about their experience as an officer with the Anti-Terrorist Squad. You'd fit the bill perfectly. At the same time it would make a change for you, get you out of the office and put you in touch with like-minded people. Hopefully give you a firmer idea of what you want to do next.' Another pause. 'Besides giving you time away from Harry.'

'I am already away, or rather he is. He went home to Mother last Thursday.' Tessa's infectious giggle broke loose as did her ever-present sense of the ridiculous. 'Normally it's the wife who does that, but in my case . . .'

'Harry will always turn to a woman,' Ian told her bluntly.

For a while each rode their own train of thought, then Tessa asked: 'You are convinced I would stand a good chance with the Selection Board?'

'I am positive.'

Tessa nodded, mind made up. 'Then I will apply. Maybe it will provide the necessary catalyst.'

'Good. And Bramshill?'

'When is it?'

'You should go down next Sunday ready for the Monday morning start.'

'Short notice.'

'Can't get away?'

'I don't see why not. We're not exactly snowed under just now.'

'Then have a word with Dave Hawkins.'

'Yes.' Tessa made a second decision. 'I will.'

'Excellent! Bramshill will give you the change you need.'

Tessa stretched a hand across the table. Warmly she said: 'Thanks, Ian. I needed to talk to someone, and who better than you, my mentor?'

'Any time,' he assured her contentedly. 'Any time at all.'

9

Bramshill had not changed since Tessa's last visit. It was still the same medieval manor house set amidst the gorse bushes of the Hampshire countryside, where the men and women destined for the upper echelons of the country's police forces took Advanced Promotion or Refresher courses or underwent some kind of specialised training. Tessa had enjoyed her previous times there. The group photograph taken after her first course – a must after any of them – hung above her desk at Richmond. This time, perhaps because of the miserable weather beyond the windows, her mood was as heavy as the skies, from which rain fell in an incessant, dreary drizzle.

She did not realise that she was sinking into a depression, which manifested itself as an apathetic lack of interest in anything beyond the state of her marriage. Having told Ian she would at once apply for a Board she then found herself unable to sit down and do so. She knew she ought to be dealing with her side of things; that it was vital she be free and clear of the wreckage if she was going to be able to concentrate on her future career, since there was no way she was going to be able to face a circle of high-ranking invigilators probing for candidates' weaknesses without a cool mind and a clear conscience. Still she see-sawed daily between opposing points of view. One minute she was racked with guilt at what she considered her welching on an obligation; the next she would tell herself that she had been as understanding, as flexible, as tolerant as any wife could be for far too many thankless years. The weight of this on her mind meant she was unable to summon either interest or pleasure in the 'good talk' Ian had known she would find. Worse, she found her concentration had also taken a turn for the worse.

She would find herself staring out of the rain-smeared windows, wondering where Harry was, why he had not been in touch, what he was planning. For he was up to something. He had never been absent for so long before. Her heart sank at the prospect of the monumental row which would result when he did deign to return. Up until the moment she had left for Hampshire he had left no message of any kind on the answering machine. She had left one for him though – should he decide to call – telling him where she was and for how long, for in spite of everything she found herself hoping that he would ring her while she was at Bramshill; show some sign of awareness that the tie that bound them was down to a single, dangerously frayed thread; agree to talk about the now inevitable divorce. But he did not. He was leaving her to flounder. Since in his eyes she was the one to blame for their present predicament, she would have to do all the dirty work. That way he could say virtuously: 'None of this is was what *I* wanted.'

Why do I keep on expecting from him what he is not

capable of giving? she asked herself despairingly, even while she found herself calling the flat daily, hoping to hear his voice saying: 'All right, when you come home let's sit down and get this lot settled once and for all. I'm as sick and tired as you are of all this argy-bargy.'

He had been gone two whole weeks now. Surely he had to have gone home some time, if only for a change of clothes? He must have listened to her messages yet had not bothered to answer any of them. Selfish bastard! A lightning bolt of anger seared away every shred of guilt. Slamming the receiver down after her latest, futile call: 'That's the last time,' she resolved aloud. 'He can go to hell. And I'm not going back to Richmond. If he can stay away, so can I.'

She made a second decision as she flung her bag in the boot of the Golf late on the Friday morning her week's course ended. She would send in her application for a Selection Board this very day; do her damndest to see that she was one of those selected for promotion to Chief Inspector. And if he did not like that then he knew what he could do. Which would be to dump her. Please God.

But in the car her resolve faltered as guilt counter-attacked, told her she was not being fair. Oh, God, what am I going to do? she said aloud, as she laid her head on the hands holding the wheel. God, somebody, give me strength . . . I have to make a difficult decision involving hurting someone who once meant everything to me, and I was taught never to hurt if I could avoid it. If only there was some other way, but there isn't. Please, God, somebody, give me a sign and the strength to do what I must do . . .

It was raining when she drove out of the gates, but as she left Bramshill behind the skies cleared and a watery sun appeared, the sight of it serving to lighten her mood somewhat.

No, she would not go back to Richmond; she would spend the weekend with her parents. Even her mother's raised eyebrows – sufficient condemnation in themselves – were preferable to an empty house and a silent telephone. Sarge would be all right because she had made the usual arrangement with her first-floor tenant to keep him provided with food and milk until she returned from her course. He had access to the flat through his cat-door.

Feeling better for that small decision she took the minor roads, content to tool through country lanes where the strengthening sun – which she took as an omen after the drizzle and gloom of the preceding ten days – gilded the leaves and made them glow at the edges.

She was almost to Cerne, one part of her mind still turning its treadmill, the other minding her driving down a narrow, winding, tree-arched country lane, when a deer suddenly leaped down from the high bank on her offside to run right in front of her. She braked hard, hauled on the wheel and managed to avoid hitting it, but as it bounded up the other high bank to disappear through the trees she was left with only the nearside wheels of the Golf on the road. The other two were in a ditch at least a foot deep.

'Oh, no!' she groaned, as she clambered out to inspect the damage. 'How the hell do I get out of this?'

Getting back into the tilting car she did her best, but the back wheels spun in the thick mud at the bottom of the ditch; the more she revved, the deeper they sank. She tried switching gears; forward, then reverse, then forward again, trying to rock the car on to the road again, but when she got out to inspect progress she saw that the back wheel was up to its axle in thick, viscous mud. The only way to get the car out of the ditch would be via a tow-truck.

'Damn it all to hell!' The words exploded from behind clenched teeth as she kicked the wheel in pent-up rage. Would nothing *ever* go right? This was all she needed.

Looking both ways, she saw the silent road was deserted; when she listened she could hear nothing but the sough of the wind in the leaves. Climbing the bank, she scanned the countryside for signs of habitation but saw only a vista of rolling fields. Cerne, she knew from the signpost she had passed not long before, was some five miles away. She could either sit and wait (why, oh why, had she not installed a carphone as Harry had urged) until someone came along, which could be a long time for she had not encountered another car since turning on to this B-whatever country lane, or she could set off and walk until she came across a telephone box.

Walk, she decided. She was up to here with sitting and waiting in general. But as if the heavens heard her, as she was locking the car heavy clouds obscured the sun and it began to rain again, this time heavily. She would be soaked after a hundred yards. Muttering under her breath, she got hurriedly back into the car.

'Somebody up there has definitely got it in for me,' she glowered, as the sky proceeded to flush every cloud in sight.

Sunk in dark thoughts, oblivious both to the streaming windscreen and the loud drumming of the rain on the roof, she was unaware of the Range Rover which drew to a stop behind her.

It was not until somebody tapped on her window, making her all but jump out of her skin, that she rubbed a clear patch in the steamy glass – she had turned the heater on – to see the blurred outline of a man standing there. Rescue at last. But she was a police officer. Cautiously she let her window down, but not enough to allow a questing hand to be inserted, while keeping a finger on the button. The gap was enough to allow her to see the face of the man who bent to look through it.

When she recognised it her stupefaction must have shown because he laughed. Enjoyably. 'We have got to stop meeting like this,' said Nicholas Ould.

But he proceeded to deal with her predicament in the way of a man used to disposing of problems. Ignoring the pelting rain as if it were no more than a light shower he made a thorough inspection of the stranded Golf, before returning to say: 'It will have to be hauled out, I'm afraid. In the meantime, I suggest you come back to the house with me and wait in comfort while I call my garage and set the wheels in motion, so to speak . . . Are you in a hurry?'

'No,' Tessa replied dazedly, her mind still reeling from the unexpectedness of it all.. Then: 'You live around *here*?'

'About three miles away by road – just across those fields if you walk, which I would not advise in this rain.'

'Which is exactly why I was sitting here,' Tessa pointed out with poisonous sweetness.

'By your reaction to my appearance, I take it you don't see me as a countryman?'

She regarded his Barbour, Tattersall check shirt, sweater and cords, topped by a tweed cap, and thought he looked for all the world like one of those men who congregate at point-to-points or game fairs.

'You don't strike me as a son of the soil,' she answered pointedly.

Opening the door of the Golf to help her out, 'How did you get into the ditch?' he asked.

She told him about the deer.

'Oh, then I must apologise since it was probably one of mine.'

'*Yours!*'

'I have a small herd which grazes in my park. My great-grandfather bought a few pairs and they obeyed the biblical canon to go forth and multiply. These days they number more than fifty and now and again one tends to stray.' The dark voice became a purr. 'But then, don't we all?'

When she did not answer he said helpfully, 'Fate does seem to be putting us in each other's way, doesn't it? This is our third encounter. Do you think somebody is trying to tell us something?'

For no good reason Tessa remembered her silent prayer not long before, which provoked a knee-jerk response. 'You don't really believe *that*.'

'Ah, you forget I am half-Spanish . . . rumour has it that an ancestress of mine was a *bruja* – a witch, in English.' Now that I can believe, Tessa agreed silently.

Opening the door of his gleaming, racing green, top-of-the Range Rover, he paused.

She looked up at him questioningly.

'I merely wish to assure you that is quite safe to ride with me. Every vehicle I drive is now thoroughly checked before I get into it.'

The policewoman in Tessa came to the fore.

'You've had no more warnings?'

He shook his head. 'I don't expect any. That is why I take precautions.'

'They told you that the origin of the bomb was Spanish?'

'Yes. And that the terrorists were probably of the same nationality.'

'Had you done anything to incur the wrath of the Separatists?'

'I refused a sizable loan against securities which, I was warned, were highly suspect, offered by a man who later turned out to be deeply involved with ETA. The bomb was, I suppose, their way of telling me not to be so cavalier in future, but I would have expected them to blow up one of the Spanish branches of the bank – we have one in Barcelona and another in Madrid. I confess I am somewhat shocked that they took my refusal so personally.' His voice was bland as unsalted butter: 'It must be my Spanish blood, and not unconnected with the fact that my mother's brother-in-law was blown up in his car a year or two ago. However, he was a member of the *Cortes* – the Spanish Parliament – and a well-known opponent of separatism. I, on the other hand, have never expressed any opinion one way or the other.'

'Very sensible of you.'

'Oh, I am ever sensible,' he assured her gravely, 'to so many things.' His eyes touched her like fingers. 'And I can assure you that the experience has taught me a valuable lesson.'

Warily, for she was never sure when this man was being serious, Tessa asked: 'And what is that?'

'Life is short, therefore waste not, want not a single moment . . .'

As their eyes met and held Tessa was left in no doubt as to just exactly what he was thinking of.

You must be joking! she wanted to say as she climbed into the Range Rover. With what *I've* got on my mind?

'Where were you bound when you went into the ditch?'

he asked, settling himself in the driver's seat and fastening his seat belt.

'My parents' house. Just outside Dorchester.'

'Going home for the weekend?'

'Yes.'

Silkily: 'Alone?'

'My husband is working.'

'Again?'

'Policemen tend to work long hours.'

And it's none of your damned business, her tone said.

'What brought you this way *en route* to Dorchester?' he asked casually, manoeuvring the big car carefully around the Golf – which he had disabled to prevent anyone trying to drive it away – before making speed.

Tessa explained.

'Bramshill . . . that's the police college, isn't it? Are you one of those people they call "high fliers"?'

'Bramshill is intended to help police officers develop command skills,' Tessa responded neutrally.

'As an Inspector, do you command?'

'Yes.'

'Men?'

'And women.'

'And do you always get your man?'

Tessa ignored his sub-text. 'That is the motto of the Canadian Mounted Police, not the Met, but yes, a good part of the time I have done.' They drove in silence for a while, beginning to descend a hill into a valley at the far end of which Tessa saw a lovely old house set amidst formal gardens. Almost idly, Nicholas asked: 'Did you join the police force for ideological reasons?'

'I felt it offered a worthwhile career.'

'Are you a career woman?

Oh no you don't, she thought, instinct warning that the less this man knew the better. 'I was brought up to believe that any job worth doing is worth doing to the best of one's ability.'

She felt rather than saw his smile, and knew with baffled unease that he was seeing exactly what she was trying to conceal. Well, he is a womaniser, isn't he? she thought snottily. He probably knows more about women than any ten psychologists.

They were passing a high brick wall, and he slowed the car preparatory to turning right, driving through a pair of ornate iron gates which he opened with a small electronic gadget that looked like a keypad. They closed behind the car as it turned on to a long, straight drive ending in a sweep before a lovely old Elizabethan house.

I would have passed this without a second glance, Tessa thought. Her initial unease tightened its grip. Could he be right? Was Fate throwing them together?

Nonsense! she answered herself forthrightly. Coincidence, that's all. Didn't Daddy explain that 'so-called' Fate is the working of God's will?

True, but didn't he also say that people come into your life for a reason, and though you may not be able to discern that reason at the time, what is certain is that it is all part of God's divine plan?

And then she remembered again, with a swoop of the stomach, how only a couple of hours ago she had prayed for God – *somebody* – to help her.

Assisting her down from the Range Rover, Nicholas felt her shiver and asked with concern: 'Cold? You can warm yourself at the fire once we are indoors.'

Not the one you would like to light, Tessa told him silently.

He ushered her up a flight of shallow stone steps and into a high, wide and handsome hall with a magnificent oriel window at its far end. His shoes rang on the stone flags with which it was floored as he led her across it and into a big room walled with books where the promised bright fire was burning.

'Get warm and then help yourself,' he said, nodding to the large butler's tray which was set with bottles and glasses. 'I'll be back in a minute. Mine's a gin and tonic, by the way. One-third gin, two-thirds tonic, lots of ice and a slice of lime, not lemon.'

Throwing her one of his white-hot smiles, he closed the door behind him.

As Tessa busied herself with the Tanqueray and opened a fresh bottle of Schweppes, she could not drag her mind away from Nicholas's remark about Fate, and her own plea for help. The only kind of help a man like him was likely to offer a woman, she reasoned, would be to undo buttons and draw down zips. On the other hand, she had no doubt as to his ability to hinder. Especially a woman's logical thought processes . . .

It is no more than coincidence, she told herself irritably. They do exist, you know.

Coincidence, my foot! that other self retorted. To be rescued from a ditch by this particular man on a minor road in the depths of the Dorset countryside is a hell of a sight more than coincidence.

Absent-mindedly she gulped her drink only to find that in her bemused state she had failed to add tonic so that she took a hefty swig of neat gin. Grimacing, she made amends and carrying her glass to the fireplace, sat down in front of it on a long, wide footstool covered in a lovely old brocade. In a rack by its side was a selection of papers and magazines. The *Financial Times*, of course, and the *Economist*, along with the rest of the heavies plus a couple of tabloids. Obviously he believed in sampling a wide variety of news.

Picking up a tabloid – all her jittery mind was capable of dealing with right now – she leafed through it until she came to the horoscope page which, like everybody else, she always read but never admitted to. Under her own sign of Virgo it said: 'Someone from outside your normal social circle is about to add a special sparkle to your life. Saturn and Jupiter are urging you to turn your back on the demands and pressures you have been experiencing lately and acknowledge your own needs. Even though by nature you tend to be cautious, it is time for you to set in motion a complete change: of pace, of outlook and, most of all, of mind.'

She almost dropped the tabloid. Instead she managed to lay it down before reaching for the second one. This time her forecast said: 'It is make or break time for those born under the sign of the Virgin. You know only too well that somehow or other you have got to find the determination to rid yourself of unhappy ties and associations which are holding you back. Go for it.'

Utterly taken aback by now, she put both papers down then sat staring unseeingly at the wall of books. Dead to rights, she thought incredulously. Both of them. Me *and* my situation. Absolutely dead to rights. Nicholas Ould is way outside my normal social circle. He is also eminently capable of adding not only a sparkle but a positive dazzle to any woman's life, while my desire to rid myself of unhappy ties is what has got me in this particular situation in the first place.

Gulping her drink: Been there, done that, she counter-attacked. The last thing I need in my life right now is another womaniser.

Just then a voice behind her said affably: 'Yes, I do have a great many books, don't I? A lot of which I happen to have read.'

Steeling herself, Tessa turned to see him pick up his glass. He sipped, smiled and said: 'Perfect . . .' in a way which stirred an idle finger around her vital organs.

'The rescue of your car is in hand,' he was saying. 'It will be delivered here once fixed, which will be a couple of hours, since I told them to check it thoroughly afterwards. Which gives us plenty of time for a nice, leisurely lunch – or are you expected home?'

'No,' Tessa found herself answering, 'I intended to surprise them.'

'Whereas instead you have surprised me – pleasantly, of course.'

Again Tessa found herself unable to meet those disturbing eyes. For God's sake, act your age, she reminded herself. You are thirty-two not twenty-two!

A tap at the door heralded a white-coated manservant who announced: '*La comida esta servida*.'

'I hope you like Spanish food?' Nicholas said.

'What? Oh, yes . . . yes, I do.'

'Good.'

He conducted her to a small, cosy dining room on the other side of the hall, where they were served by the same manservant. Spanish-style, there were *dos platos*: two plates. The first a perfectly chilled, perfectly judged *gazpacho*, smooth and thick, pink with tomatoes and redolent of cucumber and garlic, eaten with crusty, fresh-baked bread. The second was a whole fish which he told her was *besugo* – bream in English – poached with onions, tomatoes and garlic and accompanied by creamy potatoes and tiny mange tout. That was followed by a salad of crisp lettuce, peppers and spring onions in a pungent, also garlicky dressing, and another of tomatoes drizzled with olive oil.

The pudding was one Tessa had encountered many times in Spain when on holiday: *flan*, but this one was covered in a caramel as rich and smooth as Nicholas Ould's voice, sliding over the tongue and down the throat without the need for any effort. With it they drank Spanish wines.

And talked.

He was no strain to talk to. He was even better to argue with. As the good wine relaxed Tessa and loosened her tongue they engaged in a spirited discussion as to the current state of the economy, about which he had an insider's knowledge. Using it, he proceeded to demolish a great many of what he uncompromisingly called her misconceptions. By the time he'd finished she had a much clearer picture of just how complicated the economics of running a country were. There was a great deal more to him than his reputation as Playboy of the Western World.

It turned out that he had indeed read ninety-five per cent of the books in his library. 'Those I haven't read are those I find I can't. Either too dull, too badly written or just plain unreadable.' As it was for her, reading was one of his great pleasures in life. He shared her taste for biography and they had a stimulating argument as to the merits of Michael Holroyd versus Peter Ackroyd. He was also an *aficionado* of the American thriller: 'not the bloodless, endless red herrings

English detective puzzle but the true thriller; blood and gore, mayhem and mean streets.' This led to Tessa's telling him about some of her own real-life experiences, like the time she had been called to a punch-up in a pub.

'There were at least twenty people milling around, all thumping and kicking each other, and we had to wade in and calm them down. We had just about done so but there was still a sizable bunch of them clustered together when I saw this arm in a sheepskin coat pick up a credit card from the floor and put it in his pocket. Another man nearby had his back to me but he was on his knees stuffing the contents of a wallet back inside it so it seemed logical to assume that Sheepskin had picked up a card that did not belong to him. So I arrested him and he flatly denied it. He said he did not own any credit cards. Somehow or other he had got rid of this one because it was not on him when he was searched, but I knew he had taken it; there was no mistaking his sheepskin and nobody else was wearing one. I saw it plainly as he bent down to pick up the card. So it was his word against mine.

'The lawful owner confirmed that one card was missing, and though we searched the place it was not found. By the time the case got to court it had been replaced by the bank, and as the accused's witness was his best friend, who swore uphill and down dale that I was lying with the intention of fitting up his friend, the judge dismissed the case. But I knew he'd picked up that card and must have passed it on to the friend who had either parked it somewhere or scarpered. No doubt that's why the latter said to me, as we were leaving the court: "You'll get yours, you bitch!"'

Nicholas did not say a word. He had his chin on his hand

and his eyes fastened to her face in a way that was insidiously flattering, as though she held him spellbound.

'Anyway, a few weeks later I was coming to the end of my shift – I was late turn and it was about a quarter to ten and I was on my way back to the station. There was a short cut through a housing estate, using a passage between two blocks of flats. It was not quite dark but the place was deserted, not a soul around, and the light in the passage was broken, as they always are. I was about halfway down the passage when I saw a man coming towards me. As we neared each other I saw it was Best Friend. He stopped dead and said in a menacing voice: "You're the one who tried to stitch up Barry," and the next thing I knew he had me backed up against the wall, holding me by the neck with one hand while making a fist with the other. I knew I was in for a thumping so I closed my eyes and braced myself, but the blow never landed. The next thing I knew he had released me and walked off. Two men and a Rotweiler had come through the other end of the arch.'

'A narrow escape.'

'I shook for a good hour afterwards.'

'Do you often run into situations like that?'

'I've had my share.'

'But you are taught to defend yourself, surely?'

'Oh, yes, but when you are only five feet six and your opponent is six feet and built like a brick-building, you can only do the best you can.'

Nicholas regarded her thoughtfully. 'What is it like to be a woman in such a masculine occupation?'

'You can say macho,' Tessa told him dryly. 'And it can be difficult. My very first Chief Superintendent, for instance, conducted his appraisal interviews of WPCs by – and I quote – "the size of their tits". I was told by the Admin Sargeant that he'd see me early on in the morning.'

She saw his well-shaped mouth twitch but he said nothing.

'I was also told, when I applied to join the District Support Unit – a sort of roving public order patrol and just the sort of policing I wanted to do – that it was Men Only. But it's not only policemen who think that way. I was once asked by a very snotty male defence counsel: "Is it *Miss* or *Mrs* Sansom?" I told him it was Detective Sergeant Sansom actually.'

'Yes,' murmured Nicholas. 'I can well believe that.'

Warming to her theme Tessa asked: 'How about this then? When I was a uniform PC I was once out patrolling with a Sergeant. We stopped a vehicle which had been reported as stolen not long before. There were two men in it and they got out and ran off in different directions. The Sergeant had a personal radio but I didn't – not enough to go round, they said, so all I could do was chase one man while the Sergeant went after the other. The Sergeant, who was a good bloke, called up for assistance, giving my location and direction, saying I didn't have a radio. As luck would have it, the Station Duty Officer happened to be driving past the top of the road about a quarter of a mile from where I was pelting after my suspect. His reply was: "She reckons she can do the job. Let's leave her to get on with it, right?" He neither attended the scene nor came to look for me. However, I eventually found my suspect hiding behind a garden wall getting his breath back, so I nicked him.'

'Did the Sergeant tell you what the Duty Officer had said?'

'Oh, yes. He was steaming! He thought the DO was a prat anyway, but the PC who'd told him had been in the car and was of like mind. Those two were much more typical of male attitudes at that time than the Sergeant.'

'But the status of women police officers has improved over the past few years, has it not?'

'It has indeed. We are not called *women* police constables for a start. Now that the Met is an Equal Opportunities Employer, everybody is a police constable.'

'Are you a feminist?'

'Insofar as I regard myself as in no way inferior to any man, then yes, I am. But I don't go along with the extremists.' Her dimples flashed. 'Like joining the Society for Cutting Up Men, for instance.'

'I am relieved to hear it. The only thing about a woman that should be sharp is her tongue . . .'

Something in the way he said it made her heart thud and her skin crisp, but he did not change the subject.

'What do you think about arming the police as they do in other countries?

'We already go armed in certain situations.'

'I mean the constable on the beat.'

'No,' Tessa said without hesitation. 'It's too dangerous. It's not unknown for a policeman to lose his gun and have it used against him by the very people he is up against.'

'But with criminals going armed more and more . . .'

They were off again on another non-acrimonious argument, he putting his experience in Spain and America up against hers in the UK, and this time she was able to straighten out a few of *his* misconceptions. He laughed uproariously as she told him about some of the people she had worked with, like Treasure.

'Because she was worth her weight in gold?' he hazarded, as she knew he would.

'No, because they had no idea where she had been dug up.'

As he relished that she wondered fleetingly whether or not to tell him the origin of the nickname TCP but decided against explaining it meant That Cunt Perkins. He obviously shared her sense of humour and was deeply interested in her work, but she decided that it was better left unsaid. In spite of their incredible *rapport*, she really did not know him well enough. Nevertheless, she was aware that she was enjoying herself on a scale such as she had not experienced in . . . My God! she thought blankly. I can't remember when. Gone was the depression that had afflicted her at Bramshill. This man had replaced it with euphoria. It was so long since she had talked so enjoyably, laughed so wholeheartedly. She did not want this lunch ever to end. Poor Davina, she thought, not pitying her in the least, you don't know the half.

And all the while she was emptying both her plate and her glass.

A woman who appreciated good food, Nicholas judged. Which pleased him. He had no time for women who counted the calories in every lettuce leaf. The relish with which she savoured the soup and the fish whilst appreciating the wines he took as an indication that her other appetites would be equally developed.

Although she had made no impression on him at their first meeting – he was under par and she was under cover – she had aroused an acute and acquisitive interest at their second encounter. She was out of his usual way yet eminently worthy of his attention. Made up to best advantage hers was a lovely face; large eyes deeply, vividly blue, fringed by long, thick lashes, nose straight and short, a mouth – ah, yes, that mouth. The kind to inspire a man to incredible fantasies as to what it could do to certain parts of his anatomy. But it was the striking personality and the mind – all her own – lying in wait behind the fragile exterior which had struck his favourite chord. Her sense of humour, for instance, and the way she effortlessly returned the conversational ball. He liked her lack of the archness shown by so many women, and the fact that she never went fishing for compliments. Her crisply confident manner had made it plain she'd had enough of them and to spare and did not need any from him, thank you very much.

But what had come across more than anything was her cool sensuality; his sexual radar had detected a V-8 engine under that beautifully designed bonnet. The minus was that at the wedding she had made it plain she was not interested. Curiosity as to why had sent him in search of Drear Davina, who told him spitefully – in great detail – that he would get no joy there. Tessa Sansom happened to be well married to a handsome stud, added to which she was the last woman to indulge in hole and corner affairs.

'Never in holes, my dear Davina,' he had protested, 'and corners are much too uncomfortable.'

But he had found out what he needed to know, so regretfully relinquished the prospect. Yet here she was, crossing his path for the third time. Perhaps Fate, in a state of petulant boredom, *had* decided to take a mischievous hand. What was it they said? Once was coincidence, two was happenstance, but three times merited investigation.

So be it. He would investigate.

It was as he watched her scrape up the last smear of caramel from her second helping of *flan* before emptying her glass of the luscious desert wine that had accompanied it, that he saw how best to do it.

'You do like Spanish food,' he approved, as she placed her spoon on her empty plate.

'Your kind of Spanish food I do.'

'What kind do you not like?'

'Well, in Spain you use parts of a chicken that we normally throw away . . . and I can't face squid cooked in its own ink though I love it fried in batter. And I don't care for chickpeas – what are they called in Spanish?'

'*Garbanzos*.'

'Yes. Them.'

'You know Spain well?'

'I've only been three times, each time on holiday. The first time was a tour by car from Barcelona to Cadiz. The second was two weeks in a villa in a lovely unspoiled little place called Nerja, not far from Malaga, and the third was in another village just north of Alicante – Javea.'

His strategy was working. Memories of Spain had her glancing out of the window at the still heavily falling rain to sigh: 'Oh, to be there now, where the sun is no doubt hot and high and the temperature is even higher.'

He stirred his nicely simmering mixture. 'It was eighty-five degrees when I talked to our branch in Madrid by telephone at ten this morning; a bright sun in a cloudless sky.'

Tessa could not repress an involuntary moan at the picture his words conjured up.

Raising the heat: 'I have a house on the Costa Brava, just south of Cadaques; it's name is *Aguas Frescas*, Fresh Waters in English, because it is built over a stream that comes down from the mountains.'

'Mmmm, sounds wonderful,' Tessa sighed dreamily,

replete with good food, her tension unwound to limpness by the sheer pleasure she was experiencing.

'Oh, it is, I assure you. The house stands above a tiny bay where you can swim in water that is so clear you can see the pebbles on the sandy bottom and the fish swimming above them.'

He saw her close her eyes as if she were seeing it in her mind's eye, unconsciously tilting her head back as though to the sun, a dreamy smile lifting the corners of that tantalising mouth, heard the long sigh that escaped her.

He had learned she possessed imagination, but this was remarkable.

'Mmm,' she breathed.

She would never be more ready, so he administered the *coup de grâce*. 'I am flying there this very afternoon. Why not come with me? Leave this awful weather behind and soak up some Spanish sun instead.'

Tessa's eyes flew open as she sat bolt upright, but his easy, conversational tone did not lose its momentum. '*Aguas Frescas* is the perfect place to relax, and I get the impression that you are in need of both rest and relaxation.'

Tell me about it, groaned Tessa to herself, even as she found herself saying automatically: 'No, I'm afraid that's not possible.'

'Why not?' He raised his eyebrows. 'Is it that you think you do not know me well enough?'

'Well, I don't do I?' she replied with blunt honesty. 'We haven't spent more than a couple of hours in each other's company.'

'That can be remedied, but I think you already know much more about me than I do about you. Didn't Davina tell you?'

Tessa had the grace to blush.

'Or is it that you doubt I am capable of wanting a woman purely for the pleasure of her company?'

He saw that sink in its teeth down to the bone before pressing home his advantage.

'I have thoroughly enjoyed our lunch, and I think you have found it equally pleasurable. Why not continue the enjoyment over the weekend? I can provide you with more good food and wine, you may sleep as long as you wish, and if it pleases you to do no more than lie in the sun, then by all means do so.' A pause. 'You may do whatever you wish.'

Oh, do stop! Tessa was imploring silently, finding the temptation worse than anything St Anthony had undergone. Which, of course, Nicholas damned well knew.

Why not? her inner self rose up to demand rebelliously. Loosen up, Tessa. Subjugate that common sense. Live a little. Get a life. I mean, why the hell not? Harry is God knows where with God knows who except it is bound to be a woman. Has he rung you? Has he left a message? Has he hell! And what does it matter anyway if you and he are finally through with each other? You can see your parents any time, but Spain – Spain, Tessa – sun, heat . . .

Sex.

My God! she thought, shocked rigid that she could even *think* of sex with anyone but Harry. Besides, she reminded herself smugly, Old Nick might have the reputation of a sexual virtuoso but hadn't she been married to the Metropolitan Police's Prize Stud for the past eleven years? There were only so many things a man and woman could do to pleasure each other and Harry knew them all. According to him he'd written the manual. Never mind about Harry, her baser self ordered ruthlessly. He isn't minding about you.

You'd be a fool to turn this offer down. Even the Godfather never made an offer like this.

Nicholas Ould watched her struggling, confirmed in his estimation of her as a woman who took her responsibilities seriously. Long experience of married women had taught him that if everything in her garden was as perfectly lovely as she no doubt wanted him to believe, her refusal would have been as nicely put and firmly indicated as it had been at the wedding. Now her hesitation betrayed the true state of affairs. Which was that she was ready for one. Besides, when he had come across her stranded car, the depression had been greater inside than out.

As he watched her, she suddenly raised her head from contemplation of her plate to chill him with the cool, almost calculating expression in her lovely eyes. Now what? he thought, instantly on the alert. She's up to something . . .

This was confirmed when she asked cannily: 'Just what exactly are you offering?'

Got her! he thought, before replying, with just enough surprise in his voice to make her squirm: 'Exactly what I said. Rest and relaxation in a beautiful house on the edge of the sea in a country whose climate is infinitely superior to this one.'

Tessa stared hard at him. He stared back. Is it that she does not want to be treated as just the latest in a long line? he wondered.

She was still gazing at him, but meditatively now. Look, her inner self was arguing, it is really quite simple . . .

I know that. It's the complications that could ensue which worry me.

Why should there be any? Unless . . .

Come on, remember Davina's blow-by-blow account.

Ruthless, she said. Discards them with the sheets, she said. So turn the tables. Use him – and to prise Harry loose. If your anything-but-better-half were to get wind of you swanning off to Spain with Nicholas Ould he would go spare. His own catting around he regards as nothing more than exercising his rights, but where his wife is concerned he locks the cat-flap every night. Let him get wind of this and he'll have you in the divorce court before you can spell cuckold!

She lowered her lashes to hide her eyes, aware he was watching her closely, feeling excitement roil. Could this be the help I prayed for? The means to cut myself free . . . Is Nicholas Ould my knife?

Anything I wish, he said. So take him at his word. That's the beauty of it all. You don't *have* to have sex with him, you only have to go to Spain with him. That will be enough for Harry since he is not capable of believing that a woman could go away with a man for the weekend and not spend every minute in a state of rampant carnality. He judges everybody by his own standards.

'Well?' Nicholas pressed, deciding she had had long enough to make up her mind, pushing back his cuff to look pointedly at his watch. That always set the spurs to their decision. He never asked twice, and he had given her long enough. Besides, even if his instincts were giving him the thumbs up, there was the still niggling doubt as to what had finally tipped the balance in his favour. He only knew it had to do with that coolly assessing look she had given him. Well, he would have the whole weekend to find out. Which was his firm intention.

'Whatever *I* wish?' she repeated, as if asking for final confirmation,

Ah, he thought. So that's it. 'Whatever *you* wish,' he agreed, confident that once he got her there he would soon have her doing whatever *he* wished.

'In that case . . .' her smile broke through, 'if you will allow me to make a phone call first?'

'Of course. There is a telephone on the desk in my study. The second door on the right.'

If Harry is in or if there is a message from him I won't go, she told herself as she stabbed out the numbers. If there is no answer and no message, then Spain it is.

The phone rang and on the second ring the answering machine clicked on. She heard her own voice: 'Hello from the Sansoms. Sorry we are not here right now to take your call, but if you leave your name and number, one of us will call you back as soon as we can. Please speak after the tone.'

Switching on her remote control Tessa played back the messages that had been left. There were two of them, both for Harry. But there were none from him.

So be it, she thought, replacing the receiver with a steady hand before walking back to join her host.

'All squared away?' he asked.

'Yes,' she replied, striking the match that would burn her boats to the waterline. 'No problems.'

10

As Nicholas and Tessa walked out of the back of the house and across the lawns to where a bright red and yellow Sikorsky S-76 helicopter waited: 'I have no passport with me, you know,' Tessa reminded, in a sudden, last-minute bid for common sense, 'and the clothes I took to Bramshill are not the sort of things one takes to Spain.'

The mercurial eyes ranged over her Calvin Klein jeans, her Next pale blue cotton shirt, and the Marks & Spencer navy blue blazer with brass buttons – the off duty clothes she had donned to leave Bramshill – before he said: 'You look fine to me, but whatever you need you will find at *Aguas Frescas*. I so often have unexpected guests that I have no choice but to cater for them. As for your passport, Spain is an EC country and entry as my guest is easily arranged.'

Wanting to needle that unshakeable confidence, Tessa observed tartly: 'You obviously wield a great deal of clout in that country.'

'They know who I am,' he agreed equably.

Entering the helicopter she found it comfortable, even

luxurious, but as the door was shut and secured she knew a moment's sheer panic at her foolhardiness. Where was her normal caution? What had possessed her to act so out of character? Oh, for God's sake, her inner self snarled. When will you realise that there are doubts, fears, even compulsive drives that are *not* fuelled by your beloved rationality but can still exert a powerful influence on your life. Sit back and accept that this is one of them.

But she still had to clamp her mouth shut so as not to shout: 'Stop the engines! I've changed my mind!' Pride helped her keep silent. That and the thought of Nicholas's contempt, for he would undoubtedly think her all sorts of fool. Then the engines started up and it was too late anyway.

The helicopter ferried them to Gatwick, where Nicholas kept his Grumman Gulfstream II, and at 5.30 p.m. they were passing over the Sussex coast. It was 7.20 Spanish time when the jet touched down at Gerona airport.

Formalities were brief, because Nicholas handled them. Obviously, that was what he'd been doing when he made that telephone call from the plane, for some kind of minion came on board, carrying a briefcase from which he took a sheet of official-looking paper which Tessa saw bore the logo of Ould & Sons. Nicholas scanned this while the minion, having produced a small Polaroid camera, took Tessa's likeness, which he then affixed to the paper before asking her to sign across it. He explained that it allowed her to enter the country for forty-eight hours, vouched for by Don Nicholas. The uniformed official who had accompanied the minion then scrutinised the document, after which he examined Tessa before stamping the permit with a flourish. He did not examine Señor Ould's passport, which Tessa noticed was a British one. Instead he smiled, bowed, wished them '*Buenas Tardes*' and then both men left.

'The name Nicholas Ould seems to invoke the same sort of respect as that of King Juan Carlos I,' Tessa marvelled. 'But then, I expect he is a friend of yours?'

'As a matter of fact, he is.' This was said so pleasantly it left her feeling cheap and resolving to keep her needle in its case.

Waiting for them at the foot of the aircraft steps was a car which Tessa, who was a fan of James Bond as played by Sean Connery, recognised as an Aston Martin.

'We have about an hour's drive to *Aguas Frescas*, so should be there at around nine o'clock,' Nicholas told her as she settled herself in her glove-leather seat. Take as long as you like Tessa thought. This is luxury upon luxury . . . I could get used to this.

When they had boarded the Gulfstream she had been under attack from her regrouped conscience so that her replies to her companion's best efforts at easy conversation were terse, to say the least. Taking the hint he had left her alone, which instead of pleasing her had produced contrary feelings of disappointment, only to have her mood turn yet another somersault when she got a good look at the interior of the plane. Sumptuous was the only word capable of doing it justice, with its leather-upholstered club seats, sixteen-channel stereo system, twenty-four inch television screen, VCR, well-stocked bar, and four analogue clocks which told the time in London, New York, Hong Kong and Tokyo.

When *aperitivos* were served by an attentive steward, she accepted a glass of sherry and proceeded to make inroads into the bowls of stuffed olives, salted almonds and *crudités* such as celery, peppers, carrots and onions, which she dipped into a selection of more-ish dips, turning to food for comfort as she always did when something was gnawing at her peace of mind.

As he made a telephone call, lounging back in the armchair opposite hers, Nicholas Ould monitored her from under his lashes, smiling to himself as he watched her hoover the bowls clean. Still struggling, he thought. She wants, yes, but what is it she wants? Not me. Not yet, anyway. She is not yet *aware* of me. So just why *is* she here? What made her look at me so calculatingly before deciding to say yes? Ten to one it has to do with what was on her mind when I found her sunk in gloom this morning. Still is, for that matter. How fortunate I have the whole weekend to find out.

It was a prospect he found intriguing, not to say stimulating. Tessa Sansom was, quite simply, a challenge he could not ignore.

Now, as the big, powerful car took the road north to Figueras, Tessa finally acknowledged that she was being manipulated by what one of her instructors at Hendon had called 'the three Fs': the Fickle Finger of Fate. For no good reason that she could divine, it had casually pointed in her direction and said: 'That one there . . . the blonde . . . yes, her.' She, Tessa Sansom, had been chosen to be the recipient of a once-in-a-lifetime, twenty-two carat gold, gift from the Gods. There had to be a reason; there always was, but for now, the night air was warm, perfumed with what she always thought of as the scent of Spain, a heady combination of the colognes everyone wore, pungent Spanish tobacco and the ever present fragrance of the pine trees which grew everywhere on the Costa Brava, the car was unbelievably comfortable, and driving it was a man right out of Her Favourite Fantasy. It was a case of '*che sera, sera*', she decided, and having done so, felt her tension drain away.

They did not talk much, but the silence was not in the least strained. When he put a tape in the Blaupunkt radio-cassette she was conscious of disappointment, until the first seductive strains of Manual da Falla's *Nights in the Gardens of Spain* – which she had once heard played in the gardens of the Alhambra on a never-to-be forgotten summer night – made her draw in a sharp breath of delight. The music stole onto the heavy night air, the limpid notes of the piano glittering like crystal before merging with the quivering strings to dissolve slowly, like sugar on the tongue.

Closing her eyes she let the music take her where only music could.

Glancing at her, Nicholas Ould unwrapped another layer from her inner core. So, music was another of her pleasures. It was obvious from the way she was lying back in her seat, eyes closed, body all but vibrating, that her response to it was intensely subjective. Good. Something else they had in common. It augured well for her eventual response to him.

By the time the car reached Figueras and turned off the main highway, heading north-east to Cadaques, Tessa was in a state her mother was wont to describe as *in alt*. The music had drawn her even deeper into the spell, and when they turned off again, this time on to a narrow lane where pines crowded the slopes on either side, their scent filling the air and mingling with another she recognised as that of the sea, she was totally under the influence.

Her first sight of the house was under the molten glow of a setting sun which had painted the sky every variation of the colour purple; from bruised lilac through pinkish mauve deepening to red-gold and on to majestic royal, paling away to the most delicate of greys, all slashed with fiery streaks edged in gold, brushing the white walls of the house with deeply mysterious shadows. The large single-storey villa was double-terraced, the lower level ending in a balustraded walk to a cork-covered landing stage which could also be used as a diving platform. The Mediterranean was incredibly blue, hardly ruffled by the breeze, which was too languid to move the blossom-laden bushes of jasmine and oleander surrounding the house, their scent heavy on the warm air.

'I am so glad you like it,' Nicholas Ould said suavely, surveying the ecstatic face, the no-longer-dark-with-misery eyes, now transformed into star sapphires. Of course, she would naturally be as responsive to beauty as she was to music. Better and better. 'We are on Cap de Creus. It is mostly rocks, but there are a few secluded sandy coves. You do swim?'

'Oh, yes.'

'Good. The water is warm and the sea floor slopes gradually. Now, let me show you the house.'

It was tile-floored, open plan, with wide arches between large, lofty rooms, all of which had vast expanses of windows, hung in filmy white voile, overlooking a paved terrace set with lounging chairs and swings upholstered in brightly coloured linen. It was all white – floors, furniture, flowers, round tables covered in silky damask – but in every room the corners held fresh and spreading greenery, interspersed with ornate Spanish candlesticks of wrought iron bearing thick, tall candles, and on the walls were carved and gilded 17th-century mirrors.

The terrace was obviously used as the dining room in summer, for it contained, under an awning, a long table big enough to seat a dozen or more.

A white-coated manservant, a dead ringer for the one they

had left behind in Dorset, had come forward to greet them with a soft: '*Buenas Tardes*'.

'This is Rafael; he looks after things,' Nicholas said. 'He speaks excellent English, as do all the servants.'

'He looks like the man who served our lunch.'

'Not surprising. They are brothers. All the servants do six months here and six months in England. They speak both languages.'

Oh, the pleasures of riches, was Tessa's response. I must be careful not to get hooked on this . . .

When finally he ushered her into a bedroom, saying: 'This will be yours,' it was a veritable honey-pot; apricot, peach, pale and deep gold, with splashes of white and zingy turqoise. En suite was a positively sybaritic bathroom lined with floor to ceiling mirrors. Behind one wall was a fitted wardrobe, while on the glass shelves above the double basins was a selection of soaps, talcs, bathoils, emollient lotions and perfumes, all by Guerlain, as well as several unopened bottles of differing kinds of shampoos. In a drawer was a complete range of matching cosmetics. The plain white towels were thick and fleecy, big enough to use as sheets. Hanging on a hook was a towelling robe and there were slippers to match. On the floor behind the door were the latest electronic scales.

I have a feeling I am about to gain more than weight, Tessa thought on an inner giggle, the spurs of her conscience having lost their spikes.

'There should be a selection of swimsuits here.'

Nicholas slid back the mirrored doors and, sure enough, each on its own padded hanger, hung some half a dozen swimsuits, both bikinis and maillots. One she instantly marked as hers: a deep violet maillot, cut high at the front, pared away at the back.

'And clothes in here.'

Pushing back another mirrored door, he revealed a rack of brightly coloured shirts, the kind to be worn over a swimsuit or one of the various pairs of shorts and trousers which hung next to the shirts. Everything was casual, all with designer labels, and the sizes ranged from an eight to a fourteen.

On the racks below awaited a range of flat-heeled sandals of various kinds, along with *alpargatas* of every colour.

'Use anything and everything as and when you wish. It is all for my guests.'

As old-established and successful brewers the Nortons had never been short of a bob or two, and her father's family had been comfortably off. Tessa was therefore no stranger to the things money could buy, but this man was *seriously* rich; here was luxury on a scale she had hitherto associated only with the likes of Aristotle Onassis, Gianni Agnelli, the Rockefellers and the Rothschilds.

'As we are in Spain we keep Spanish hours; dinner will therefore not be until ten o'clock,' he was saying, as he closed the mirrored doors. 'Can you last out until then? If not, I can always provide you with a *bocadillo*.'

Tessa had the grace to blush at the laughter in his voice. She had eaten like a stevedore at lunch and consumed God knows how much on the plane, but she had been under stress. Now that the stress was gone so was her hunger. Nevertheless she made the gesture of glancing at her watch.

'I think I can wait,' she assured him, demurely.

'A drink beforehand at about nine-forty-five, then?'

'Yes, please.' In fact, yes to everything, was Tessa's fervent response. All this was turning out to be far, far – well, *more* – than she had expected.

He smiled down at her, 'If there is anything lacking, all you have to do is say so.'

I'll bet, thought Tessa.

When he had gone she looked down at her arm. The almost invisible golden hairs on it were positively quivering.

At the same time as she was stepping into the shower Harry Sansom was turning the key in the lock of his front door. As he opened it, he sensed at once the flat was empty. Sarge came to meet him, only to make a strategic retreat when he saw it was not the person he wanted. Harry heard the clatter of the cat-flap.

Scowling, he went to check on the answerphone, found, amongst the others, the message about Bramshill as well as several calls that were obviously message checks. No doubt Tessa wondering where he was. Good. He had intended her to do just that, deliberately staying away so that his non-presence would bring her to her senses, make her miss and want him. She must be well aware by now that he was seriously displeased. If this longest of all absences didn't convince her she had better do the right thing then he would have to take some really drastic action.

As his mother had advised.

'You've got to make yourself master in your own house,' she had told him. 'I don't hold with all this feminist claptrap. Women need men and men need women and it don't matter that it's for different reasons. Men are the breadwinners and it's not natural that your wife should be earning more than you. Tilts everything off balance. She should be at home with a couple of your kids by now, and if you can't make her see that, then my advice is to get rid of her and find a woman who will.'

'You never liked her, did you?'

'Because she wasn't right for you – nor for the family neither. She's not our sort. To tell the truth, I never thought it would last this long.'

'I'm not going to be the first Sansom in the divorce court,' Harry had flared, sensitive in the only area he was capable of being: his own status. 'We were perfectly happy until she went and took that Accelerated bloody Promotion Course. All she has to do is go back to putting me first, and we'll be the same as we were.'

His mother had shaken her head, sceptically. 'Chance would be a fine thing. You've let it go on far too long, son. It's got to the stage where your wife is wearing the pants. Get rid of her while you can and find yourself a *female* woman, one who'll be content to be a wife. That's always been enough for us proper women.'

As always, his mother could make him feel he was letting the family down by not exerting his authority as a male. Your father would never have allowed it, she was saying. Nor do your brothers. So what's wrong with you?

What the hell more he could do? he thought, aggrieved. His mother was right about Tessa being different. For a start she was not the kind he could subdue with a slap. She'd turn round and knee him in the balls. Before packing her bags. All the same, there was no way he was going to allow himself to be divorced when he had done nothing wrong. She was the one at fault because she had relegated him to the back burner. His mother was right in her judgment. Tessa did lack respect for his authority and standing as a male. In fact, sometimes, when she looked at him with that blue stare of hers, he could have sworn she thought herself his fucking superior. All right, so she had brains. He had always known that; in spite of his reservations he'd even been proud of them until she let them go to her head and spoil everything. But being clever also meant she was smart enough to take him on and show him up without so much as a by-your-leave. Like dragging him through the divorce court. No doubt with that clever-dick lawyer uncle of hers handling her case. Her class had never shrunk from using the law for their own ends.

He scowled round the flat, immaculate except for the faint film of dust that had collected during her absence.

Shit! If he had known she was going to Bramshill . . . He had intended her to be alone here, waiting and wondering and worrying as she came to realise how angry he was. If her course was supposed to finish this morning why the hell wasn't she here? He had expected to find her anxiously waiting, not only ready but wanting. Tessa was the last woman in the world to go looking for it. If she had been he wouldn't have been able to use sexual starvation as a weapon.

Mind you, he had not meant to be away so long, but on his second night, on going with his brothers for a drink at a club they frequented, he had met Mandy, obviously looking for action. One look at her red hair, those 38D-cup beauties and that bandage of a skirt, and one thing had led to another. More particularly to her flat on the river at Wapping. She was something in the City, one of those yuppies who worked as a broker, and she made a lot of money. Mandy was a goer. Game for anything. He could get really dirty with her – and had, especially in her jacuzzi.

It made him hard just to think about it. From the off she'd been willing to try anything, unlike Tessa. It had taken him months before he could get her to handle him never mind take him in her mouth. Mind you, once she got the taste for it . . .

So why the hell wasn't she here, then, frustrated as hell and ready to beg? He felt anger build. Probably gone off somewhere with those poncey friends of hers. People he had no use for. Stuck-up bastards. Thought they were a cut above everybody else because they'd been Noticed by Those On High. Sod that for a lark. If that was the way she wanted to play it, he would go back to Mandy and invent some more games of his own . . .

The front door slammed behind him.

11

Tessa took a last, considering look in the mirror and decided that not only would she do, she would do very well.

She had showered, washed and dried her hair, anointed herself with handfuls of silky lotion perfumed with Mitsouko, then donned a matching lacy bra and briefs from the bag she had taken to Bramshill – the only things of her own she was wearing. From the wardrobe, after lengthy consideration, she had chosen a pair of white crêpe palazzo pants and a pure silk organza shirt the colour of pink carnations, patterned with a design of that flower in white. It was a colour which both suited and flattered her, enhancing the newly minted gold of her hair, intensifying the vivid blue of her eyes. Yes, she thought in smug satisfaction, doing a 360-degree turn so as to examine her image reflected from all sides, I will do very nicely. What exactly she would do was something she put to the back of her mind, but the nervous excitement she was feeling was undoubtedly responsible for the flags of colour flying in her cheekbones.

It was a long time since she had taken part in the games

men and women play and she was rusty, to say the least. The best way to handle it – him – was cool assurance; that should carry her through the early play-offs while she watched, listened and learned. Like whether or not he had been telling the truth when he had said 'Whatever you want.'

One thing she had learned long since was that a man in pursuit of a woman would say anything to achieve his ends. The trouble was that Nicholas Ould was not your average man. She had foolishly thought that after Harry there was nothing more to learn about womanisers, but she was beginning to recognise that for the mistake it was. Harry was many things but he was no sophisticate. Nicholas Ould epitomised the word. This, she lectured her reflection, is an entirely different ball-game.

Fortunately, she was no longer handicapped by the shyness that had afflicted her when she first met Harry. Not after years of working in the canteen culture, the most intensive training ground known in the Art of Coarse Sex. Not that there was anything coarse about Nicholas Ould. Far from it. Like the other side of the galaxy, for instance. She would just have to play it – him – by ear. It was as well, she reflected on an impish grin as she turned from the mirror, that he had no idea she possessed perfect pitch.

When she made her entrance on to the terrace, to her chagrin he did not see it. He was at the drinks trolley with his back to her, intent on measuring precise amounts of liquid into a jigger before pouring them into a silver cocktail shaker. Still, it gave her the advantage of being able to give him the once over. Informality prevailed at *Aguas Frescas*, he had informed her earlier, which was no doubt why he was wearing a beautifully cut cream linen suit, its unstructured jacket unbuttoned over a crisp pale blue shirt. Armani, obviously. She had noticed that before: his elegance. It came from a lean body without an ounce of surplus flesh and a length of leg that could carry clothes with the sort of *élan* to which Harry had aspired but never managed to reach, though he spent a lot of money trying. It was in uniform that he turned most heads.

Just then, Nicholas turned his, looked at her, and all of a sudden Tessa was rooted to the spot, feeling his eyes like probes as they went over every inch of her, leaving a tingling sensation in their wake.

Eventually he smiled, releasing her. '*Buenas noches*', he greeted, before asking, *à propos* her carnation pink shirt: 'Is that a compliment to my Spanish half? *The clavel* – which is Spanish for carnation – is to this country what the rose is to England.'

Tessa only smiled, allowing him to think so, before registering what was hanging low in the sky. 'But – the moon is red!' she exclaimed.

'We are that much further south. Were we on the Costa del Sol it would be even bigger and the colour of blood.'

'Now there is a word that appears all the time in things Spanish. *Blood and Sand*, *Blood Wedding*. Even *Sangria*, a variation on the Spanish word for blood, isn't it? And the bullfight entails the shedding of blood.'

Tessa was aware she was babbling, but after that look her scruples had staged a counter-attack with massive reinforcements.

'Have you ever seen a bullfight?' he asked.

'No.' She forbore to say that Harry had, and raved about it afterwards. 'But I have read *Death in the Afternoon*.'

'And?'

'It was reading Hemingway that first made me want to come to Spain.'

Looking up from the drinks once more he again pinned her with his eyes before saying softly: 'Whatever the reason, I am very glad you did.'

Tessa had to turn away to regain her composure.

Wow! she thought, taking in deep breaths. When he gets going he's something and no mistake. She could feel him concentrating on her in a way that totally undermined her self-control. In an effort to appear casual she leaned on the still sun-warm marble of the balustrade, apparently fascinated by the enormous moon, whose reflection formed a shimmering ladder of spangles on the cellophane surface of the wine-dark sea. No wonder he brings his women here, she thought muzzily. This place is an aphrodisiac in itself.

She turned back to him as he came across to her, carrying two cocktail glasses. As he held hers out to her, he did not take the opportunity to allow his fingers to brush hers. No, not this man. He would never be so obvious. Examining her glass she saw that it was rimmed in salt. 'A Margarita?', she identified. 'But I've not had one like this before.'

He raised his eyebrows questioningly.

'I had my first one when we were in San Diego a few years back. It came in a huge glass with a straw and was so cold it gave me a headache.'

'That would have been a frosted Margarita, made with lots of crushed ice. This is the classic version as taught me by a bartender in Cuernavaca. Try it, see which you prefer. I can easily make you the one of your choice.'

He watched her raise her glass before matching her, saying as he did so: '*Salud y pesetas*.'

He missed out the *amor*, Tessa thought, perversely disappointed, realising in the next instant that when it came to playing the games men and women play, this man was World and Olympic Champion. Not looking at him, she sipped experimentally, then was unable to stop herself from taking a greedy mouthful. 'Mmmm . . . nectar.' It slid over her tongue and down her throat, leaving her tastebuds swooning.

'Potent nectar. I will allow you one only before dinner. Two would put you under the table rather than at it.'

Tessa giggled.

The magic was working, Nicholas noted with satisfaction. Not that he had ever known it to fail. The devastatingly romantic combination of climate, situation, and a liberal application of wanton luxury had toppled many a woman from her virtuous pedestal. When this one had come on to the terrace he had seen at once that it had already dusted off whatever it was that had earlier dulled her spirits, revealing a glow at which a man could warm himself. Watching her sip her Margarita he was confirmed in his assessment of her as a woman of appetites. Which suited him just fine, since he intended to develop them – especially the one which interested him most – to the point where she was positively ravenous.

When dinner was announced they went not to the big table at the far end of the forty-foot terrace, but to a smaller, round table set in the curve of the house under a white wall against which a magnificent fig-tree had spread itself, already laden with ripening fruit. They sat facing each other over a dark green glass bowl in which freshly cut camelias floated. Tall candles burned in glass storm lanterns, the latter not needed since the night air was too enervated to stir itself. The table cloth and napkins were of exquisitely embroidered lace-edged linen, the glasses of crystal so fine they were almost invisible, while the cutlery had the heaviness of solid silver. Everything bore a crest which Nicholas said was that of his mother's family.

'*Virtus sola nobilitat*,' read Tessa. 'Virtue and nobility are all?' At his surprise she came clean: 'My father read Classics at Oxford. He reads – used to read – both Latin and Greek.'

'Of course . . . Bishop Paget is a well-known scholar. In fact, it means "Virtue alone enobles".' His voice was dry. 'Something an ancestor of mine did not wholly believe, because when Philip II offered to make him a *Marques*, he accepted like a shot.'

'Do your parents live in England or Spain?'

'My father died some years ago. My mother divides her time between Madrid – she is a *Madrileno* – and London, according to her mood.'

'And you?'

'I live and work in England, but I come here as often as time and my schedule will allow.'

'I suppose running a bank calls for long hours and hard work,' Tessa said.

'It is not nine to five, five days a week,' he agreed.

For no good reason she found herself telling him what she had never told anyone, not even her husband: 'I have money on deposit with your bank.'

He looked up in surprise.

'My brother left it to me.'

'Left?'

'He was murdered twelve years ago.'

She saw the dark eyes flood with the quick comprehension that was so much a part of him. 'Yes,' she confirmed. 'That is why I joined the police force.'

Their first course arrived. As Rafael began to serve it,

Nicholas Ould said: 'As we are in Catalonia, where the fish is superb, and remembering you told me you loved all kinds of shellfish, I told them to prepare *veneras* – scallops, in English, done in the Galician style, which is chopped up with buttered breadcrumbs, parsley, onions and peppers, and served on their shells.'

Tessa sampled and closed her eyes in bliss as the succulent combination completed the rout of her taste buds that the Margarita had begun. How Harry would have loathed these, she thought as she tucked in. Fish to Harry was cod, haddock or rock salmon, preferably in batter, and while he adored jellied eels, he regarded shellfish as unfit for human consumption. Then: I am *not* going to think of Harry, she resolved firmly. The last thing he will be doing is thinking of me.

With the scallops they drank, Spanish-style, a *Manzanilla*, which was dry and refreshing to the palate after the richness of the shellfish.

When Rafael had left them alone again Nicholas asked: 'What sort of an account with Ould & Sons do you have?'

Tessa told him.

'And you have done absolutely nothing with it since your brother left it to you?' He sounded not so much incredulous as appalled.

'I was too upset at the time to do anything about it, and afterwards – well, I had other things on my mind.'

Frowning, he said: 'The bank takes pride in doing the very best with the money our clients deposit with us, but without any discussion as to the optimum way to utilise market forces you have probably earned much less than you should have had the account been properly managed. Did nobody ever write to you about it? We don't see it as our job to pester clients, but we do monitor what we call dormant accounts.'

'Back at the beginning, yes. I told them just to leave it where it was.'

'Money should always be made to work for you,' he said severely, 'not left to languish where it will not only lose its lustre but its value. Would you like me to take a look at your account and advise you how best to utilise it in future?'

'Would you?' Tessa found herself asking gratefully. If she was going to leave Harry she was going to need all the money she could get; for lawyer's fees if nothing else, except that she was sure that there would be an additional expense: financial compensation. If Harry thought he could get a settlement as recompense for hurt pride he would do his damnedest to do so. Besides, she was no longer the virginal innocent she had been when the money had come her way. Since then she had seen far worse things than that which had shocked her rigid one afternoon in Rupert's flat. She would use his legacy and be grateful.

Nicholas had been watching her as she pondered what he had said, noticing the shadowing of the brilliant eyes. Her brother's money obviously held unpleasant connotations, not surprising considering the manner of his death and the ensuing scandal. But he was glad to have a second string to his bow: her account with the bank was a means of keeping in contact.

Their second course was baby lamb, cooked in an old-style baker's oven over a wood fire, arriving at the table crisp and tender and served with a *purée de patatas con setas*, creamed potatoes with bacon and fungi, and a dish of *guisantes y alcachofas a la Catalana* – artichokes and fresh peas. With it they drank a 1970 *Gran Reserva* Rioja from the *bodega* of the

Marques de Murrieta. Feeling its rich, deep, earthy darkness steal its way through her bloodstream, Tessa made her second glass last, so that she would be able to enjoy the luscious dessert wine which accompanied the pears poached in red wine.

When she asked what the wine was he told her it came from a village just outside Granada and recommended that as she liked it, she should try a local liqueur with her coffee. Its name was *Aromas de Montserrat* since it was made in the monastery of that name just outside Barcelona.

'I've never been there,' Tessa said.

'Where? Montserrat?'

'No. Barcelona.'

'Oh, then you must let me show it to you. The next time I have to visit Barcelona I will let you know, and if you are free, you can accompany me.'

'Hang on a minute,' Tessa protested woozily. 'I've only just arrived on the Costa Brava, and unlike you I am not my own boss.'

'Would you like to be?'

'I hope to have the chance, one day.'

'Back to that again, are we?'

'Sorry?'

'Chance – about which we talked earlier. The way that chance, Fate, call it what you will, seems to be throwing us together.'

'If I eat many more delicious dinners such as the one I have eaten tonight, it will take more than Fate to throw me anywhere!'

As she had hoped he threw back his head and laughed, revealing a long brown throat. Tessa let out a relieved if silent sigh that he had followed her diversion. She had drunk too much glorious wine to be in the condition needed to defend her title as put-down champion of this or any year, though she had kept up her end of the conversation during dinner. They had sparred all through the scallops, for instance, on the merits of French vs Spanish wine, and she was not in the least surprised to learn that he owned a vineyard, in Rioja country. Over the lamb they had discussed Spanish vs English culture, whence it became clear that he knew a great deal about both. Over *postre* – dessert – they explored history, a liking for which he also shared.

By the time dinner ended she was high on a combination of wine and pleasure. As the ever-attentive Rafael pulled back her chair, she found that her legs had suddenly become very heavy. It was quite an effort to put one foot in front of the other, but she managed to make her way to where the coffee tray had been placed, on a low table in front of one of the deeply cushioned loungers. She had to be careful not to fall into it.

As it was, the moment she leaned back against the comfortable cushions she was hit by an overwhelming desire to close her eyes. Her lids seemed to have been weighted and proved incredibly hard to lift. Desperately she drank two cups of good Spanish coffee, hot and strong and black, refusing more than one thimbleful of *Aromas de Montserrat*, constantly blinking wide-eyed to keep her lids from closing. But she was fighting a losing battle as the heady combination of Nicholas, the place, the ambrosial food, the glorious wines and her own high, combined with her earlier exhausting emotional struggle – the sheer excitement of this whole incredible day – had the effect of sand bagging her.

Perhaps if I close my eyes for a minute or two, she thought . . . A few minutes is all I need . . .

★

She woke up in her own bed, disoriented at first until the computer of her memory flashed up text on the screen of her mind that had her sitting bolt upright. She had gone and fallen asleep on him! She put her head in her hands. Oh, God. All she had meant to do was close her eyes for a moment. That moment had lasted, according to the digital clock on the bedside table, some twelve hours, for it was now 11.22 a.m. and sunlight was filtering through blinds that were not entirely closed.

'I'll bet he's never had anyone go to sleep on him before,' Tessa said out loud, and giggled in spite of herself.

So? her cooler self asked. Didn't he say you looked as if you needed some rest? Well, you've had it. Further laughter threatened. He's the one who has had to go without his recreation . . .

She exploded into giggles. What on earth was the matter with her? She should feel awful; guilty, ashamed, at the very least apologetic, yet all she could do was laugh about it.

And why not? Hadn't he also said: 'Anything you like'?

Yes, he had, but I doubt he meant anything like falling sound asleep on him, she told herself. Well, what's done is done, even if what he had in mind was doing me. Which brought on another fit of irrepressible giggling.

Truth to tell, she realised as she stretched to her muscle-cracking limit, she felt *good*; no hangover, rested to a fare-thee-well and aware of a decided edge to her perceptions. Her body, for instance. She looked down at it, saw she was wearing a white silk nightrobe that tied at the waist. Somebody had put her to bed; in this house, no doubt one of the many maids. She had no memory of it; no memory of anything beyond sitting down on that unbelievably comfortable lounger and closing her eyes. 'All I can do is apologise,' she said out loud. 'It's not as though I meant to do it. Well . . . maybe subconsciously, as a form of defence.'

Forget Bramshill psychology, she warned herself as she left the bed to pad to the windows. Pressing the button that raised the heavy *persianas*, she let in sparkling sunlight and the brilliance of a glorious morning with the sky and the sea in perfect harmony, singing a rousing chorus of 'Am I Blue?'

She was in the shower, adjusting taps to find the perfect mix of hot and cold, when the phone rang. Sliding back the glass door of the shower stall, she reached out to lift the receiver from its cradle on the wall.

'Good morning,' an amused voice said. 'I hope you slept well?'

His tone was dry, teasing even, not in the least put out. Oh, clever, Tessa thought admiringly, before answering in the same vein: 'All I meant to do was close my eyes for a moment. It was not my intention to fall asleep on you. I can only apologise and say I must have been more tired than even you realised when you said I was in need of rest.'

'Obviously you needed much longer than a moment, and I must say you sound much better for it,' he said smoothly, not in the least put out by her pointing the finger.

'I feel it too.'

'Good. Then come and have some breakfast.'

'How did you know I was ready for it?'

'You raised your *persianas*.'

'Now that's what I call service!'

'It gets better.'

He rang off.

After a tingling shower, her new-found confidence had her taking down the violet maillot, which she topped with a crisp, whiter-than-white cotton-voile shirt which skimmed the tops of her thighs, slipping her feet into a pair of leather thongs. As she brushed her hair she was pleased to see that she was what her mother would call 'in looks'. This enchanted place was obviously working its magic on her, though she was willing to bet it had that effect on everybody. Every woman, anyway. Especially when dealing with a magician like Nicholas Ould. There had been no hint of reproach in his voice just now. Had Harry been expecting to get his oats last night his fit of the sulks this morning would have obscured the sun.

Well, she thought, agog with anticipation as she left her bedroom, let's see what today brings . . .

It brought visitors.

They had breakfasted – or rather she had since he had been up since eight, but joined her in a cup of coffee while she demolished a selection of various Spanish *pasteles*, warm from the oven and eaten with butter and apricot jam.

Afterwards, he had taken her round the gardens, which were in the process of evolution, being created on land won by blasting rock from the mountain. When they were finished there would be pools, fountains – thanks to the stream – and shaded walks. 'My inspiration is the Alhambra,' he told her with mock solemnity. 'You must come and see my poor imitation when it is done.'

'Imitation, perhaps. Poor never,' Tessa mocked back.

She had the obscure feeling that mockery somehow helped keep him at the proper distance, which instinct was telling her should be arm's length. He was the most physically disturbing man she had met since Harry had bowled her over, and whereas she had been an impressionable nineteen-year-old virgin then, she was an experienced married woman now, even if that experience had been with only one man. All the same, taking everything plus Harry into account, she reckoned that the Nicholas Ould effect merited every bit of its reputation.

After their walk they had gone swimming; racing each other to the floating platform anchored about a hundred yards off-shore, where they sprawled breathlessly, letting the hot sun dry them, lying in companionable silence.

In brief black trunks, though he was not as beautifully built as Harry – few men were – Nicholas was nevertheless in very good shape, surprisingly wide of shoulder, narrow of waist and hip, all of it without an ounce of flab. When water cascaded from those wide shoulders as he used his arms to push himself up on to the platform, Tessa felt her body make an unbidden response, and she had to look away when he raised his arms to squeeze water from his black hair.

Unlike Harry's, his bathing slip was not designed to display what it pretended to conceal, but as he lay down on his back, it was impossible not to be aware of its existence.

Or him. Without warning, awareness of him had begun to hum about her like an force field. Not even with Harry had she known awareness of such intensity. Will you for God's sake stop with the comparisons! she seethed at herself, flouncing over on to her stomach. It serves no purpose. Just accept once and for all that coming here was ordained, like he said – and no, that does *not* mean declining responsibility. Daddy was right. This man is in your life for a purpose. Why else were you Duty Officer that day? Why else was he at that wedding? Why else did your car go into that ditch? He is the knife you asked for so why are you still debating with yourself as to whether or not you should use it?

'Has something displeased you?' Nicholas asked. He had

levered himself up on one elbow and was regarding her quizzically.

She started: 'What? Oh, sorry . . . I was miles away.'

'Without hope of rescue, from the look on your face.'

'No.' She pillowed her head on her arms, her face turned towards him. 'Thanks to you. You were right. I did need this. How did you know?'

'Your light had dimmed.'

'Not surprising. I had things on my mind.'

'Now resolved?'

'How can you tell?'

'It's been re-lit.'

Something in the way he said it had Tessa stiffening, her eyes losing focus as she saw his face coming nearer. He was going to kiss her, she knew it, and found herself powerless either to move or speak. Just as his lips touched hers a telephone bell rang. He rolled away, sat up violently, snarled something in Spanish that left her in no doubt as to its meaning, then yanked up a section of the cork matting to reveal a hollowed-out section containing a cordless telephone.

'*Digame!*' he barked into it, making Tessa hope it was a hell of a sight worse than his bite. As he listened she saw him draw his brows together in a thunderous frown. Slamming down the receiver and closing the lid of the box he drew a deep breath, his expression so grim that Tessa felt her heart sink to think of the kind of bad news he must have had. But his voice was calm, even resigned, when he turned back to her to say: 'Unexpected visitors, I am afraid. My mother and some of her friends are on their way, about ten minutes' drive away.'

'Your *mother!*'

Tessa's sense of the ridiculous got the better of her and she convulsed. First she went to sleep on him; now his *mother* was about to descend on them.

'This just isn't your weekend, is it?', she said unsteadily. For a moment she saw fury flash, making it plain that his bite was indeed to be feared, then as his own sense of humour got the better of him he too began to laugh.

'Now we are even,' he conceded, a decided gleam in these mercurial eyes.

'What do you want me to do?' Tessa asked, holding his gaze, willing to be guided.

'Do?' Something in the way he smiled set her skin pricking. 'Why, come and meet her, of course.'

She was the elegant lady in red Tessa had spotted at the wedding, but today she was in pale green linen under a wide straw hat. Her companions, two of them, were a woman of her own age, also groomed to the last eyelash, and a lovely young girl not long out of her teens. As Tessa came out from behind Nicholas and into view of the two women she saw an expression of almost comical dismay cross Lady Ould's smiling face before she and her friend exchanged a look of the kind that spoke volumes; each one with comprehensive footnotes. In the next instant Reina Ould was coming forward to embrace her son, with an ingenuous smile.

'*Tesoro* . . . I said to Mercedes that you would not mind giving us lunch. We left Andorra after breakfast and as we were passing so close to *Aguas Frescas* . . . Besides, Mariano needs a break from driving.'

Tessa watched with fascination as with perfect courtesy, giving no sign of anything but pleasure, Nicholas kissed first his mother's hand then her cheek before turning to the older woman to salute her in the same way. With the younger woman he only bowed over her hand. He then presented Tessa, first to his mother, then to the Marquesa de Condeverde and her daughter Maria del Carmen.

'But – I remember you,' exclaimed Reina Ould, after eyeing Tessa with a mental magnifying glass. 'You were at Jorge's wedding . . . wearing such a lovely yellow hat.'

Nicely done, Tesssa thought admiringly, but you remember me only because your son singled me out.

'Yes,' she replied, just as nicely. 'My mother and the bride's mother are cousins.'

'Of course, the Bishop's wife. Who stands in relation to Caroline's mother as I do to Jorge's.' She gave a trill of laughter. 'Always the family ramifications.' Her tone was creamy with contentment. She had placed Tessa, if not to her entire satisfaction then at least in the scheme of things, but Tessa sensed that it was not the scheme Reina herself would have chosen.

'What a pleasant surprise,' Nicholas said to his mother, in tones that made it plain to Tessa, at least, that it was anything but. 'You never tire of giving them, do you, Mama? Of course I shall be delighted to give you lunch, but first you must excuse us while we go and put on some clothes. We were swimming when your imminent arrival was announced. We shan't be long. In the meantime, Rafael will see to your needs.'

Taking her arm, he bore Tessa away at the trot.

'What's all the hurry?' she queried. 'I thought you said they were staying to lunch.'

'They are, but before that I want to do this . . .'

Before she knew what he was about she found herself held with the most perfect strength and lightness, being kissed in a way that rendered her mindless.

Eventually Nicholas moved his lips from her mouth, to her eyelids, to where her crisp short hair sprang from her temples, to her ear, the lobe of which he bit gently, making her quiver, to her throat and then back to her mouth again, after which, holding her away slightly, he looked into her eyes again.

'I always finish what I start,' he said, 'but it will have to be later. Take this as a statement of intent.'

Tessa could only nod before she reeled away. In the shower, she stood for ages under a powerful combination of jets in order to cool her suddenly fevered body and imagination. She felt all of a heap, quivery inside, legs trembling. Standing with her arms braced against the tiled wall, she slowly slid down until she was sitting on the floor, letting the water cascade down on her.

She had not felt this way since Harry. And look what *that* led to, she warned herself. This is another powerfully sexual male, Tessa, so for God's sake be careful, since that is obviously where your weakness lies. Just as well you are no longer like that poor young girl out there, who from the way she looks at Nicholas is suffering from a bad case of adoration. She never took her eyes off him for a moment.

And then the penny finally dropped. This was a fishing expedition, and the bait was that delicious young girl.

Tessa sat up abruptly. Now she understood his anger . . . This 'happened to be passing' bit was obviously a regular occurrence. Lady Ould was an incorrigible matchmaker.

I must have come as nasty shock, Tessa realised. No wonder I sensed chagrin at finding yet another transient in the place she obviously hopes the young and virginal Maria del Carmen will eventually occupy – permanently. Did she really think to find him on his own? Ah, but didn't he say he came here as often as he could? Perhaps he does come alone every now and again to get away from it all. This place does have the most amazing effect on one. God knows it has totally captivated me.

Over lunch, her hunch was proved right. She was watching the latest in a long line of candidates being dangled before a man who had no intention of choosing any of them. Why on earth could not his mother see that? She was by no means stupid. Could not she see – feel, even – that her son's scrupulous politeness concealed an iron-clad indifference?

Why does she do it? Tessa wondered, until it became patently obvious, as lunch progressed, that to Reina Ould her son was the centre of her life, and that she desperately wanted what *she* considered best for him. The right wife.

The fact that he went his own way, continuing to choose what *he* wanted, was something she stubbornly refused to accept.

Though the two women were at opposite ends of the female spectrum, Tessa was reminded of no one so much as her mother-in-law, whose passionate influence on her own son was far more powerful. Dolly Sansom was the only woman Harry had ever listened to. It was obvious that Nicholas Ould also listened, but with his deaf ear.

Tessa sat and marvelled. Oh, how I would love to see you handle Dolly Sansom, she told him silently. What is it with mothers and their Benjamins?

As for Maria del Carmen, she said little and ate less. While Tessa demolished every morsel of her *coctel de Aguacates* – avocado with *jamon se serrano* and quails' eggs – the girl played with hers. Nor did she take more than a morsel of the delectable poached salmon trout with its *mayonesa*, or the delicious *bartolillos* – pastry cream wrapped in a pastry shell and fried before being dredged in sugar and cinnamon.

Unrequited love? Or disappointment at finding yet another woman *in situ*. Poor bitch, Tessa pitied. I'm glad it's not me.

As the meal wore on, her newly sensitised antennae began to detect the slightest fraying of their host's imperturbable patience, and when, towards its end, she caught a hard glance between him and his mother, she was not surprised when only fifteen minutes after coffee Reina was sweeping up her friends in an orgy of light-hearted chatter and laughter, giving absolutely no indication of her true feelings. There was a flurry of kisses on hands and cheeks – Tessa was reminded of nothing so much as a cageful of brightly coloured parakeets – before Lady Ould bore her friends off to the big grey Mercedes. As if she had not suffered yet another defeat, Reina held out one magnificently jewelled hand to Tessa.

'I am so pleased to have met you. I hope you will come and see me when we are both back in London. Nico will bring you, won't you, Nico?'

'Don't push, Mama,' he told her calmly.

She trilled out a laugh and shrugged appealingly in Tessa's direction. 'Someone has to.'

As they watched the big car drive away, Tessa looked up at Nicholas and saw him staring after it with an expression which gave her goosepimples. The other side of his character? she wondered uneasily.

Sensing her watching him, he looked down at her. 'I'm sorry about that,' he said abruptly, and she knew he meant it.

'You were not to know,' she consoled.

'One never does with my mother. She means well but it does not always turn out that way.'

'You haven't met *my* mother,' Tessa said.

He laughed, and she sensed a lightening of his mood, but the warning was implicit when he said impatiently: 'Let's forget about mothers, shall we?'

She felt him take her hand, weaving her fingers through his own long, strong supple ones, pressing the firm warmth of his palm against hers. Instantly she was overwhelmed by a surge of feeling so intense it made her ears ring. He smiled down at her and she smiled back. When he bent his head to kiss her he met a response so sudden and complete it brought home the realisation of just how great her reserve had been, though he had known better than to mistake it for coldness. But first he had to rid himself of his irritation with his mother.

'Let's walk,' he said.

Arms about each other's waists, they walked the mountainside, he surprising her once again by his knowledge of the native plants, flowers and birds. They walked until the drumskin tightness had faded from his face and the tension left the long body. By the time they got back to the villa he was loose and pliable again. All traces of lunch had been cleared and the house was drowsing in the late afternoon sun, the water in the small bay looking coolly inviting. Warm from their hike up and down the mountainside, he asked: 'Want to swim?'

'Oh, yes, please.'

As she went to change, Tessa was atingle with expectation. Without doing anything untoward he had somehow contrived to tighten the sexual tension between them. Her awareness of him was now such that it had begun to constrict her ease of manner, causing her to feel her way like someone who could no longer see it.

He took her to a tiny cove where the water was so clear they could count the grains on the sandy bottom after they had dived from the rocks above. Afterwards, they spread themselves on a big flat rock, hot from a day's sun, and let its warmth dry them.

Tessa closed her eyes and drifted off into a light doze. While she did so, Nicholas watched and wondered about her. What was a woman like her – cultured, educated, intelligent – doing married to a man like Harry Sansom who, if his informants, of whom he had made enquiries, were to be believed, was a serial adulterer of monumental proportions? Why did she stay with him? It did not fit. From what she had told him of her work, Tessa was both competent and capable and not one to suffer fools gladly. Yet Harry Sansom was a fool: he had to be to cheat on a woman such as this. Perhaps a case of opposites attracting?

Nicholas had been there himself. The trouble with instant flare-ups was that they burned out just as quickly, and she had married young. So why was she still Mrs Harry Sansom? Reluctance to admit failure? Somehow he doubted it, though that steel-willed resolution of hers was something she had obviously acquired with maturity. But surely Harry Sansom was the reason not only for her recent depression but for her being alone at the wedding and again yesterday morning.

Was he the reason for her sudden decision to kick over the traces – because it had been sudden, he was sure of that. Perhaps they had already been loosened? Whatever, he was glad she had come his way. Overcoming her initial reluctance, not to mention her guilty conscience, had revealed a naturalness and charm he found enchanting. He liked the way that once having made up her mind, she had ceased to be a nervous bird of paradise, poised to fly at the first sign of danger; instead she had folded her wings and hopped down beside him to eat from his hand, eager for her first taste of what was obviously a new and exciting experience. He was under no illusions, though, as to the sharpness of that pretty beak.

When they got back to the house, its silence was that of emptiness. Wordlessly Tessa turned to him, a query in her face and eyes.

'I have given the servants the night off. We are on our own. I thought we might be even less formal tonight.'

Under his eyes Tessa felt her body constrict, but her voice was steady when she asked: 'Is that wise? I know we are in Spain but they have terrorists here too.'

'I think you are exaggerating my importance to ETA. I did something they did not like and it caused them to attempt to punish me, but I doubt they lie awake at nights wondering how to do it properly next time. I need no more lessons. Rest assured I have learned – am learning – a great deal from the last one.'

'Just so long as you don't underestimate them.'

'I don't, but to put your mind at rest, the house is protected by the very latest in state-of-the-art infra-red beam security systems. Rafael switched it on before he and the servants left for the village. If anybody comes within fifty yards of the place except for those with a deactivator like this' – he showed her the small car alarm look-alike he carried – 'it activates all sorts of bells and beepers, both here and in the police station at Cadaques. Satisfied?'

'Yes.'

'Good. Now let's go and wash the salt off.'

As she soaped herself, Tessa kept expecting to see a shadow on the glass, heralding a long-fingered hand sliding the door aside, but it never materialised.

He knew how to put her emotions through hoops.

When she went out on to the terrace it was empty, though music was coming from somewhere. Hidden speakers, no doubt. A piano, a guitar, a double bass and the voice of Ella Fitzgerald singing soft, low, and very slow. Seduction music.

Right, she thought, feeling her skin prickle. This is it. He has set the stage beautifully, so do you perform or not? Feeling slightly hysterical, she thought on a giggle: Come in number 797, your time is up.

She was standing by the balustrade, body tense, heart beating an anticipatory tattoo, when he came up behind her in his silent way, sliding his arms about her before turning her into his arms. The moment she felt his body against hers, hard and ready, all indecision fled. She wanted this man, and this was her opportunity to have him. This was a time out of time, all reality blurred, all edges softened, all dreams within reach. Throwing off the last of her reservations, unhesitatingly she reached out for them.

As she had known he would be, Nicholas was a beautiful dancer, light on his feet, perfectly balanced, skilfully guiding her so that she followed him unthinkingly. He made her feel like a feather. Oh, yes, she thought dazedly, there is no doubt about it, Tessa, your time *is* up. Remember the old song 'You and the Night and the Music'? They are all present and accounted for and ganging up on you . . . Closing her eyes she surrendered herself to the potent combination and allowed it carry her away.

They danced through one slow and dreamy song and into

another, then a third, the atmosphere saturated with the mind-bending drug known as sexual awareness, of each other and what was about to happen between them. They did not speak, just drifted over the stone flags of the terrace, she conscious of the hard breadth of shoulder under her hand, the pressure of long, muscular thighs; he of the scented softness of her and the way her breasts, unconfined under her sleeveless, vest-like T-shirt, pressed against him. He held her close but not in what in canteen-speak was known as a crotch-squeeze. She was aware of his erection, but he did not thrust it at her. She hid her smile in his shoulder. That was for later.

When the last track had ended he stopped but did not release her from his arms before asking: 'Drink?'

She shook her head. Unsmilingly they looked long and deep into each other's eyes. What was between them needed no words.

Taking her hand he turned it palm upward and kissed it, pressing his tongue against the scented softness of her skin for a moment. Her ears rang and she swallowed hard to clear them. She was in no state to resist when he took her by that same hand and led her into the house, where, on the firm mattress of the king-size bed in his surprisingly austere bedroom, he showed her what the act of mutual passion delayed could be.

Tessa had believed there was nothing more she had to learn about sex because Harry had taught her everything, but she had been wrong. Nicholas showed her that Harry was expert only in its mechanics; of the concomitant emotions he simply had no idea. Nicholas demonstrated to Tessa what the words 'reciprocal possession' meant. Nothing Harry had ever done had prepared her for the heights this other man took her to, where she experienced a storm of pleasure so intense she thought she would die of it, biting the back of her hand so as not to cry out. Never before had she felt so gloriously enjoyed, so frankly worshipped. Harry had always seen to it that she climaxed, but it took Nicholas to make her perceive at last the ulterior motive behind Harry's intensity; it was to feed his own ego. Her pleasure had been a by-product. It was only later, when thinking about it – as she was to do incessantly – that she understood the essential difference between the two men. Harry fucked. Nicholas Ould made love. Through him, Tessa became aware for the first time of sexual generosity. Harry was not generous, just greedy. Nicholas Ould brought her to climaxes which broke her apart, after which he lovingly and tenderly put her together again only to break her once more. Over and over and over again.

She lost all track of time; she lost track of everything – where she was, who she was, what she was – as her ecstasy was prolonged beyond all imagining. He seemed to draw fresh vigour from every peak she reached. Only when he detected – how? – that she was tiring, did he allow himself to take his own pleasure, not in triumph at still being Undefeated Champion, the way she had become used to with her husband, but with a joyous, stunning pleasure as intense as her own that set her nerves tingling before fulfilment claimed them both.

12

When Tessa arrived at Gatwick it was raining, but as she descended the aircraft steps, an elegantly dressed, grey-haired man stepped forward with a sheltering umbrella.

He bowed as though greeting royalty. 'Good evening, Mrs Sansom. Mr Ould has instructed me to offer you every assistance in his absence. I am to see you through customs and passport control. Your car has been rescued, repaired, and once all formalities are over will be waiting for you. I trust your flight was trouble-free?'

What would happen if I said no? Tessa wondered but had not the heart to ask since he looked so concerned. After all, he had been sent to look after her. That Nicholas had made it his business to arrange it all gave her heavy heart a lift. Somehow it made her seem more important to him; a case of 'out of sight, but not out of mind'.

'Everything was just perfect,' she assured him.

Truth to tell she had hardly noticed what was going on; she had been too busy reliving every single, incredible minute of the night before, pasting them all in her mental scrapbook, still feeling their heat as she did so. Once back in London and reality she would have to put them away. For what she had to do now she must have an unfettered and uncluttered mind. Last night had been a close encounter of the incredible kind. Now she had to return to earth.

'Is there anything you require?' her escort enquired deferentially.

'Not a thing,' Tessa answered. She had more than enough to be going on with, thank you very much.

Even without his presence the name Nicholas Ould was enough to ensure that the magic carpet came out, on which Tessa floated through passport control – her companion producing some kind of paper which lowered all barriers – and customs. As they left the Arrivals terminal her Golf – looking as if it had come straight off the assembly line – was drawing to a stop by the kerb. The man driving it got out, took her bag from the porter who had carried it, put it in the boot, then held the driver's door open.

Do I tip? she wondered, as she thanked them both, before deciding that it would be sheer *lèse-majesté*. But she would have to find out what it had cost to bring her Golf back to such perfection, then send its rescuer a cheque.

Back to the mundane indeed, she thought on a sigh, as she made for the M23, teetering between misery and the residue of magic, the latter having held her in its grip since waking up that morning.

When she had opened her eyes, having slept deeply and dreamlessly, it had been to find herself alone, still in Nicholas's big bed, the hands of the clock telling her it was 10.58 a.m. An early riser himself, he had obviously left her to recover the energy she had squandered so prodigally the night before. For the second day running she had felt like a million dollars – no, today it was ten million at least! Truth to tell, she had thought luxuriously, today I am beyond price!

Because that was exactly how Nicholas had made her feel. In all her years with Harry never had she known such a glorious morning after, awoken filled with such a sense of well-being, physical and emotional. In a word: fulfilment. Or should that be metamorphosis?

Leaping out of bed, she went into the bathroom where she examined her naked body in the mirrors. It was unmarked. His passion had been searing but what made it so memorable was his tenderness. Harry had never been tender. His kind of machismo saw tenderness as weakness and invariably left bruising in its wake.

Not so Nicholas Ould. It was his tenderness as much as his passion that had rendered her down to a pool of undiluted eroticism. Never before had she lost herself so totally in another human being. Last night had been some kind of a watershed. Nothing would ever be the same again. Unbidden, the words 'Thank God' sprang into her mind.

As she stepped into the shower she wondered happily what he had planned for today. Hopefully, more of the same. This place was full of secluded nooks and crannies where two people could lose themselves in each other. The very thought had her body leaping in response. I'm hooked, she thought. One cast was all it took . . .

She was towelling herself when someone tapped on the bedroom door. '*Momento!*' she called, hastily looking round for her shorts and silk singlet. Nicholas had taken his time undressing her, kissing and caressing what he had revealed with mouth and hands, in such a way that by the time she was ready for him she was bedewed with moisture and mindless with desire, but there was no sign of the clothes he had removed, only the white silk robe lying across the foot of the bed. Wrapping herself in it, she called: 'Come in.'

It was one of the maids, carrying a tray on which was a coffee pot, cup and saucer and a frosty glass of fresh orange juice. As she laid it down Tessa saw that propped up against the coffee pot was an envelope.

'*Buenas Dias*', the maid said with a smile, showing no surprise whatsoever. '*Quiere usted algo mas, Señora?*'

Having listened and learned Tessa understood that she was being asked if she required anything more, so was able to answer: 'No, *gracias*.'

When the maid had gone she picked up the envelope: thick, heavy, cream-laid paper; no name on it but obviously intended for her. She opened it. A single sheet bearing a brief hand-written message dated and timed at 8.30 a.m. No salutation. Cool or clever? she wondered with a sudden sense of disappointed unease.

> My apologies but a very early call from Frankfurt necessitates my immediate departure. I really am sorry, but I am in the hands of others on this one. In spite of all the little things sent to annoy us I did enjoy our brief time together. May we do it again? I promise I'll do it *perfectly* next time. You can reach me at my private number. I hope you will try.
>
> *Hasta pronto*.
>
> N.

Enclosed with the note was one of his cards, the bank's telephone number crossed out and his private number written in.

Tessa sank down on the side of the bed, conscious of a disappointment so savage it verged on the edge of pain. Gone! No more of him? Desolation knifed her. Then she read his note again. Until soon, it said. That was what *hasta pronto* meant. He wanted to see her again. Ah, yes, but as much as she wanted to see him? Passionately, desperately, longingly.

The trouble was, she couldn't. It was far too risky.

Last night may have served to make up her mind, but she had hoped to make of today the most glorious finale, take all she could of him because it was all she would ever have, and give as much of herself as he wanted.

Then never see him again.

After all, she had not fooled herself into thinking she had more than a temporary visa to his world; it was just her lousy luck that her stay had been curtailed.

Look, she told herself, fate arranged all this for you, as a means of obtaining the freedom you want so much. So, this is probably all you are meant to have. God knows it is a hell of a sight more than you expected. So long as you remember that what it has not given you is the right to involve a man who is no more than an intimate stranger in what could well turn out to be the most acrimonious divorce of all time. How often were you told by your mother, when you desperately wanted something, that what you want and what you get are invariably two different things?

Folding the note, she put it back in its envelope then tucked it away in her wallet behind her credit cards. When she got home she would burn it.

She found she had no appetite for breakfast, so went for one last swim. Might as well wring out to the last drop what solitary pleasure she could. On reaching the raft she lay there, her mind rapt in memories of the previous night, reliving every look, every touch, every kiss, every unbearably pleasurable peak. When it got too hot on her back she turned over on to her front.

On returning to her own room an hour later to shower she found her bag packed and the clothes she had travelled in washed, cleaned, pressed, and ready to wear.

At twenty minutes past two, after a brunch of smoked salmon and scrambled eggs, accompanied by hot buttered toast, Rafael came to tell her that the car was waiting. He took her bag and she followed him. Before getting into the car she looked her fill at the house, the sea, the sky, the mountains.

'You like *Aguas Frescas*, I think', Rafael smiled, observing the look on her face.

'Oh, yes, I like it,' Tessa assured him fervently.

At Gerona she was met by the Spaniard who had greeted them on arrival. She returned the entry permit he had provided after which he bowed her on to the Gulfstream, and after an uneventful flight they had touched down at Gatwick to find it was raining.

Of course, Tessa thought now, as she switched on the windscreen wipers, hearing the growl of thunder overhead as the rain began, back to reality with a vengeance. But, oh, how nice it would have been to be able to live in fairyland for a little while longer . . .

Sarge came to meet her when she let herself into the flat, tail high, purr loud, wreathing himself round her legs until she picked him up to stroke him lovingly, burying her face in his fur as he head-butted her to show how he had missed her, his rough tongue laving her hand.

'I'm back, Sarge. Sorry I have been away so long, but I won't be going far in future.'

She fed him, giving him an extra large helping, before unpacking her bag, finding to her delighted astonishment that the white silk robe had been included. Packed by accident or design? Whatever, she was not going to give it back. This fragile piece of silk would keep her memories bright for a long, long time. She held it against her face; it smelled of the Mitsouko she had worn. Carefully she placed it in the bottom of her lingerie drawer, then put everything else away in its proper place, after which she checked the answering machine. Harry had been back home: he had replayed all the messages but had left none, nor were there any fresh ones. It was obvious he had merely called in because the place was as tidy as she had left it. Still nothing to say, she thought, not caring any more.

She went to tell her neighbour she was back, taking with her as a 'thank you' the bottle of gin she had bought in the Duty Free shop at Gerona Airport. On returning to her own flat she made a pot of tea then sat down to go through the pile of mail which Harry had tossed on to the coffee table. It was either bills or junk. Taking out the household cheque book she set to and methodically paid those bills that had been lying around for the past ten days, then she got out her writing paper, and after chewing the end of her pen for a while and discarding several attempts, finally gave Nicholas Ould his *congé*.

> Thank you so much for a fabulous weekend, one I shall never forget, but I am afraid it will not be possible to repeat it.
>
> You were right in saying that I needed rest and

relaxation, and you gave it to me in full measure.
Thanks to you and *Aguas Frescas* I can now put my life in order.

If you will send me the bill for the repairs to my car – which, again thanks to you, is as rested and ready to go as I am – I will send you a cheque.

She hesitated over the final salutation, finally adding only: 'Tessa'.

Straight from the shoulder, she thought, as she addressed the envelope to Eaton Square. Polite but firm. Nothing remotely like the way she felt, but that was something she would just have to cope with.

That unpleasant duty done she firmly turned her attention to drafting her letter of application to the Selection Board which would assess candidates for promotion to Chief Inspector.

Again she discarded several drafts before the letter was composed to her satisfaction, after which she wrote it out properly and added it to the pile. After that she stretched, and checking her little carriage clock, saw with surprise that it was almost nine-thirty. Going into the kitchen, she took a bottle of wine from the chill compartment of the fridge, and as she poured herself a glassful shut her ears to the clamour of memories bent on reminding her what she had been doing this time last night . . .

I'll fix you, she thought desperately, heading for the telephone.

Normally she rang home every Sunday, but being at Bramshill she had missed a week, so now she spent ten minutes listening to Dorothea tell her there was no change in her father's condition. 'How are things with you?' her mother asked, finally, which blanket question was meant to cover anything and everything. 'Fine,' Tessa lied.

'Will you be down next weekend? It's your father's birthday on Sunday.'

'Yes, of course,' Tessa answered quickly, guiltily aware that she had forgotten. 'I'll come down straight from work on Friday.'

'Good. You can meet the new Archdeacon. Not what your father would have approved of, but like everything and everybody else today, the Church does not seem to know where to take its stand.'

Speak for yourself, Tessa thought, as she replaced the receiver. I've finally taken mine, except standing did not come into it . . . Going into the kitchen, she refilled her glass before investigating the freezer. She had not eaten since her brunch, more than seven hours ago, but nothing took her fancy. Too bad, she told herself unsympathetically. You have been spoiled. You are back in the real world now.

She took her wine and, picking up the *Radio Times*, was happy to see that an old and favourite movie was on: *The Thomas Crown Affair.* But when it came to the chess scene, she found she could not watch what she had always considered to be one of the most erotic scenes in any movie. It reminded her too much of the eroticism of the night before. As Faye Dunaway and Steve McQueen began to kiss each other she jumped up and switched off the set. *This will not do!* she lashed herself. It was a one-night stand; end of story. Do something, keep busy, occupy your mind.

With what?

For God's sake, there must be something . . .

But there isn't. With Harry away the washing is up to

date, so is the ironing. I have dealt with Nicholas, written my application, called my mother, paid the bills. There is nothing more *to* do.

Oh, yes there is, she told herself grimly. Picking up her glass, she emptied it before heading for the fridge.

She was deeply asleep, felled by the entire bottle of Sancerre, Sarge curled up in the crook of her legs, when Harry quietly closed the front door of Mandy's dockland flat and made for the lift, leaning back against its panelled wall when it came, yawning prodigiously, bronze hair tousled, blue eyes bleary, carrying his jacket over his shoulder. He was early turn, and felt like anything but. What he wanted to do was an about-turn to Mandy's flat, to climb back into her warm and rumpled bed where he had spent the last four pleasurable hours, none of them in sleep. Now he wanted nothing more than a good kip to recoup his spent resources. She was a goer was Mandy. His groin was sore and he felt shagged out, but he had to go home to Millwall and change before heading for Battersea and an eight-hour stint. Checking his watch he saw it was just coming up to 4 a.m. Yawning again, he stepped out of the lift into the parking area which was set under open arches in what had been the cellars of the former warehouse. He made no sound as he walked towards the bay where he had left his treasured Ford Sierra Cosworth which had replaced the XR3i. The car park was always brilliantly lit in an attempt to deter car thieves, so when he turned the corner he saw them at once: two teenagers in street-cred uniform – unlaced sneakers, torn jeans, baseball jacket and baseball cap, worn back to front – one watching the other working busily with a screwdriver to force the doorlock of

Harry's pride and joy, not expecting to be disturbed at this hour of the morning.

Disbelieving rage flooded him. The Cosworth – known as The Beast – was as much a part of his image as his nickname, and as lovingly preserved. That some snot-nosed kids should have the nerve even to *think* of using it for a joy-ride flicked the safety-catch on his hair-trigger temper. Roaring king-of-the-jungle style: 'Get away from there, you thieving bastards! Nobody nicks my car . . .' Harry took off at the run.

They looked up, saw him, big and red-faced with temper, barrelling in their direction. The look-out, smaller and younger, not much more than fifteen, took one glance and did a runner. The other, older and bigger, about seventeen, clenched his hand round the sharpened half-inch chisel he had been using on the lock, then as Harry came nearer, changed his mind at the expression on his face. But he had left it too late. Harry did a flying tackle – he was renowned for them on the rugby field – and brought him down. They hit the concrete, Harry on top, the boy banged about and breathless, struggling frantically beneath him.

'Let's have a look at you, you little shit!' Harry snarled, lifting himself off his captive, clamping a hand on one shoulder so as to turn him face upward. But the boy beat him to it. Bruised from his fall, squashed by Harry's weight and panic-stricken at the prospect of what he knew would be a custodial sentence this time, as Harry dragged him off the concrete he twisted himself face upward, the hand holding the sharpened chisel coming up as he did so, all his strength behind it as he pushed it into Harry's chest, which it penetrated like fingers through face cream.

A look of astonishment came over Harry's face. It was still there when he fell backwards. Then there was only the sound of running footsteps which rapidly faded, leaving nothing but silence.

13

Tessa was listlessly working her way through her in-tray, still struggling to free herself from the sticky-sweet web of memory, when her internal phone rang.

'DI Sansom.'

'Tessa, can you spare me a minute?'

Sitting up straight and brightening her voice, 'I'll be right there, sir,' she answered.

With thankful alacrity she closed the file she was supposedly working on and replaced it in her tray before getting to her feet, straightening her skirt and reaching for her jacket. She hoped her line manager wanted to see her to give her an interesting assignment. She was finding it very hard trying to fit herself back in the groove. For a start, this wet Monday morning, in spite of a slight hangover, her mind would keep trying to make a break for it in the direction of Nicholas Ould. She kept having to haul it back and shove it in its customary groove. As she made her way down the long office she prayed for a complex case which would necessitate her nose being soldered to the grindstone; lots of witnesses to question, information to be sifted and hours to work. She tapped on her Superintendent's door.

'Come in.'

Closing the door quietly behind her Tessa smiled and said: 'You sent for me, sir.'

Dave Hawkins turned from the window. 'Ah, yes . . . Tessa.'

The moment she registered his tone of voice her smile first became fixed then faded, even as her face lost colour and her stomach lurched. She knew that voice, recognised the particular facial expression he was wearing; they always went together. She had used both too many times herself not to know what they meant.

Leaving the window, Dave Hawkins came towards her. 'Sit down, Tessa.' That confirmed it. She shook her head. 'It's Harry, isn't it?' she heard herself asking. 'Something has happened to Harry.'

How could she not sense it? Dave Hawkins thought helplessly. She had been in the job long enough to know how it was done. 'Yes,' he confirmed in the dispassionate tone he had learned to adopt after handling his first 'sudden death'. 'Harry's dead, Tessa. His body was found this morning in the parking bay of a block of flats on the river at Wapping. He'd been stabbed through the chest. We think he interrupted somebody trying to steal his car; the lock had chisel marks, and from the wound, we think it was inflicted by that same chisel. I'm so sorry . . .'

He saw her take a deep, jolting breath, as if to steady herself, but her voice was not shaking when she asked: 'When?'

'The post mortem will establish that for certain. All we know right now is that it was some time in the early hours of this morning. Unfortunately, he was not found until the occupant of one of the flats came down to collect his own car at 8.20 a.m.'

Tessa nodded, her eyes unfocused. 'Have you told his mother?' she asked finally.

'Wapping has sent someone. You know the drill when a policeman is murdered.'

'Yes,' Tessa answered. Then: 'Wapping?'

'They're doing a door-to-door to find out who he'd been visiting,' Dave Hawkins lied smoothly, this information having been ascertained within half an hour of the police arriving on the scene. There were only twenty flats in the former tea warehouse, each enormous floor having been quartered. In time Tessa would find out about Mandy Barrett, but not until she was over the first shock. If she did not already know. Everybody else seemed to. Harry Sansom had been a randy sod who had been unable to resist living up to his nickname.

'Best thing you can do is go home and leave it to us to sort it all out,' he said, controlling his anger and frustration at the stupidity and waste of it all, especially the loss of a damned good copper. 'I can arrange for someone from the Enquiry Team to talk to you there. You know we will do our best. I'll have someone drive you. Is there anyone you would like to be with you?'

Nicholas Ould. The name materialised in Tessa's mind as silently as he had a habit of doing in a room. Suddenly her longing for him was so acute she almost cried out, but she stifled it. He must have nothing to do with this. In any case, she had no idea where he was.

'No, sir,' she said.

'Then I'll arrange for someone.'

'I don't want to go home,' Tessa said. Realising from the way he looked at her that she must have used a tone of voice not normally adopted towards a senior officer, she added in more conciliatory tones: 'If it's all right with you, sir, I'd rather stay here and keep busy . . .'

'Best not,' Dave Hawkins was kind but unyielding. 'You need time to come to terms with this.'

Knowing better than to argue, 'Yes, sir,' she said dutifully.

As he reached for the telephone someone knocked on the door. It was Sergeant Dace, known as Ma because she was plump, matronly and had a marvellous way with shocked witnesses.

'I thought Inspector Sansom might like a cup of tea, sir.'

'Good thinking, Ma.'

Tessa felt someone take her arm, push her gently but firmly into one of the chairs in front of the desk.

'Here, love, drink this.'

Obediently Tessa took the mug that was put into her hand, lifted it to her lips, sipped and grimaced as she tried to hand it back. 'It's got sugar in it . . .'

'It always does at times like this. Go on, get it down you.'

But there was no way Tessa could drink tea with sugar in it. So she just sat and wrapped her hands around the mug. It was hot and warmed them. They were cold. She was cold. All but numb with it. *Harry* is dead, she said to herself. Harry *is* dead. Harry is *dead* . . . But the words meant nothing. Not until, like a lightning bolt, other words breached the wall of her shock. *And I am free.* I don't have to struggle to free myself. No need for a divorce. Harry is gone. No more waiting for him to come in from work, wincing at the slam of the front door. No more shirts and underpants flung on the bedroom floor, no more uncapped toothpaste and damp towels left lying, no more stubble hair in the basin. No more head-banging, heavy-metal so-called music blaring. No more sulks. No more rows.

No more Harry.

She suddenly became conscious of a burning sensation on her thighs and discovered that she had somehow snapped the handle off her mug, because it and its contents were lying in her lap. Clucking like a mother hen, Ma Dace had Tessa up off her seat in an instant.

'I'm sorry,' she apologised numbly, feeling ashamed.

'Not to worry. Just let's get you out of that wet skirt . . .'

As she shepherded Tessa out of the door, Dave Hawkins said into the telephone: 'Ian? Dave Hawkins here . . . you've heard? Yes, of course . . . It's always the same when a policeman is murdered . . . You and me both . . . Harry Sansom of all people . . . Off duty in one sense but on in another, if you know what I mean. Yes, I've just told her . . . very shocked, but you know Tessa. Pure carbon steel backbone. Look, Ian, I was wondering . . . Her mother is miles away, and you are such a close friend . . .' A relieved smile lightened his face. 'That's why I thought of you . . . Yes, soon as you can. Come up to my office. And thanks, Ian.'

'Well?' Ian McKay asked as Ma Dace re-entered the sitting room of Tessa's flat.

'Nothing, sir. Not a word. Stiff as a board. I've given her a couple of tablets – nothing mega, just sedatives. I've found them very useful in situations like this. Best if she's out of it all for a while. Has she got any relatives we can contact?'

'Her parents live in Dorset. I'll call her mother. I don't know about any other family members.'

'What about the Sansoms?'

'They'll have enough to contend with.'

'Well, somebody ought to be here for her, sir.'

'I will be,' Ian said. 'It's all been arranged.'

Ma nodded, then shook a disbelieving head. 'Flash Harry Sansom of all people; the last copper you'd think of to die in such circumstances. Did you know him, sir?'

'I was his Inspector at Haringey.'

'I worked with him at Battersea a few years back. A good copper.'

And a lousy husband, Ian thought. Stupid son-of-a-bitch. Bed-hopping with anything in a skirt when he had a wife like Tessa at home, and all because he was jealous of her. What an idiot! Goodbye, Harry, and good riddance.

When Tessa woke up she felt thick-mouthed and muzzy, as if her mind had been packed with gauze. The clock-radio said 19.12 and there was a thin line of light under her bedroom door. No doubt Ian was still playing 'Someone To Watch Over Me'. He had been there when Ma had knocked her out with whatever she had put in that cup of tea, but there really was no need for him to stick around. She did not want anybody. She wanted to be alone to think. She had to think because there was so much to think about, to sort out. If they were worried she might in her grief do something drastic they need not worry; that was the last thing on her mind. She had already done something drastic. And, as things turned out, unnecessary. Now she would just have to deal with the consequences.

Moving in slow motion she managed to weave her way – as if through a fog – into the bathroom, where a sluice with cold water and two minutes with the electric toothbrush prodded her back to some sort of life. Putting on her slippers and dressing gown, she brushed her hair without the aid of the mirror before making her way down the corridor to the sitting room where she found not Ian but her mother, sitting straight-backed and upright in the Georgian wing-chair, watching Channel 4 News with the sound turned low.

'Mummy! When did you get here?'

'Tessa . . .' Dorothea flowed to her feet before surging forward to enfold her daughter in an embrace, an indication of her awareness of the gravity of the situation. 'I came as soon as Superintendent McKay rang to inform me of your husband's unfortunate demise.' She made it sound as though Harry had committed yet another execrable lapse of taste. 'I have left your father in Riggs's capable hands. He takes very little looking after these days, and Mrs Hobbs does the lifting anyway. I have arranged to be away for as long as you think my presence is needed.'

'Where's Ian?'

'If you are referring to Superintendent McKay, I sent him away. There was no need for him to remain once I was here, though he very kindly offered to. I told him that since you have a family there was no need of his offices, kindly meant though they were. He seemed rather put out.'

Tessa sank her teeth into her lower lip at the thought of Ian being disposed of like a discarded wrapper.

'Have there been any calls?'

'The telephone has hardly stopped ringing, but I left all calls to be dealt with by the answering machine.' She eyed her daughter critically. Pale, no doubt from shock, and somewhat heavy eyed, but that could be the result of the sleeping tablets she had been given. Her voice was steady, her manner calm, but then, Dorothea would have expected nothing less from *her* daughter.

'Now then, I have put a chicken casserole in the oven which will be ready in – ' she checked her wristwatch – 'about an hour. Are you hungry? Thirsty? One usually is after taking sleeping pills.'

'Do you know, I would love a drink – but not tea. People seem to have been thrusting cups of tea at me all day. What I would like is a gin and tonic.'

'What a splendid idea. I'll just go and get a lemon.'

As her mother made for the kitchen Tessa sank into the other Georgian chair and let out a shaky breath. In the midst of her tangle of mixed emotions was a hard-core of relief at her mother's presence, knowing that the cold douche of her practicality and common sense were just what she needed to lift her clear of the morass into which she seemed to have fallen, emotions that would, should she let them, drag her down to the depths, like quicksand.

When Dorothea handed over a large gin and tonic, Tessa drank hers thirstily. 'Oh, I needed that. Has there been any news while I've been out of it?'

'There may be fresh information in one of your calls, but there was an item on the BBC News to the effect that they think your husband interrupted an attempted car theft.'

'Yes,' Tessa said, leaving well alone.

As she resumed her own chair, Dorothea handed down judgment. 'I will not play the hypocrite and say that his death is of great import to me. I hardly knew him, did not like what I did know, and nothing will ever alter my opinion that the marriage was a foolish one entered into without proper thought on either side.' She paused, then floored

Tessa by continuing: 'But I think you had already come to that conclusion.'

In the face of her daughter's dropped jaw she continued: 'I may not be a demonstrative woman, but that does not mean I do not understand what is demonstrated to me. It is many years now since your husband accompanied you on one of your visits home. In fact, I cannot remember the last time I saw him. Nor did you ever talk of him to us. You may have lived in the same house but I do not think yours had been a true marriage for some time.' She locked on to her daughter's astonished eyes. 'Am I not right?'

'Yes,' Tessa managed to answer, awed by her mother's unsuspected insight.

'It was not my business to interfere, but had you asked my advice I would have given it. However, it has been a rare occasion when you solicited any form of counsel from me; your father was always your guide.' This was said without rancour, as a simple matter of fact. 'I am afraid you will have to make do with me from now on.'

'You have never approved of my becoming a policewoman, have you?'

'I did not then and do not now think it a suitable occupation for a woman. Crime is for the most part committed by men and should therefore be dealt with by them.'

'You had much more in common with Harry than you realised. He thought exactly the same way.'

Dorothea raised her eyebrows. 'Indeed?' she said, that one word capable of depressing the highest pretentions. 'I never had enough conversation with him to be aware of what he thought.'

'He had opinions every bit as firmly held as yours,' Tessa found herself defending.

'Which quite obviously differed markedly from your own. Is that why your marriage failed?'

Tessa was staggered yet again. Over the years, she had come to accept the commonly held opinion of Dorothea Paget as being a woman who had the sensitivity of a Sherman tank, occupying her time in rearranging other people's lives to her own satisfaction. Now here she was revealing herself to be a closet example of the old Yorkshire type: 'See all, hear all, say nowt'.

'Yes,' Tessa answered again, relieved to get it off her chest at last.

'Well, he's gone now,' Dorothea said, practical as ever, 'so you'll be able to go your own way, which had become your objective, had it not?'

Tessa sat back and regarded her mother with frank amazement. 'Why have you never said any of this to me before?'

'Because you tended to regard even the mildest criticism as an attack on your judgment, from which I deduced that you were only too well aware of your mistake.'

'It seems it takes a death in this family to provoke any real exchanges within it,' Tessa observed tartly, stung by the truth yet at the same time relieved not to have to hide it any more.

'I am of that generation which regards such probing as bad manners.'

'But you must have talked to Daddy.'

'Your father has always found it easier to commune with his God rather than his fellow men, but all marriages have their difficulties. My own were caused by the life and death of your brother.' Dorothea paused. 'It was a blow from which your father had no hope of recovery.'

'What about you?'

'I am not so easily overset. That is not to say that I shall not grieve for Rupert to my dying day. He was my son and I loved him. Harry was your husband but I do not think you had loved him for some time. Therein lies the difference.'

'True,' Tessa admitted, able to at last. 'I was going to divorce him, but it's all academic now – except I would rather it had been done by divorce than death.'

Something in Tessa's face and voice had her mother rising majestically to her feet. 'I should go and take a look at the casserole. Would you prefer potatoes or rice?'

'Oh . . . er . . . um . . . rice, please.'

And there was I thinking she neither knew nor cared, Tessa thought. I should have realised that even though my mother is the product of a family not given to displaying their emotions, she has them all the same. Didn't I catch a glimpse of them when Rupert died? Which thought brought to mind the welter of emotion that would be flooding the Sansom household right now. A product of her upbringing, she preferred her mother's dispassion.

Perhaps that's where I went wrong with Harry, she thought. He was so terribly sentimental, while I am not. Ah, yes, but sentimentality is not the same as emotion. I was the one moved to tears by music or great beauty. She heaved a heavy sigh. Well, it's too late now, and so easy to be wise after the event . . .

Funny, this past weekend seems to have been a case of 'you in your small corner, I in mine'. Both of us playing away.

No! She bit down hard on the thought of Nicholas Ould.

I will *not* think of him, except to thank God that he is now safe from anything Harry might have done.

Since Dorothea regarded eating in the kitchen as something only servants did, they ate in the dining room, Tessa pouring the wine while her mother served the casserole, – richly fragrant with red wine, mushrooms, olives, peppers and garlic – and added the saffron rice. It was twelve hours since Tessa had eaten, and then only a slice of wholemeal toast and marmalade, and she discovered she was hungry. As they began to eat, the telephone rang again but the answering machine clicked on after the first ring.

They ate in silence for a while then Dorothea asked: 'What about the funeral? It is something that must be thought about and properly planned. Or do police funerals, like military ones, follow a specific pattern?'

'Yes,' Tessa said. 'They do, but I don't think you need worry about it. It won't be me who will do the arranging. Normally it is the widow's prerogative but it is his mother who is doing the real mourning, so let her do it in her own inimitable way. Weddings and funerals are Sansom specialities. She did not get the chance to arrange her son's wedding, so I shall tell them to let her arrange his funeral. I have no doubt it will be as big a production as she can make it.'

Dorothea pursed her lips. 'Have you heard from her?'

'No, nor do I expect to. The Sansom clan never welcomed me as a member – even an honorary one. I don't expect to be consulted or required to do anything except play my walk-on part as Harry's widow.'

Dorothea's brisk refusal to don the weeds of hypocrisy, plus her unhesitating acceptance of her daughter's own lack of the 'expected' feeling, were just what Tessa needed, so she was able to continue: 'Just because I no longer loved

Harry does not mean that I do not regret his death, even if it has given me my freedom. It is all such a pointless, purposeless waste. He should have lived, agreed to the divorce and gone on to marry a woman who would been the kind of wife he wanted.'

'And what kind was that?'

'The kind who insists on having the word "obey" in her marriage vows.'

Dorothea pursed her lips again. 'You were always a biddable child,' she said, 'but the police force brought out the independence which was latent in you. Something, I have to admit, I did not see was there.'

'Don't they say you only see what you want to see?'

'They do, and it is an accurate assessment.' She paused. 'Which was your husband's trouble, was it not?'

Tessa shook her head in baffled admiration. '*You* saw a lot more than I ever gave you credit for.'

Dorothea's smile was perfunctory, her mind intent on what they were discussing. 'While the fact that you did not kept you in an unhappy marriage?'

'Yes. It was my mistake so I had to pay for it. But in the end, I thought I had paid enough. Over the odds, in fact. I wanted my freedom more than I wanted Harry, something I never thought would happen.'

'He did at one time have you in some kind of thrall,' her mother observed, making it sound like a communicable disease.

'A sexual one. Where I went wrong was in believing it was love.'

'A common enough mistake in this day and age.'

Dorothea's tone disparaged both.

'Well, I won't make the same mistake again,' Tessa said,

thinking of Nicholas Ould. 'I will be very careful in future to know a man's character before – if – I commit myself to him. Unfortunately, I was nowhere near as grown up as either I or Harry thought when we married.'

Tessa closed her eyes as her numbed feelings cracked and gave way under a sudden and irresistible wave of emotion. 'Oh, Harry, I'm so sorry . . .' She bent forward as though in pain, putting her hands over her face as she burst into racking sobs. Instantly, Dorothea rose from her chair to go round the table, where she did something she had not done since Tessa was a child. She put her arms around her daughter and drew her close. The moment Tessa felt her mother's ample bosom beneath her cheek her self-control went completely. 'It's my fault he was at Wapping with some other woman,' she sobbed. 'If I hadn't been such a selfish bitch he wouldn't have felt the need to look elsewhere . . .'

'Men always have and always will look elsewhere,' Dorothea dismissed. 'It is their nature. I trust you are not being so foolish as to blame yourself for your husband's adultery. He went of his volition, not the first nor the last husband to blame his own excesses on some supposed lack on the part of his wife. Disabuse yourself of any sense of blame. In fact, I will go so far as to say that he seems to have gone to some pains to make you think the fault was yours.'

Tessa was again amazed, amazed by her mother's perceptiveness. 'Yes, when he went over the side it was not just for his own gratification – it was to punish me because I was not behaving as he thought a proper wife should. I always knew to the minute when he began an affair by his lack of interest in me . . .'

'But you did not feel deprived because for you the fire had gone out?' Dorothea observed astutely. 'Not very intelligent of him, but then, like so many members of the male sex, he was ruled by what he carried between his legs rather than what he carried in his head.'

Tessa's sobs wobbled into laughter. 'Oh, Mummy, Mummy . . .' she gasped when she could, 'you know exactly how to reduce things to their proper size. What could ever withstand that juggernaut practicality of yours?'

'It has stood me in good stead all my life,' her mother acknowledged. 'We Nortons are known for our common sense. You, however, are both Paget *and* Norton, and the Pagets incline more to sensibility than sense. Your father is a perfect example.' Tilting her daughter's chin she examined the tear-blotched face, the drowned eyes. 'At times like these a cup of good strong coffee is called for, accompanied by a small brandy.'

She made to disengage herself but Tessa held on tight. 'Thank you, Mummy', she said with passionate gratitude. 'For coming and for being all that you are . . . much more than I ever gave you credit for.'

'Ever a human failing,' Dorothea allowed on a dry smile. 'Now, you go and listen to your calls while I make the coffee.'

Ian's was the first one, no doubt made as soon as he got home.

'I rang to tell your mother about Harry and she must have left for London immediately because within three hours she was on one side of your doorstep and I was on the other.' He sounded rueful. 'That's some forceful lady, Tessa. Now I see where you get it from . . .'

His voice changed, deepened, making her frown uneasily. 'If there is anything you want, anything I can do, you have my number. Please, Tessa. I want to help. You know how fond I am of you . . .' He became brisk again. 'No news about the investigation, except that the post mortem confirms that it was a chisel; it pierced the aorta and Harry died at once. No other wounds. No blood except on the body, no signs of violent struggle apart from some dirt on his shirt and trousers. No sign of the weapon. No sign of anything. One smeared palm print on the car door, not enough to be of any use. Nothing but scratches on the door handle. No witnesses. Nobody heard anything. It's one of those 3N cases. Nobody knows nothing, which makes finding the culprit very difficult. However, if I should hear anything I'll let you know at once, and if you want me to come over, all you have to do is call.'

No, thought Tessa, subliminal instincts ringing all her alarms. I'm not ready for that from you, Ian. Come to that I never will be.

The other messages were from friends in the job; either hers or Harry's. Mostly Harry's for he knew far more people than she did, having been as gregarious as she was reserved. There was nothing from the Sansoms.

'Do I ring them?' she asked her mother, when she came in with the coffee. 'I'm not sure of the form.'

'Would Mrs Sansom welcome a call from you under the present circumstances?'

'I don't think she would accept a call from me in any circumstances now that Harry is dead. But if I don't call her it's going to look awfully callous. The thing is . . . I haven't the slightest idea what to say to her.'

'People always loathe what they fear,' Dorothea observed shrewdly, 'but you may leave Mrs Sansom to me.'

Tessa poured her brandy into her coffee, which she sat and sipped while she listened and marvelled as her mother, displaying all the lofty high-handedness of a tenth-generation Norton, dealt with the Sansoms.

'Who was it you spoke to?' Tessa asked, when Dorothea finally put the phone down. 'One of the sisters?'

'Cissy, I believe she said her name was. She told me her mother is – and I quote – "under the doctor".' Dorothea raised eloquent eyebrows. 'The mind boggles.'

Tessa whooped with laughter again which, precariously balanced as her emotions were, once more changed to tears. This time she wept for her dead marriage, for her lost illusions, for the way what had started out so bright and shining had ended so tarnished and broken. She wept for an idol revealed to be fashioned from her own imaginings.

Dorothea let her get on with it. Better out than in was her philosophy. Unshed tears rusted the workings of the mind. But helpfully, at regular intervals, she held out the box of tissues.

When finally she gained control of herself, Tessa blew her nose and asked: 'Did she mention me?'

'She asked – somewhat cursorily, I thought – how you were, but she did not express any desire to see you or invite you to join the family in their mourning. When I asked about the funeral she said to tell you that they have all the necessary arrangements in hand. No doubt you will be informed as and when those arrangements are completed.'

'I want to see him,' Tessa said, in tones that brooked no argument. 'For the last time. I have the right.' She paused. 'I also feel I must. Anything else would be dishonourable.'

'Of course,' her mother agreed unhesitatingly. 'Shall I come with you?'

'Would you?

'Of course,' her mother said again.

The official identification had been made by Harry's father while Tessa was still under the influence of Ma Dace's tablets, but the body was still in the mortuary, the Coroner not yet having released it for burial.

Since identifying her brother all those years ago, Tessa had seen many dead bodies, so the next morning, after the necessary arrangements had been made, the sight of Harry's did not come as any shock, except for the deathly whitness of his ruddy skin. Gone was that effortless glow of health which had been so much a part of him. And he was cold.

'I'm so sorry, Harry,' she whispered desolately, as she bent to kiss his marbled handsomeness. 'I wish it could all have been different.'

Ten days later, Harry's body was released by the Coroner. Though his murderer was still unknown, the case was not regarded as having ongoing complications since there were no other persons involved. The Sansoms were therefore able to bury him with all the pomp and ceremony due to a murdered Sergeant of the Metropolitan Police, while the investigations carried on.

The funeral was held at Millwall, and so many people attended that the service had to be relayed to the neighbouring church hall as well as the crowds unable to gain admittance either there or to the packed church. The latter was a sea of blue uniforms with a cohort of Tessa's colleagues from the CID and SO13, the Anti-Terrorist Squad. Harry's coffin was draped in the Metropolitan Police flag, his helmet atop, and the horse-drawn hearse which carried it at a snail's pace through the crowded streets was accompanied by a motor cycle escort. His pallbearers were uniformed policemen. The Commissioner was there with his wife, as was a sprinkling of other top brass. Dolly Sansom was a heavily veiled figure in black supported by her husband and eldest son, her other children forming a protective guard of honour around her.

Since Dorothea Paget was not the kind to allow her daughter to be overlooked, on the Paget side of the church, in the front pew, sat Dorothea's brothers, each accompanied by a wife in elegant black. Dorothea's sister and her husband were also there with their son and his wife. The Pagets were outnumbered ten to one but they were nevertheless a presence to be reckoned with.

Eulogies were spoken, tributes paid, colleagues read lessons and prayers, and through it all Tessa sat unveiled and unmoving, her face blank, only her bright hair shining from under her small black hat. One of her aunts had offered her a couple of tablets which, she said, 'render you most marvellously null and void at times like these', but she had no need of them for she felt nothing anyway. None of it was real to her. It was a theatrical performance, and she had always preferred the movies.

She looked across the church at her in-laws and thought: In his death they shall be divided. Not one of them had spoken to her, but all had looked at her with cold hostility. Your fault, their accusing gazes said. Our Harry should never have married you. You were All Wrong for him.

The flowers were many and varied; from the two-foot-high name HARRY spelled out in white chrysanthemums, sent by his parents and siblings, through all the piles of various wreaths and sheafs of blooms from family, friends and colleagues. Tessa had sent a double ring of red roses surrounding a cushion of violets. Back at the beginning, roses and violets had been the very first flowers Harry had ever sent her, the card accompanying them reading: 'Roses are red, violets are blue, do I need to tell you that I love you?' Her card read simply: 'In remembrance, Tessa.'

The interment was private; only family and close friends. As in the church, the Sansoms and their allies ranged themselves on one side while on the other Tessa, flanked by her own family and friends, faced them across the open grave.

As the committal ended and the Sansoms turned to go, Harry's mother twisted her head to stare at Tessa. She had raised her veil, and all the anger and hatred she felt had carved deep lines on her ravaged face, the burning eyes silently accusing. I wish to God my son had never set eyes on you, they said. He's dead because of you. He wouldn't have been at Wapping if it wasn't for you. *You* did for my son. All this is *your* fault . . .

Dorothea, who had also felt the heat of the animosity as it scorched across the grave, now moved deliberately, interposing her body between her daughter and those Medusa eyes, murmuring something in her brother's ear as she did so. Taking Tessa's unresisting arm, gently saying, 'Come along, my dear, there is nothing more to be done here,' Gerald Norton led her away in the direction of the waiting cars.

14

Three days later, Tessa opened the front door to find the eldest of her sisters-in-law standing on the top step, wearing a face that looked, as Harry had been wont to say, like a smacked bum.

'Hello, Cissy!' Tessa said in surprise. For Harry's sister to have come to Richmond portended something serious. A cease-fire? An offer to bury their differences along with what had caused them? Whatever, if there was an olive branch in Cissy's capacious bag, Tessa was not going to throw it on the fire. She was about to say 'Come in' when Cissy beat her to it.

'I've come for Harry's things,' she announced peremptorily, her voice as aggrieved as her stare.

'Things?'

'His clothes, his possessions – everything. You're not likely to keep them, are you? You wanted a divorce, didn't you? The last thing my mother wants is for them to be dumped at the nearest Oxfam shop!'

Tessa's breath hissed as she drew it in. 'What gives you the right to think I would do such a thing?'

It was as though an invisible finger had poked itself into Cissy's chest, forcing her to retreat to the second step.

'Well,' she blustered, 'you wanted rid of Harry, didn't you? Served his purpose, hadn't he, by giving you the benefit of his experience so that you could go on to higher things and leave him behind! So why would you want to keep anything that reminded you of him?'

'What I want to keep has absolutely nothing to do with you, or any of the Sansoms.' Tessa was white with rage. 'It was made plain enough at my husband's funeral that you want nothing more to do with his widow. Tell your mother I am quite content to leave it that way.'

Stepping back, she hurled the front door shut with a slam.

'Hard as nails, she was,' Cissy reported back indignantly. 'I never so much as got over the doorstep!'

When Dorothea returned from the House of Lords, where she had been lunching with her brothers, she found her daughter in the marital bedroom, still seething, cupboards open, drawers gaping, her late husband's personal possessions in various piles on the bed.

'The nerve! Coming here and demanding that I hand over everything that belonged to Harry – most of which I bought anyway! His watch, for instance!' She flourished it at her mother, its having been returned to her, as his widow, with the rest of the possessions found on the body.

'I *gave* him that Tag-Heuer for our seventh anniversary, along with the ivory back scratcher in the shape of a curved hand. To scratch his seven-year itch, I said . . .'

Her voice faded and her face changed, all the fight going out of it as she slumped down on to the duvet. 'What is the matter with me, Mummy?' she asked despairingly. 'For someone who has just obtained the thing she wanted most, why do I feel so wretched about it? I thought we had fought all our battles, so why do I feel that I am still at war?'

'Because you are,' her mother pointed out in her ruthlessly rational way. 'With yourself. You had made your decision, wanted your freedom, but you wanted it done cleanly, legally, with no torn edges. Instead, the way it was done has left you not only torn, but bleeding.'

'So what do I do?'

'Endure. You are strong. These past few days have proved how strong.' She turned to the matter in hand. 'Do you wish to keep any of the things that were your husband's?'

'Not the clothes,' Tessa answered. 'Let somebody else have the use of them. But I will keep his watch, his gold cufflinks, and the silver-backed brushes I bought him. Everything in this pile here. The rest can go.'

'I do not see his uniform.'

'He was living at his mother's when he died; had been for some weeks. All his gear was there.'

'I see . . . In which case, why not let her have the rest of it?'

'Why not?' Tessa agreed, the last of her anger draining away, wanting only for it all to be over and done with.

'Let's pack everything up then, after which we can arrange for it to be collected and delivered.'

Once the last details connected with death and a funeral had been dealt with, Tessa found herself deeply and utterly exhausted, on a scale so profound she could do no other than give way to it, so when her mother went back to Dorset she went with her and spent a great deal of time sleeping – at least ten hours every night, as well as a nap in the afternoon

– or sitting at her father's bedside with a book. Officially, she had been given a month's compassionate leave. Dave Hawkins had told her: 'Take as long as you feel you need, Tessa. I want you back, but it has to be one hundred per cent of you. Come back only when you think you are capable of giving that not only to me but the job.'

'Very sensible,' commended her mother when Tessa told her. 'Sudden bereavement exacts a heavy toll on the emotions. Stay here as long as you wish. I am glad of your company.'

Tessa stayed in Dorset a fortnight. Then she rang her boss.

'Are you sure?' he asked.

'Yes. I want to get back to work, sir. Back to normal.'

'Then why not ease yourself into things gradually? Come in for a couple of days a week until you feel sure you are up to full-time duty.'

'All right,' Tessa agreed, experience in dealing with superior officers dictating her answer, knowing that all it took was a foot in the door. 'I'll do that.'

Within two weeks she was back full-time, working at the Pisa-like tower of files containing the paperwork she hated yet was glad of now; it kept her mind occupied and her days filled. She was still in bed by nine each night with a book, turning her light out by ten and not waking until the alarm sounded at seven-thirty. Sarge, now that he knew there was no one to kick him off, shared the big bed with her, usually curled up on top of the duvet in the crook of her legs.

She regularly saw Ian Mackay, and knowing it was kindly meant, that he was genuinely concerned for her, agreed when he suggested they meet every two weeks instead of every four. It was after the third such meeting that she realised the change in his attitude towards her. It was no longer that of old friend and sympathetic mentor. He acted now as a would-be suitor. In fact, she realised with stunned surprise, he was courting her; asking her out, bringing her little gifts: a book they had discussed, a CD she had heard and commented on. Her first instinct was withdrawal. She had no emotional feelings for Ian, never would have; he just did not appeal that way. On the other hand, she did not wish to lose a valued friendship. Good and true friends were harder to come by than lovers. As well as that, with the new sensitivity with which her encounter with Nicholas had endowed her, she too knew what it was to long hopelessly for something. She was therefore at her most tactful when she indicated that she was not in the market for a replacement Harry; that after her experience of marriage she was content to be a single woman until such time – if that ever came – she met a man she could not do without.

Ian was not upset. On the contrary. 'I have jumped the gun,' he said remorsefully. 'It is far too soon, I see that now. Of course it will take time to get over Harry. Even if you no longer loved him you did so once, and very much. You were together eleven years. Having waited that long I can wait longer. It gives me the chance to prove how good I would be for you; the right kind of husband, light years away from what Harry was. Just so long as you know that I am here – will always be here. I know you, Tessa. I don't want you to brood.'

'I am not brooding, Ian. I have accepted the situation. There is nothing I can do about it after all. But coming to terms with that acceptance takes time. Harry has only been dead a couple of months, after all.'

'I just can't help being concerned for you. It has been a habit of mine for a long time now.'

How well he had hidden it. 'I had no idea,' Tessa said.

'There was no point – then. Things are different now.'

Not where you are concerned, Tessa thought. It's no use, Ian. You are not what I want. Never will be what I want as a lover. But her new understanding made her loath to inflict hurt. That night, getting ready for bed, she pondered aloud on the problem to Sarge, already on the foot of the bed performing his own ablutions.

'Why is it,' she asked him, 'that the men we want never want us, while we never want the men who do?'

Sarge blinked his large yellow eyes at her and offered no opinion.

15

'For God's sake, Nicholas, say something! You're sitting there like a graven image and people are beginning to stare.'

Sibella Lanyon's voice, though low, had an edge to it. She had her reputation to think of. Having been Nicholas Ould's London Mistress-in-Residence for eight months now she was not about to have questions raised as to the pending expiry of her lease. She was well aware that their prime position table was being pinpointed by the avidly curious eyes of the people at the other tables; that clientèle who came to see who was with who and why and for how long and 'Haven't you heard, darling?' It was bad enough that he had been away eight whole weeks – and she still did not know where – she was damned if she was going to allow him to sit there sunk in abstracted thought, hardly eating a thing but drinking plenty, leaving her to smile and chatter vivaciously as though everything was as perfect as ever. Under the table she kicked his ankle viciously.

'What? Oh, sorry, Sibella. Do forgive me . . . I was miles away.'

'Obviously.' Archly, as if it did not matter: 'With whom is what I'd like to know? What is it with you these days? Since you came back from this last trip you've been like somebody once removed; present but not really there; not nearly so amusing, and definitely no way near as light hearted. If I didn't know you better, I'd say you were in love.'

'Would you?'

He sounded so interested that Sibella looked at him and wondered uneasily. Since his return she had also begun to wonder if he was slowly but surely distancing himself from her prepatory to cutting her loose. He was no longer focusing himself on her in that insidiously flattering way he had; his warmth was definitely somewhat cooler, and though he had taken her to bed on the night of their reunion and been as skilled and inventive as ever, she had sensed that while his body was with her his mind was not. Something new. And unwelcome.

She had always known it was not permanent, his affairs never were, but the past eight months had been of a quality and calibre she had never known before, creating an unexpected dependency. Another addict, she thought bitterly. The very thought of his withdrawal from her life made her want to get on her knees and beg.

So she drawled lightly. 'You must be joking! I know you better than that. But something is on your mind. I think it all goes back to that bomb.'

'I have been pondering on my life,' he admitted, 'especially since, if the old song is right, it is just about to begin. I shall be forty in a few weeks' time.'

A gigantic burst of relief had Sibella bursting into laughter.

There was no replacement on the horizon! It was pure male vanity! 'Is that all!'

'You never find your own birthdays so funny,' he pointed out mildly.

'Of course not!' she retorted cheekily, lifting her glass. 'When they are your own they are occasions for sorrow, which is why I am sorry I did not realise you were in mourning. Let me cheer things up by being the first to wish you Happy Birthday.'

Gravely he replied: 'Not while I'm wearing sackcloth and ashes.'

Sibella's glass went down with a thud. 'It's not your damned birthday, is it?' she asked flatly. 'It's something else.' She took a chance. 'Me?'

'No. Not you.' The quality of his smile was further cause for relief, but then he sighed before continuing. 'Me.'

'You! What on earth have you got to worry about?'

'My own mortality?'

'I knew it! It is that damned bomb. But I was there too, you know, and it has only made me more determined than ever to get the best out of every minute of every day.'

'And are you?'

'Of course I am! Aren't you?'

'No,' he said deliberately.

At a loss, she stared at him.

'I don't know what to say,' she said finally and not a little irritably. 'Maybe you should seek professional help. After all,' she went on, 'it was you they were trying to kill; I was just an innocent bystander'. Her demure smile was a tease. 'Well, not-so-innocent and not standing, but you know what I mean . . .'

He laughed, leaned over to pick up her hand and kiss it,

pushing back the diamond and emerald bracelet he had given her only hours before. Sibella all but purred. That would show the cats she still drank nothing but cream. Then, seriously she went on: 'That bomb must have been much more of a shock to you than it was to me, and I found it bad enough! You're still not over it, that's what it is. What you need is a nice long holiday, away from it all; the bank, the world, everything. Why don't we go to *Aguas Frescas* for a week or two?'

'No.'

It was so abrupt her jaw dropped. 'But – '

'I have to go to New York,' he said easily, softening the blow, 'and after that to Singapore. A holiday is out of the question, I'm afraid.' His further smile smoothed the edge of her disappointment. 'Later on, perhaps.'

Her heart resumed its normal beat: 'Yes,' she said eagerly, 'later on. Whatever you say, darling.'

She could have sworn he murmured: 'Chance would be a fine thing . . .' then decided she must have misheard him. Nicholas never left anything to chance.

Bending to pick up the morning's post, Tessa spotted the buff envelope at once and tore it open eagerly. It asked her to be available for interview by the Selection Board which would be considering candidates for promotion to Chief Inspector. She was to report to the above address, Room 213, on Friday 29, October, at 2.30 p.m.

'Yes!' she yelled delightedly, punching the air with triumph.

Her application had been delayed first by Harry's death, then her own leave, finally being postponed until such time as they decided to call her. Now, at last, they had. And she was ready for them.

In the weeks since Harry's death her scarcely human detachment had worn off. She had begun to feel again, lighter of spirit and less heavy of heart, beginning to enjoy work once more, even if she was still doing purely administrative duties: 'Good training for a Chief Inspector,' Ian had warned her mercilessly, 'unless you can get yourself on a Crime Squad or AMIT. Want me to see what's up for grabs pending your Board?'

'Would you?' Tessa had accepted with alacrity. Ian himself had recently become Chief Superintendent McKay, taking over command of a brand new police station at Brondesbury, and thus was no longer able to be Tessa's mentor: 'But still your friend.'

'Oh, yes, always that,' Tessa assured him, taking the opportunity to make one thing clear. 'I cherish our friendship, Ian. Let's never lose it.' She was also uncomfortably aware that neither did she wish to lose his twenty-odd years of widespread contacts.

He had looked at her, hesitated, then decided against whatever he would have liked to say, saying instead, equally firmly and with a confident smile: 'I don't intend to. In the meanwhile, let me see what's on the grapevine that would be suitable for an up and coming Chief Inspector . . .'

'*Ojala!*' Tessa said fervently.

'What?' He looked at her in surprise.

'Oh, sorry . . . Spanish for "I hope to God!"'

'I didn't know you spoke Spanish.'

He sounded put out, as though he ought to have been told, she thought irritably. 'You are forgetting, Harry and I spent three wonderful holidays there.'

Not to mention – to you, anyway – the most glorious weekend of her life. Where she had learned what *Ojala!* meant.

'Yes,' Ian said, using the flat voice he always used when she spoke of her late husband. 'I had forgotten.'

His 'Why haven't you?' hung on the air like smoke.

It was not Harry Tessa had taken to remembering of late. Truth to tell she hardly thought of him at all any more or the failure to find his murderer. But she had begun to think about Nicholas Ould a lot, especially at night when, as she lay in bed, she would find herself going over and over, with total recall, that one, marvellous, unforgetably passionate night, re-living his ardour, his unabashed sensuality, his enormous – and unfeigned – tenderness, until it became a kind of anguish. But better that, she told herself, than the slow calcification of all fond recall.

She had not heard from him since her return from Spain. He must, she told herself, still be abroad, knowing nothing of the culmination of their climactic weekend. Were he not he would have been in touch, she was sure. He was not the kind of man to hold a grudge against a woman just because she had turned him down. Not when he knew damned fine that all he had to do was stand there and another would be along in a minute. She had taken to searching the financial pages, finding only a mention of his bank in an article about venture capital. When she went to the hairdresser she went through the glossies which covered the kind of social life he led, but there was nothing there either, though she did come across a picture of the woman who had called on him at the hospital. The one who, according to Davina's gossip, he had been in bed with when his car was blown up. His London mistress. She was with her husband in the picture; a tall, fair, boyish-looking man said to be the Hon. Edward Lanyon. Nowhere was there so much as a mention of Nicholas Ould.

It was coming up to ten weeks now. Surely he had not been abroad all that time? He had told her he travelled a great deal but that the major portion of his time was spent managing the family bank. What could be keeping him out of the country for so long? Biting on the bullet: perhaps another woman, she thought, one he cannot bring himself to leave. My own fault, she lacerated herself. I turned him down, didn't I? So she was glad of Ian's companionship; knowing she was using him; that she should be cruel to be kind and put an end to hopes she could see putting out shoots, but selfishly she could not bring herself to dig them up. Better to be with him than alone with a longing never to be satisfied. They were both losers, and losers always sought their own kind.

Then, one morning, at around 7 a.m. she was awoken by a phone call from her mother, sounding calm, almost relieved. Her father had died, as unobtrusively as he had lived, some time during the night, letting go his grip on life without disturbing anybody. When Riggs had gone in to attend to him as usual he was already cold. Within the hour, Tessa was in the car heading for Dorset.

'You look peaky,' was Riggs's sour greeting when she arrived. 'Far too pale and far too thin. You need feeding up.' He was always grumpy and sharp-tongued when he was upset, and one look at his face told Tessa just how deeply distressed he was. Riggs had never married. He had little use for women. The then Major Hugh Paget had long ago appropriated all the fierce loyalty, and committed devotion Corporal Herbert Riggs was capable of. He probably feels as though he has lost some vital part of himself, Tessa thought, so she overlooked his rudeness, answering lightly: 'I've had a bit of tummy trouble.' Which was only a slight variation on the truth. Her periods were acting up again. Twice she had thought she was coming on only to have the bleeding stop after a while. She had also had the occasional brief but sharp stabbing pain in her lower abdomen, nothing like the slow grind of a period pain but not enough to make her go to her doctor since it never lasted long.

After all, she had been through it all once before. When Rupert had died her cycle had gone completely out of whack and she had not seen a period for three months, due, her doctor had told her, to a hormonal imbalance brought about by the stress of her brother's death and its traumatic aftermath. Harry's equally sudden death, coming how and when it did had been no less a traumatic upheaval. And now that her father was dead – the second death within less than three months – it would probably play even more havoc with her hormonal responses, although the only one she was conscious of right now was one of gratitude for a happy release. The gentle father she had loved had not been alive in the real sense of the word for a long time now.

When she embraced her mother it was obvious she thought the same way. 'He slept from this life to the next,' she told Tessa. 'Just the way he would have liked, and from the way he looks, it was.'

It was true, Tessa thought, when she went in to her father later. Death had restored him to his former state, even though his drastic weight loss had rendered him gaunt. His familiar, sweet smile was on his lips, as though he had just received some wonderful news. Which Tessa did not doubt for a moment he had.

She bent to kiss him. 'Goodbye, Daddy,' she said lovingly. 'God bless.'

His funeral was well attended, the Cathedral packed, not only with parishioners but the County and a goodly sprinkling of his fellow Bishops. He was buried in that part of the transept where all the former Bishops of Dorchester lay. Eventually a marble slab inscribed with his name and the dates of his Bishopric would be laid over his tomb.

Dorothea was magnificent afterwards, greeting people, never forgetting a name or a face or, very often, the occasion of the last meeting, no matter how long ago.

Tessa helped her mother stoically even though she had not felt one hundred per cent since getting out of bed that morning. A feeling of nausea had taken hold and would not go away, though when she tried to be sick she found she could not. Her skin felt clammy, and as the day went on so it wore her down until all she longed to do was go up to her bedroom and lie on the bed. But there were people to attend to, though much as she saw that empty glasses were re-filled and food was handed round, she could not face either herself. She did manage to slip away and take a couple of Panadol, but they did not work.

Several people put her drawn appearance down to grief. 'Poor darling,' her Aunt Charlotte murmured. 'But it really is the best thing, you know. Hugh had not really been with us for so long. What makes it worse is its coming so soon after the other . . . This has been a ghastly year for you. What you need now is to have a good, long rest. The one you did not take after your husband's death. Why don't you come with us to Florida? It's glorious there at this time of the year.'

'I'll see,' said Tessa evasively.

'I have persuaded Dorothea to come. She needs the break too.'

'Now that I do approve of,' Tessa said. 'Get her to stay as long as you can. She has not had a real holiday for years.'

'I know. But we'd love to have you come too. We've plenty of space – the villa has six bedrooms.'

'I can't promise,' was all Tessa would say.

By the time people started to leave she was hanging on by her fingernails.

'Are you all right,' her mother asked in concern, as she and Tessa crossed paths. 'You don't look at all the thing.'

'I don't feel it,' Tessa admitted wearily.

'Then leave the rest to me. Go on up and rest. You have done enough today.' She bent to kiss her daughter's wan cheek. 'I'll come and see you when I've speeded the last departing guest.'

Tessa managed a grateful smile but as she turned to go pain stabbed her, doubling her up. For a moment she could not breathe as it racked her, starting in her abdomen and spreading to her shoulder blades.

'What is it?'

Tessa saw her mother's face through a haze of pain. 'My stomach . . . Oh, God . . . . I think something just burst . . .' As she clenched her belly she felt something inside her pulsing, and when she looked down it was to see blood running down her black-stockinged legs.

'Oh, my God!' Dorothea exclaimed in horror. 'James! Riggs! Somebody . . . quickly! Call an ambulance! I think Tessa's appendix has burst!'

16

'*Por Dios, Nico!*' Reina Ould switched on the lights in the darkened room to see her son sprawled in his big chair by the windows overlooking Eaton Square. 'Why are you sitting in the dark? And that music! The violin sounds as though it is weeping.'

'It is,' her son told her. 'It's playing a blues.'

'Blues!'

'This particular Ravel sonata exactly reflects my mood,' her son told her succinctly, before pressing the remote control lying to hand and switching off the CD player.

'Do not think it has gone unnoticed!,' his mother retorted.

'I am sorry if my reflective mood displeases you, Mama, but all I am trying to do is sit and think in peace and quiet in my own home.'

'Why? You never used to do it before – well, not where anyone could see you, anyway. What is it that troubles you? For you are troubled. I am your mother and I know your every mood. Is it the bank?'

'No. The bank is fine.'

'What, then?'

'My life. My past. My present. My future.'

'Your past! Your future! And what is wrong with your life, may I ask?' She put a hand to her throat. 'You are not ill? You are not suffering from some terrible disease?'

A sigh. 'No. I am not ill.' He paused. 'No, I do not have some terrible disease.'

With fervent relief his mother crossed herself. '*Gracias a Dios.*'

'You worry too much.'

'Mothers always worry. And when I find you sitting in the dark, listening to music which wails, I worry even more. What is it that is not as it should be? For something most certainly is.'

Her eyes searched her son's face, monitoring his expression – subdued and thoughtful – and the stance of his body, slumped rather than occupying his big chair with its usual grace. The word 'defeated' came into her mind. No! she rejected. Nico? Nobody could possibly topple such a tower of strength. Then it came to her.

'*Por Dios!*' Exultation rang in her voice. 'I never thought to see the day. It's a woman! Who is she? What is her name? Do I know her? Where did you meet her? Is it serious? It is so long since you had a serious *affaire* . . .'

His voice was without inflection when he replied flatly: 'I am not seriously involved with anyone, Mama.'

Her face fell. 'Then . . . I do not understand. Why do you shut yourself up and brood? What has turned you so – so solitary? What happened while you were away, for it is since you came back that things are – you are – different. Please do not try to deny it to me, your mother.'

'Of course something has happened. A bunch of terrorists tried to assassinate me, remember?'

'But that was months ago! And you did not brood then. You shrugged it off. Besides, nowadays you have minders, your cars and your houses are equipped with all kinds of alarms. Is that why you have been hiding yourself away since you came back? I thought you believed that a man had to be dead to be tired of Society.'

'I am not tired of "Society", as you call it. I merely wanted some peace and quiet in which to consider my future.'

His mother frowned as she sorted through reasons why, her face clearing as she finally found another hook on which to hang her concern. With crisp certainty she stated, 'The answer to any worries about your future is simple: marry. You have had a long bachelorhood, Nico. At forty a man's future should be settled on his wife and children.'

'It is not given to all men to have either one or the other or both.'

'Of course it is! Why should you be different?'

Very softly, almost to himself, her son murmured, 'Why indeed?'

'Nico, I have presented you with a dozen or more candidates over the past few years; extremely eligible, pretty, well-brought-up young women who would make you the perfect wife. Surely, by now, with all your experience, you must know what you want in a woman?'

'Yes, I do.'

'Well, then?'

'She must also want me.'

'Are you trying to tell me that a woman has turned you down?' Reina Ould's laugh dismissed even the thought. 'No . . . that is not possible.'

'I'm not telling you anything,' her son said, in a voice that had her expression tightening.

'Does that mean I may continue to hope?' Sarcasm dripped.

'Oh, hope comes free.'

Baffled, and angry because of it: 'I do not understand you,' Reina Ould said petulantly.

'Never mind. Just so long as I do.'

Losing her patience, knowing that in this mood she would get nothing out of him, 'Thank God somebody does,' she snapped. The door slammed behind her.

Almost immediately it opened again. 'You made me forget what I came to tell you.'

In the act of using his remote control: 'And what was that?' Nicholas controlled his impatience.

'I have just had a lovely long chat with Isabel on the telephone and she gave me all the news as to what happened while I was away visiting Elena. Jorge is to become a father in seven months' time; her third grandchild! Everybody is delighted, of course, on both sides of the *matrimonio*. She also told me about the Bishop's daughter – the one who was at the wedding and was with you in Spain when I called at *Aguas Frescas* in August.'

'What about her?'

'Her husband was killed – murdered – that very same weekend she was with you! Imagine! Isabel says he tackled some ruffians trying to steal his car and was knifed for his pains. As I was in Mexico City for so long, this is the first chance Isabel has had to tell me. Her daughter-in-law's mother is, as you know, first cousin to the Bishop's wife . . .'

'Yes, yes, I know. What else did Isabel say?'

'Why, nothing. That was all, but that was why I came by

– to ask you for Mrs Sansom's address. The least I can do is write to her. We met twice, after all.'

'No need,' her son said. He had risen to his feet. 'I will tell her myself.'

17

There were five names, with a bell beside each one, to the right of the front door of the fine old Regency house standing on its bluff above the Thames at Richmond. Nicholas Ould pressed his thumb on to the bell marked SANSOM. The wind off the river was sharp and he shivered under his cashmere top-coat, but it was not from cold so much as tension.

He had found her stiff little note among the pile of non-urgent mail waiting for him on his return to England. He had not recognised the writing, but on seeing the postmark had opened the envelope with a sense of anticipation, only to receive a disappointment that surprised him by its sharpness. He would have sworn he had read her right. The way she had abandoned all reserve, for instance, opened to him in a way that opened up unrealised depths in himself . . . In pondering on it later – and at length – he'd recognised that in Tessa Paget he had encountered his kindred spirit, possessed of a sensuality that matched his own but allied to other qualities that, for the first time in his experience of women, loomed equally large.

But she also had a husband who obviously meant more to her than he had given her credit for. Enough to make her go back to him. What else could her words mean? Yet he would have sworn he had made an equally profound impression on her. The two of them had, almost literally, gone up in flames . . . The last thing he had wanted to do when that phone call had woken him was leave her. Which was why he had left his invitation, confident in his opinion that, like him, she wanted more of the same. He would have taken any odds that her marriage was not giving her what she wanted and needed. Yet here she was giving *him* the brush-off. It was all so totally unexpected that for a moment he was not sure whether to be affronted or amused. How was it that he, with all the insights and experience acquired over twenty years with twice as many women, had been so wrong about this one? Obviously he had not got anywhere near the core of Tessa Sansom. On the contrary, he had misjudged not only her but her situation in thinking she was searching for something he was perfectly placed to supply. Her note made it clear that the weekend had made up her mind not to disturb the *status quo*. Oh, well, he had self-justified, tossing the note aside, all other things considered it was probably for the best.

But his instinctive reaction to the news that she was now a widow had been so powerful he knew that he had only been fooling himself. He wanted to see her again. Very much. It astounded him just how much. As for the rest . . . well, he would tread softly until he knew just how glad she was to see him. For the first time, where a woman was concerned, he was not sure, of her or himself.

He rang the bell a second time before stepping back onto the gravelled sweep of the drive to look up at the house.

There was a light in an upstairs window, but he knew she lived on the ground floor, and that was dark. Just then a big black and white cat came round the corner of the house and eyed him warily for a moment before changing its mind and going back the way it had come.

He rang the bell again, longer this time. But there was no answer. Wherever she was she was not at home.

He was just about to turn and leave when the front door opened and a middle-aged woman, dressed for the street, came through it. Seeing him, she stopped halfway, hand protectively ready to slam the door shut should he make a false move. He came forward into the light cast by the porch lamp.

'Good evening,' he said pleasantly. 'I am looking for Mrs Sansom but she does not appear to be in. Do you know where I might find her?'

'Dorset,' the woman answered, her tone and manner easing to relief as she got a good look at him. 'Her father died yesterday and she went down straight away. I know because she left me a note asking me to feed her cat.' She clicked her tongue. 'Poor Mrs Sansom, first her husband now her father, both within three months, though her father had been an invalid for years. Even so, it is a double blow.'

'Yes,' agreed Nicholas slowly, assimilating his own inner dismay. 'I had no idea . . .' His smile was a glimmer of its usual brilliant self. 'Thank you.'

Well, he thought bleakly as he walked back to his car, at least he knew where she was, even if there was nothing he could about it. This was no time to bring his personal concerns – even if they did concern her – to a woman already overburdened with her own. He would just have to possess his soul in patience. A grim laugh escaped him. *Not* one of his virtues . . . But he could write to her. A letter of condolence and the offer of *Aguas Frescas* should she feel the need. That would re-establish the connection after which, all being well, he could take it from there . . . When he got back to Eaton Square he mixed himself a drink, then taking Tessa's note from the locked drawer where he kept his private papers (he had retrieved it from the wastepaper basket for a reason he was not then prepared to admit to himself but now not only understood but accepted) and with the benefit of hindsight and fresh information, read it again, this time between the lines. Had he interpreted her brief 'I can now put my life in order' wrongly? He cursed himself for not having given her words the consideration they merited. His then preoccupied state of mind had no doubt coloured his reaction, producing a cynical: 'What else?' Now he saw what a sad yet courageous little note it was. Re-read and reconsidered in the light of what had happened to them both since there was enough in it to give him hope. And was not 'Nothing ventured, nothing gained' the motto of Ould & Sons? He poured himself a fresh drink, sat down at his desk and uncapped his fountain pen. At that moment his private line began to purr. He checked the clock. Almost 10.30 p.m. That line, scrambled for security, was only ever used for urgent and private business calls. Something had to be afoot for it to ring at this time of night. His surmise was confirmed when after he had picked up the receiver and said, 'Nicholas Ould,' a tight voice said: 'Nicholas, it's Dick. We've got trouble.' Dick Channing managed the Hong Kong branch of Ould & Sons.

Nicholas sat up straighter. 'What kind?'

He heard Dick take a deep breath. 'Charlie Wells has

disappeared. So has forty million dollars from the accounts he was running.'

'*What!*'

'He left the bank after work on Thursday evening, saying he was going to Macau for a long weekend – you know how he loves to gamble, which is what makes him so bloody brilliant at trading – but he did not come into work this morning, out of character for a man who was always on the floor every morning by six a.m. without fail. I called his flat but there was no answer. Also unusual. That Chinese girl he lives with should have been there. So I sent somebody round and he reported back that the flat is empty but for the furniture which goes with it. Not a single personal possession, his or hers. His Porsche is gone too. Wherever they've gone – and it won't be Macau – they've got a three-day start on us.'

'What have you done to safeguard his positions?'

'Everything I can. So far as his section is concerned, things are running normally and I've put Jim Stockard in charge. They've been told he's got a touch of 'flu and won't be back for a few days. If you approve, I want to put your computer genius on to the case to see if he can find out just what Charlie has done, how he did it, and where he has put what he got from it. The systems are damned complex but Charlie knew every twist and turn.'

'So does Carl,' Nicholas said grimly. 'He wrote most of our programs. Put him on to it right away while you concentrate on a damage-limitation exercise. No police. No Commercial Section investigation. Not a word gets out. Understand me, Dick. The lid goes on tight. I will not have the bank's reputation brought into question. This is a strictly internal matter which we will handle ourselves. Our Hong

Kong reserves can easily cover a forty-million-dollar shortfall. You know what to do to fill the hole so do it, but quietly – I mean like in stocking feet. I suppose we must be grateful that it was not four hundred million Charlie helped himself to. I'll want a full explanation, though. Was he working with anyone? Somebody covering for him?'

'Not that we know of, but the possibility is being looked in to.'

Nicholas's voice was icy. 'What the hell happened to our much vaunted system of checks and balances, Dick? I want a detailed account of who and where he has plundered – every last little item – waiting on my desk when I get to Hong Kong, which will be as soon as I can.'

He rang off abruptly, swearing fluently in Spanish. Then he picked up his outside line and called his pilot, telling him to ready the Gulfstream for a trip to Hong Kong. He wanted to leave as soon as it was humanly possible.

He did not bother to pack anything; he had a flat in Hong Kong. He merely told Bates, his manservant, that he would be away for a few days and not to bother with the car but to get him a cab. He also asked him to inform Lady Ould that he would be unable to accompany her to the family birthday dinner planned for the following night.

On the plane he looked at the figures, working out first this, then that, until eventually mental exhaustion ensured he managed a few hours' sleep, waking just before they landed at Kai Tak where he was met by Dick Channing, who had a car waiting. No chauffeur, no risk of eavesdropping.

'So fill me in,' Nicholas ordered, as they moved off. 'What news since we spoke last?'

'Carl's been at his computer for a straight fourteen hours.

He's picked up Charlie's trail. Very devious, very complex and very clever. Small amounts from a couple of hundred accounts, filched and accumulated over the past year or more – a few hundred thousand here, a few hundred thousand there. Around three-quarters of a million dollars a week. Small beer when you think of the millions we deal with every day. Charlie knew his stuff and was clever enough to go for a small, steady milking; the kind calculated not to set alarm bells ringing; everything seemingly straightforward and legitimate. Except the money was transferred to a series of fake accounts he set up. From whence, according to Carl, it has disappeared.'

'And Charlie?'

'No trace, except we are sure he is not in Hong Kong. Nor did he go to Macau. We think he got on his new fancy yacht with his fancy woman and set sail for God knows where. Charlie is more than a weekend sailor and his yacht is computerised so needs no crew. That's why he spent last year's two million dollar bonus on it. Bastard!' Dick Channing was livid. 'He must have been planning this for years. Mr Prim-and-Proper himself. Never absent, never late, the best trader we had and a master thief into the bargain. Talk about appearances deceiving!'

'Did he have help?'

'Carl says there is no sign of complicity that he can discover. All the accounts were in Charlie's section, and you know how tightly he ran that. None of his boys have even the slightest idea.'

When they got to the fifty-storey building which housed Ould & Sons they went down into the Computer Centre. Carl Friedman, the computer genius Nicholas had found at MIT, was sitting at the main computer console where all the transactions carried out by the dozens of other computers in the building were logged and monitored into master files.

'A beautiful job, Mr Ould,' he said in admiring tones, turning in his swivel chair to beam at his employer. 'At once complex yet basically quite simple. Like the bank clerk who added one cent to all his daily transactions, and by putting those cents into a separate and secret account over the years, accumulated millions.'

'How did you get into his system?' Nicholas interrupted, knowing that Carl could run on for hours. 'Charlie was a whizz with computers. He would have a password within a password.'

'Oh, he did. A neat little binary code, but it left a trail. Charlie knows about computers but I wrote the programs so I was able to spot where he deviated from the norm. I also know him. All I had to do was think the way he did. Even so, he was a real Tricky Dicky. He went in and out of dead ends, dead accounts, even dead people. If I came to one dead end I went back and persevered until I found another way.' He sighed and pushed his hornrims up higher on his button nose. 'What I can't do is tell you where the money went once he finally closed all the separate accounts, except he did that gradually too, a few at a time over several months. My guess is that he has it squirrelled away in a world-wide range of accounts in small banks.'

Nicholas accepted a cup of coffee from Dick. 'Good work, Carl. You'll receive my gratitude in the form of an additional bonus.'

'Gee, Mr Ould, working on this has been a bonus in itself. I only wish I could take it further, but right now I haven't figured out how, except . . .'

'Go on.'

'Well, illegally. It's against the law to hack into other people's systems . . .'

Nicholas eyed him over his cup. 'I know,' he said, 'which of course is why I know you would never do such a thing.'

'Right!' agreed Carl, po-faced. 'Let me see if there isn't some other way . . .'

'I know you will do your best,' Nicholas said.

They looked at each other then Carl nodded. 'You bet.'

As they went back up in the lift: 'Sometimes I think the only safe place for your money is a TESSA,' Dick joked, before seeing his chief's expression and asking: '*Now* what have I said?'

'Reminded me of something I was about to do . . . Damn!' Nicholas swore from between clenched teeth before sighing, 'But I'm afraid it is still going to have to wait a while longer . . .'

18

When she collapsed into her mother's arms, Tessa also fell into a sea of pain. Each time a wave swept her under she was sucked into a swirling nightmare in which she was menaced by bottles that dripped red liquid, threatened by tubes which thrust themselves up her nose, down her throat and into her arm, and needles which kept jabbing her stomach with their fiendishly sharp points. Distant voices echoed in a blurred, indistinguishable way, a machine beeped incessantly, until finally everything faded away into blackness and silence.

When she awoke it was in a room lit by one solitary lamp. A nurse in a white uniform was in the act of checking the bottle above her head, no longer red but white.

As she opened her eyes she became conscious of a terrible backache; also her stomach was sore, and when she touched it experimentally it was very tender. Her mouth felt thick and tasted sweet and she was very thirsty. The nurse, young and pretty, smiled down at her before saying cheerfully: 'Hello, awake at last. How are you feeling?'

'My stomach is sore and my back is killing me.'

'Not surprising. They had to operate. You've got a very neat row of stitches.'

'My appendix?'

'Doctor will be here shortly. He will answer all your questions.'

'At least tell me where I am and how long I've been here?'

'You are in the recovery room of the Well Woman Clinic. You were brought here as we were the nearest hospital.'

'When?'

'This afternoon, at about half-past four.'

'What time is it now?'

The nurse turned to look pointedly at the clock on the wall behind her. 'Ten thirty-three p.m.'

'Can I have a drink? My mouth tastes foul . . .'

'Of course. Here, let me help you sit up.'

Tessa drank the cold lemon barley water thirstily before falling back on to her pillows, the effort of sitting up tiring her so much and causing such discomfort that she was glad to close her eyes again.

The next time she opened them it was to find herself in a different room: smaller, not so high-tech, and this time the light was that of the sun streaming through a big window. Standing by her bed was a tall, spare, elderly man with a fringe of white hair and half-moon spectacles, in the act of picking up her wrist and checking her pulse. The name-tag on his lapel read 'Mr Cochrane'.

'Hello, Mrs Sansom.' He spoke the kind of Highland Scots that Tessa called mouth-music. 'Sister tells me you are feeling sore.'

'Yes. Was it my appendix?'

'No. It was one of your fallopian tubes. It ruptured because of an ectopic pregnancy. That is one where the fertilised egg becomes embedded other than in the womb; the rupture was in the nature of a spontaneous abortion. You went into shock and lost quite a lot of blood. Fortunately, an ambulance was able to reach you quickly and it brought you here. We had to operate at once.'

Stunned, Tessa could only stare at him. A spontaneous abortion? *No!* That was just not possible . . . She had not been pregnant. There had been no signs. She would have known, surely. It had to be a mistake . . .

'. . . all went well,' Mr Cochrane was saying. 'We managed to save about sixty per cent of the ruptured tube and made sure the other was in perfect working order. There is no reason why you should not conceive again, but I urge you to have your IUD removed before you try, and not for some time. Your body needs to recover from the surgery before you attempt another pregnancy.'

Tessa closed her eyes as if unable to bear to look at the hideous enormity of her shock. *Pregnant! She had been pregnant!* How, after eleven long years of unbroken protection? It was just not possible! The last time she had checked, her IUD had still been there. How in God's name could she have got pregnant? It did not make sense. But, on the other hand, why should he lie?

'Just how pregnant was I ?' she asked hollowly.

'About ten weeks. I'm afraid there was no way we could save it. It is not possible as yet to save an ectopic pregnancy.'

Ten weeks! Oh, God, Tessa thought, beginning to shake as the truth hit her. I got more than I bargained for all right. 'But I thought you could not get pregnant with an IUD,' she protested, still pleading not guilty. 'I had one all my married life and it has worked perfectly. Why fail now? It doesn't make sense!'

'I am afraid we do not as yet know why pregnancies occur where an IUD is present, only that they can do, although the rate is quite low – about two for every hundred coils fitted. Unfortunately, the proportion of ectopic pregnancies in such failures is high. Did you notice any recent abdominal pain or bleeding?'

Tessa frowned, trying to chase and recover her scattered thoughts. 'Well . . . yes, a little – a sort of stabbing pain, but I thought the bleeding that followed was my hormones acting up again. I've always had trouble with my periods. When my cycle went haywire I put it down to the stress of a death in the family. Once before – years ago – my hormones went out of whack because of stress and I thought it was happening again.'

'Not this time. You were most definitely pregnant. It was fortunate you were not alone when you collapsed. But the operation went well, you are young, you are strong and should make a complete recovery. Now then, would you like a nice cup of tea?'

What I need is a double gin and tonic, Tessa thought feelingly, before saying: 'Yes, please.'

'I'll go and call your mother meanwhile; tell her you are awake. She asked to be informed at once.'

Dorothea arrived later that morning, bearing gifts. A pot plant, several bottles of Perrier, a pile of magazines and a bagful of the necessities one always needs when in hospital, even in a room of one's own. The clinic allowed unrestricted visiting provided the patient was up to it, and after coming to terms with her shock Tessa was pronounced well enough.

She was still pale, but it was not the grey pallor of the day before, and though it hurt to cough or sneeze because her stitches pulled, she felt better, though still struggling to accept what had happened to her. She also tired easily and went to sleep after breakfast, waking to find her mother sitting by her bed.

'How are you, darling?' Dorothea asked.

'Tired . . . absolutely whacked . . .'

Perhaps if she played on that her mother would not stay long. Tessa did not want to have to make any explanations until she had satisfactorily explained everything to herself.

'Of course you are tired. It is only natural. You will also find you tend towards the emotional. Both are normal after-effects of a miscarriage. So is depression, so don't worry if you feel somewhat down.'

Remembering her mother's own situation Tessa apologised: 'I'm only sorry this had to happen now, at this particular time. You have enough on your plate . . .'

Dorothea shook her head. 'Not so. I can do no more for your father, but I think there is still a great deal I can do for you. If you will allow me, of course'. The penetratingly shrewd eyes made a comprehensive scan of Tessa's troubled face. 'Which leads me to ask – do you wish to talk about it?'

Oh, God no, thought Tessa. I don't. What's to talk about? What sort of a fool I've been? Like hoping that her mother – who could add a long column of figures without recourse to a pocket calculator – would not put two and two together.

'Talk about what?' she feinted.

'The child you lost.' A long, very telling pause. 'Whose child it was.'

Tessa forced herself to regard her mother with as much of

a 'I don't know what you are talking about' expression as she could muster, only to find herself unable to maintain it in the face of that steady blue gaze.

'Had the child been your husband's, your pregnancy would have been that much more advanced. Mr Cochrane informed me it was of some ten to eleven weeks' duration. You, on the other hand, told me your husband had been "over the side", as you so colourfully put it, for a whole month prior to his death. It is unlikely, therefore, that the child was his.' Dorothea placed a hand over those of her daughter, which were lying tightly clasped in her lap. 'I am so sorry,' she said in a voice Tessa had never heard her use. 'It should be a wonderful time, the first child.'

Tessa burst into tears. Her mother reached for the large box of tissues she had thought to bring.

When she could Tessa replied: 'His name is Nicholas Ould,' before going on to relate her story, from the bomb to the bombshell.

'I see,' Dorothea said finally. 'It would seem Fate has indeed taken a hand.'

'The winning one! I'm the one who has lost everything! Not only the baby – and I'll never understand in a million years how that came about – but a whole lot else besides. All I'm left with is a whole slew of unlooked for feelings I don't know what to do with. Oh, Mummy, I've never felt like this before – not even about Harry. This is – oh, beyond anything I've ever known . . . Nicholas is so very much more than his reputation . . . not that that was exaggerated . . . you have no idea . . .'

Her mother's smile was wry. 'I was at the Maragon wedding too, you know.'

'Well, then . . . My mistake was in thinking I could

remain . . . detached. I mean, I had deliberately packed my case-of-mistaken-identity-with-Harry so as to be sure not to make the same error, but when I got to *Aguas Frescas* it was all so mind-bending and Nicholas so absolutely irresistible. I told myself that if drastic action was needed to free myself then so be it. I might as well be hung for a sheep as a lamb.'

'And so went willingly to the slaughter?'

Tessa nodded.

'Only it was not slaughter but rather life-giving?'

'Am I so transparent?'

'Only to me.'

Tessa's sigh was heavy. 'I wish you also knew why I haven't heard from him. He *must* know about Harry by now. I thought at the very least he would write and say how sorry he was, but perhaps his silence is all for the best. What do I want with another womaniser?' Then, in a burst of rage at her still-vulnerable-to-certain-men self: 'It's ridiculous really. I hardly know him yet I feel that even in the short time we spent together, I learned more about him than I ever did about Harry. Does that make sense?'

'Inasmuch as any woman in love makes sense.'

Tessa shivered. 'Oh, God, Mummy, that's what worries me. Is it love or am I just struck all of a heap by a man totally beyond my experience? I thought I loved Harry and look where that landed me. I *can't* afford another mistake.'

'I think you love this man. As to why I think so . . . you wanted his child, didn't you?'

Dorothea held her daughter's stunned eyes, watched them fill with tears of realisation.

'Yes,' Tessa answered on a sob. 'Well, I would have, if I had not lost it . . .'

'Then you must accept that for better or worse, you love

Nicholas Ould. For a woman to want a man's children is, I believe, indicative of deeply felt emotions.' Another pause. 'You did not, I think, wish to have children with your husband.'

Tessa shook her head.

'No, I thought not. I have never known that test to fail. It is the criterion by which I knew I loved your father. Unfortunately, this new loss of yours, coming so soon after your husband's death, is a blow upon a wound, but answer me this if you can. Would you rather never have had the experience, preferred never to have met Nicholas Ould and suffered the consequences of that meeting, or do you regard your brief involvement as something you will cherish for the rest of your life?'

'I don't regret a thing, except losing the baby. In spite of the way it turned out it was that once-in-a-lifetime experience they say everyone is entitled to.' Tessa sniffed, blew her nose. 'I will just have to get over it. After all, I was probably no more than number God-knows-what on his list of Thousand and One fly-by-nights . . . Perhaps this really is all for the best.'

That evening, without warning, Ian McKay turned up, carrying a large bouquet and wearing a look of concern. Tessa's reaction was a combination of dismay and irritation. 'You've come a long way,' was all she could think of to say, probably because she had subconsciously hoped the distance would prevent him. She was in no mood for him right now. She was not in the mood for any man except one and there was no sign of him.

'I had a meeting which ended earlier than expected so I took advantage of the opportunity, got into the car and came straight down. I arrived about half an hour ago but I was told you already had a roomful of visitors so I hung about until they'd gone.' He bent to kiss her cheek in what she thought irritably was far too proprietorial a manner.

'Family,' Tessa said. 'Uncles, aunts, cousins. They were already here for my father's funeral. Who told you I was in hospital?'

'Dave Hawkins. Your mother rang to tell him you would not be returning to work.'

'Oh, yes, of course . . . I'd forgotten.'

'Poor love, you have had a time of it. First your father, now this.'

For some reason his ready sympathy grated. His was not the sympathy she needed.

'Your mother said you'd collapsed suddenly and they'd rushed you in here and operated. Appendicitis, Dave said.'

'He said wrong,' Tessa said baldly. 'I had a miscarriage.'

'Oh.' Ian's face congealed on its bones, setting as stiff as paint. He was actually offended! Tessa realised incredulously.

Hurt combined with rage to knock the guard from Ian's tongue. 'Well, from what you told me a child is the last thing you would have wanted so it's probably all for the best. I mean, with your Board coming up and your sights set on promotion, a baby would have been a handicap to say the least.'

Tessa glared at him. 'I wanted *this* child,' she said distinctly. Let him work that one out. Under what she considered the merciless blows of Fate, she herself had become merciless. Let him hurt as she was hurting.

Ian looked staggered. For a moment they stared at one another, and it was Ian who first looked away.

At last he found another subject. 'I have some news to

help you get better. I was talking to Mike Newall last week and he tells me there's a vacancy coming up on an AMIT team owing to a promotion. If you get yours – and I don't doubt you will – you'll automatically be moved from SO13, so what better place to transfer to than an Area Murder Investigation Team? That will get you involved with the public . . .'

Tessa let his voice wash over her. He meant well, but she was not in the mood for him, never would be if it came to that. As a friend she treasured him, but the closer relationship he envisaged – no, took for granted now – was just not on. The way she felt right now nothing was on; not even becoming a Chief Inspector. Work, she had come to realise, was not the most important thing in her life. Lying here, with lots of time to reflect, she had discovered something else about herself: that had hers turned out to be the kind of marriage she had expected, she would not have turned from it to her job. She had done so, she realised, hindsight revealing flaws hitherto unsuspected, because she had nothing else. It had taken Nicholas Ould to reveal the limitless possibilities of that 'else'.

'. . . in here,' Ian was saying, when she brought her attention back to him.

'Sorry?'

'I am boring you,' he said stiffly.

She had never realised before just what a thin skin he had, but excused her bad manners by saying: 'It's just that I tire so easily.'

He looked mollified. 'Of course, I'm forgetting you've just had a serious operation and here am I rattling on . . . I'll go and leave you to rest in peace, get your strength back. I really just wanted to see for myself how you were. I'll ring ahead before I come again. How long do you expect to be in here?'

'I don't know. Nobody has told me.'

'Well, I've got a three-day Senior Commander course at Bramshill starting Wednesday, so I can't get back until the weekend.'

'Don't put yourself out,' Tessa said quickly. 'It's a long drive. Call me. I've got a telephone by my bed.'

'Right, I'll just take the number . . .'

He jotted it down in his notebook.

'Take care,' he said, bending to kiss her cheek. 'I want you back safe and sound. We've a lot to do together . . .'

That's what you think, was Tessa's reaction as she watched him walk away.

Her mother, sensing the depression into which her daughter was sinking, dragooned people into visiting, to chat, play Scrabble, provide company. When Ian rang at the end of that week to ask how things were going and if he could come down again, Dorothea invited him to stay for the weekend. Tessa was being discharged from hospital on Friday.

'Oh, Mummy, why? I can't be doing with Ian right now,' Tessa protested wearily.

'But I thought he was your best friend?'

'That's just the trouble. He doesn't want to remain that way and I don't want him as anything else.'

'Then this is your opportunity to tell him. It's not fair to keep a man dangling.'

Tessa was told to rest for a fortnight and do nothing strenuous, so Dorothea fixed up the conservatory as a sick room, putting in a comfortable day-bed, a table and chairs and the portable television set.

'Tessa will be at one end and your precious grapes at the

other,' Dorothea soothed the tight-lipped gardener. 'The conservatory is warm and light and gives her a lovely view of the gardens. Now don't fuss, Henry. You can still tend to your precious plants.'

'And grapes are good for invalids,' Tessa teased him.

She was lying reading and listening to Classic FM when Ian arrived, cock-a-hoop with news that he had been pulling strings and nobbling people and had arranged for Tessa to appear before another Board as soon as she was passed physically fit for duty. 'And I've discovered the AMIT vacancy is still open. Evidently they chose a candidate who was a real high flyer but she had already been earmarked by somebody at the Yard so they have to start all over again. How soon do you think you will be up and about?'

'The doctor said I was to rest at home for two weeks then go back for a check-up before resuming work.'

'Two weeks . . . hmmm . . . I could put your name forward, I suppose, with an explanation of your circumstances – not to mention my own glowing endorsement, see if they came up with any suggestions, just on the off-chance that when they take a look at your past record they will think you well worth waiting for.' He pressed her hand. 'Which you are.'

Tessa managed a smile. I can't hurt him, not when he is so kind, she thought despairingly. 'Thank you,' she said, adding as emphatically as she could: 'You really are a true friend, Ian, and I hope you always will be. Good friends are so hard to come by.'

She saw the flicker in his eyes as he recognised the line firmly drawn under the word 'friend', but made no comment, and turned the conversation to other things.

*

Riggs was washing the car when the big Bentley swung on to the drive. His eyes brightened. He had a passion for what he called 'good' cars, not those die-stamped assembly line look-alikes but hand-crafted, lovingly put together, classic automobiles. The milky-coffee coloured Bentley epitomised the word. The Rolls he was washing was forty years old, one of the early Phantoms and still going strong, good for another forty, but then, he took great care of it. The Bentley was a Turbo T. Worth a fortune but money well spent, in Riggs's opinion. He was therefore well disposed to the tall dark man who got out of it. Normally he was suspicious of uninvited strangers, but whoever this one was he had taste.

'Good afternoon, sir,' he greeted. 'That's a nice car you've got there.'

'Thank you,' Nicholas Ould said. 'I could say "snap".' He nodded at the Rolls.

'Yes, she's still a beauty, even if she is an old lady by the standards of your Bentley. The Bishop bought her when he was made Archdeacon. Can I help you, sir?'

'I hope so. I understand Mrs Sansom is still here?'

'That she is, sir. Would you be a friend of hers?'

'Yes. My name is Nicholas Ould.' He proffered one of his cards, adding casually: 'I met her and her mother at a family wedding back in June.'

After examining the card, running a calloused thumb over the three-sheet board, the beautiful engraving, Riggs enquired: 'Would that be the Maragon wedding, sir?'

'Yes. Jorge Maragon is a second cousin of mine.'

The stranger having provided the right credentials for entry over the threshold, Riggs dropped his washleather in his bucket, wiped his hands on his apron and said: 'If you'd like to come inside, sir, I'll tell Mrs Paget you're here.'

'Thank you.'

Riggs led the way into the house, which smelled of beeswax and roses, and left Nicholas in a small drawing room, comfortably furnished in best Colefax and Fowler, while he went to find Dorothea.

'Miss Tessa's not been too well lately, sir. Best if I ask her mother if she's up to seeing visitors.'

'Nothing serious, I hope?'

Riggs flicked a look at the dark face. 'She's on the mend, sir,' he answered, and disappeared through a door, leaving Nicholas to look around. Lots of flowers, lots of chintz, lots of photographs in silver frames. He recognised Dorothea Paget, the Bishop, a teenage Tessa in a *Tatler*-type portrait, and an unbelievably handsome boy who could only be her brother, the infamous Rupert.

He heard footsteps on the parquet floor and then Dorothea made an entrance, holding out a welcoming hand. Nicholas recognised her at once. The blonde Valkyrie of whom Bertie Somerset had once been enamoured. Close up he saw from where her children got their good looks, for Dorothea's burnished blondeness was enhanced rather than quenched by the black she was wearing.

'Mr Ould, how do you do? I saw your mother at the Maragon wedding but I don't think we were actually introduced, though you did meet Tessa, I believe.'

'Yes, for the second time. We originally met when she took a statement from me.'

'Of course, that terrible incident from which I trust you are now fully recovered? Tessa told me about it – or as much as a policewoman is allowed to tell.'

Ah, so she has told you about me, he thought. But how much? 'I was sorry to hear about the Bishop. Hard as it must have been for you it must also have been bad for Tessa, coming so soon after her husband's murder. I was abroad at the time so knew nothing of it until recently. This is the first chance I have had to get in touch and I am sorry it has taken so long. How is she? I understand she has not been too well.'

'She is recovering,' Dorothea said after a moment.

'I hope it was nothing serious?'

Dorothea eyed him pensively. 'She had a miscarriage,' she answered.

She had never seen a man change so quickly. All his warmth vanished as the emotional temperature dropped to freezing. His voice was a void as he said with cold formality: 'I am so sorry. In that case, I won't impose myself. Perhaps you would tell her I called, and give her my best wishes for a complete recovery.'

He turned to go, but Dorothea was not having that. Apart from Tessa eating her heart out there was something not right here, most particularly his response to her announcement that Tessa had suffered a miscarriage. His reaction had been that of a man to whom the very word 'miscarriage' had connotations he did not like, causing him to distance himself from the situation with the speed of light. Because it did not suit him? Because it meant broken rules? Not part of his *modus operandi*? Tessa had said he was a charmer and Dorothea had been aware of his charismatic personality from the moment he unleashed his first smile, but on the other hand she had never seen anyone switch off so completely. Not only her protectiveness was aroused; she was curious, for herself as well as for Tessa and if she allowed him to leave now, neither of them would never know the truth of it.

Besides, if this man was Tessa's only means of rescue then as a concerned mother she would use him for that purpose.

'Oh, after coming this far you must tell her yourself,' she insisted affably, but in her best-steam-roller fashion. 'Visitors are always welcome. She is in the conservatory with another one, a colleague of hers from London, but he has had her to himself for the past hour at least. Let me take you to her.'

Before he could demur she had slid an arm through his, and as she had foreseen, his good manners prohibited him from doing anything else but going along quietly.

Ian was still talking, but Tessa had ceased to listen. She was watching the bluetits hanging on to the squirrel-proof nutcage, squabbling with each other as to who should have the best claw-hold, when she became conscious that Ian's voice had ceased. It was the quality of his silence which made her turn her head to see he had risen to his feet, his eyes on the french windows that led from the house into the conservatory. Her mother was standing there, and beside her was Nicholas Ould.

'Another visitor, darling,' Dorothea announce blithely.

19

Tessa's heart lurched as she met the mercurial eyes which from the first had imprinted themselves on her memory, only to see, with a faint chill, that they had lost their shimmer; were instead quite opaque and decidedly inimical. His expression was equally cold, his whole stance that of a man present under duress. This is none of *my* doing, his attitude said. But your mother would insist . . .

Its effect on Tessa, who did not know what she had been expecting, was to apply the bellows to an already smouldering sense of grievance. Anyone would think that he'd had nothing whatsoever to do with her present predicament; that it was all *her* fault! But as he stood firm under the assault of her indignation it brought to mind the first time she had seen him wear that same grim expression: on the raft at *Aguas Frescas* when the unexpected and imminent arrival of his mother had been announced. She had thought then that if this was his bark she would not like to feel his bite. Now she had a distinct impression of bared teeth. His hands were thrust into the pockets of his navy cashmere top-coat, and from the way they bulged were clenched into fists. He was angry. She drew in a sharp breath. *He was absolutely livid!* Seconds out, is it? Tessa thought aggressively. Well, come on then! I've been in training for the past ten days. Let's have this out once and for all!

Sensing the crackling hostility, Ian looked uncertainly from one combatant to the other, his first instinct to protect Tessa from this obviously angry interloper who however stayed just within the french windows, like someone impatient to be gone at the first opportunity. Ian's alarm subsided into curiosity. Mrs Paget had not announced him so Tessa had to know him, yet from her expression he was not welcome. This reassured Ian somewhat. Expectantly he looked from the newcomer to Tessa and back again in the manner of one waiting to be introduced, to know who this man was and why they were staring at each other with such hungry hostility. Until it finally dawned on him that so far as they were concerned he had become the invisible man. Each was so intent on the other there was no room for anyone else. With a pang he realised that Tessa had never looked at him like that. Which was when insight hit him with a thousand megawatts. Tessa had not been thinking of Harry when she had told him passionately that she would have wanted *this* child; she had been thinking of this man. The child had been *his*. Stiff with shock, he turned a reproachful face to her – but she still had eyes only for the man in the doorway, her gaze fastened on his as though her life depended on him. That unwavering gaze also made something else quite clear. There never had been, never would be, even the slightest chance that it would ever depend on Ian McKay.

His reaction was automatic. Only when the shock had

worn off would he begin to feel angry, hurt and even more deeply betrayed. Picking up his coat, he did not say goodbye. He merely walked out. Neither was aware of his going, but as soon as he was gone Nicholas spoke.

'I came to see how you were,' he said, in the formal tones of a man reading a prepared statement. 'I didn't know about your husband's death until recently, but as soon as I did I went to Richmond, only to be told that your father too had just died, so I thought you had enough to handle and the best thing to do was give you time in which to handle it. Then I had to go abroad again at a moment's notice. I got back only last night and called Richmond again – several times. There was no answer so I assumed you were still down here. As I was spending the weekend in Somerset, and therefore only an hour or so away, I decided to take the chance and come and see how you were.' He paused. 'I had no idea you were ill.' A longer pause. 'Your mother told me you have had a miscarriage.'

His voice held all the warmth of a cold snap.

Tessa said nothing. She was damned if she was going to say a bloody word until he told her why he was so up-tight. The silence stretched, widening like a seismic fault as she waited for him to act with his usual authority, take the situation by the scruff of the neck and shake it into action, but he seemed to be waiting for her. So wait! was her rancorous reaction, accompanied by a mounting urge to hurt him as she had been hurt, was still hurting, even as she longed for him to come to her, to hold her, tell her it was all right. But he did not move; just stood where he was, his whole body a condemnation. It was as if she were contagious, she thought disbelievingly.

The silence stretched until Tessa expected to hear it snap.

Finally, when he said with the cold politeness of good manners: 'I am sorry you lost your child,' it did. For a moment sheer rage misted her eyes, but it also fuelled her tongue. '*My* child! You mean *our* child.'

'*My* child?' His sarcastic disbelief was a slap to the other cheek.

'Yes, *yours*!' Tessa repressed a wince as her stitches pulled. 'The one we created that night at *Aguas Frescas*. You do remember taking me there for the weekend back in August? I can give you the exact date of conception in case you have forgotten. Saturday, August the seventh. Surely you recall giving me the benefit of your sexual expertise for a considerable part of that night?'

'I also recall you telling me you had an IUD.'

'I did. That is why I miscarried. It was an ectopic pregnancy. Apparently IUD pregnancies usually are.'

It was a case of the irresistible force meeting the immovable object.

'What makes you so certain you were not already pregnant when I – er – devoted myself to you that night?'

'Because I can count! The gynaecologist told me I was ten weeks pregnant when I miscarried. That was ten days ago. It will be exactly twelve weeks this coming Saturday since I conceived and if you need any further proof, for the whole month before you took me to Spain my husband had been living away from home, giving his all to his bit on the side!'

The deadly anguish in Tessa's voice brought Nicholas away from the door in one swift lunge. Reaching the day bed, he pulled her hands away from her face and held them tightly between his own while he strip-searched her face and tear-filled eyes before asking, with the intensity of a man desperate to believe yet unable to make that final leap of faith: 'You are absolutely certain the child was mine?'

Tessa heard the tiny tremor in his voice but her own emotional turmoil was such that she overrode it as she shouted: '*YES! I bloody well am!* One hundred per cent certain because there is absolutely no way it could be anyone else's! Parthogenesis is something the feminists are still working on! How many times do I have to tell you?'

He drew in a sharp breath and suddenly the opaque eyes were shimmering like sequins.

'As often as you like,' he said. Bending his head, he kissed her breathless. 'As often as you like,' he repeated exultantly.

By now thoroughly rattled, not to say confused, first by him and then by her own reactions, which were now running from delight to despair and back again like a mouse on a see-saw, Tessa wailed fretfully: 'I don't understand any of this.'

Taking off his top-coat, he flung it on one chair before drawing up another.

'Of course you don't,' he soothed, his familiar smile lighting his face, warming it to the one she remembered. 'But if you are sitting comfortably, I will explain . . .' His smile turned to a frown of concern as his words reminded him of her situation. 'How are you really, anyway? How long will you be convalescent and is everything . . . all right? No . . . after effects?'

Putting the boot to his *now* obvious anxiety Tessa said nastily: 'If you mean has this spoiled my chances of conceiving normally, then no, it hasn't. My reproductive department is in perfect working order, thank you. I hope to be able to return to work in a couple of weeks.'

'Good. I know the perfect place to recuperate until then.'

Her look flung daggers which he deflected with a smile.

'Why not? Can you think of anywhere better – even at this time of the year?'

'Hang on a minute! You come in here looking like the wrath of God, more or less accuse me of fitting you up with some other man's child and then offer to take me back to the very place where you impregnated me!'

Drawing the chair as close as he could, he leaned his elbows on the bed before possessing himself of her hands again.

'For my somewhat antagonistic entrance I humbly apologise, although humble is not how I feel right now.'

'What concerns me is how *I* feel – which is anything but well disposed towards you!' Tessa shot back.

'I did come on like a brutal doubting Thomas but I had to be sure. It is of the utmost importance to me, as you will understand if you will let me explain why.'

'You think it was of no importance to me?' Tessa demanded hotly, not inclined to forgive. Well, not yet anyway.

'Of course it was,' he soothed. 'But I want you to understand what made me so bloody-minded. I *need* you to understand. Please . . . won't you let me explain?'

Tessa's look would have curdled cream, but he sounded as contrite as any woman could wish so she said ungraciously: 'So explain.' And it had better be good, her tone said.

'With pleasure – and I mean that. For a start, when I left you at *Aguas Frescas* that morning – something I had no wish to do by the way, since I had other plans for us – it was to attend to a sudden crisis at the bank; a summons I could not possibly disregard, even though the way it had been between us the night before, it was the very last thing I wanted to do . . .' She found herself helpless under those shimmering, mercurial eyes as he said uncompromisingly: 'We found each other, am I right?'

In the face of what was in his expression, eyes and voice, Tessa could only nod, his words pulling the plug on her anger, allowing the vacuum to fill with his old black magic as she marvelled yet again at his unerring ability to put his finger right on the spot where it hurt most.

'Then, while I was in Frankfurt, I had another summons, this time to Zurich, to a Swiss clinic where I had previously undergone a course of treatment. Some recent research had discovered a radical new line of treatment for what ailed me and they wanted to try it out on a suitable candidate. I happened to fit the bill.'

He lifted Tessa's hands and kissed them as he saw her alarm. 'Nothing life threatening, rather life enhancing, but all very much to do with why I doubted that you had lost *my child*.' He paused. 'Of necessity I have to be somewhat clinical.'

Tessa nodded, not wishing to interrupt, mystified, yet at the same time reassured not only by what he was saying but by the fact that he was saying it, even if it overlay a layer of unease. He was not ill, was he? Oh, my God! There was something wrong with him! There was no way he could be HIV positive, she knew that, he had told her he had regular checks, but there were other sexually transmitted diseases, and with his record . . . She reined in her fears and got them back into their cage so that he could explain.

'About five years ago,' he began, 'I had to have a whole series of tests as a consequence of being sued by a woman who insisted I was responsible for her pregnancy. They revealed that not only was I not the father, there was no possibility of my ever becoming any child's father since – ' here irony rusted his voice ' – my sperm count left a lot to be desired. In other words, I was infertile.'

At her stunned expression he continued sardonically: 'Yes, me of all people. At the time – I was thirty-five – it came as a nasty shock, but only to my pride as a functioning male, since I knew better than to confuse virility with fertility. My mistake had been to think that if you had the one you automatically had the other. I had never given any serious thought to marriage and children – I had been chased too often by women with that in mind – and I treasured my independence. Spending the rest of my life with one particular woman definitely did not appeal. So the clinic's verdict seemed to confirm me in the rightness of my decision. Without children, what is the point of marriage?'

He fell silent, as if marshalling the rest of his story. 'Then the terrorists tried to blow me up. That little brush with death exposed certain flaws in the basic structure of my life. Such as my reluctance to invest any part of my inner self in it, thus incurring the emotional wear and tear that such participation involves. It suited me to have brief but pleasurable, purely physical involvements, without any come-backs or emotional hang-ups. Escaping death so narrowly brought home to me, as only such an escape can, the fact that if the attempt on my life had been successful I would have left nothing of me behind. Oh, a few signatures on letters, some photographs, hopefully pleasant memories in the minds of a long list of women, but nothing permanent; no marker in the shape of a living human being to prove that "Nicholas Ould was here". We live on in our children and their children's children down through the generations; they are the everlasting life the Bible promises us. If I never had any offspring my death would erase my life so completely it would be as though I had never existed.' The sardonic humour flashed again. 'A blow to any man's ego. So I decided to do something to restore mine. I consulted just about every expert in the field of male infertility and was finally recommended to a clinic in Zurich which, I was assured, was the ultimate in research into its causes and would hopefully if not entirely cure me, then ameliorate my condition, because though I was infertile I was most definitely *not* sterile. What I had was worth having, they told me, I just did not have enough of it. So for eight weeks I spent every Friday to Monday at the clinic – it takes that long to learn the final result – at the end of which they told me that there was some improvement, but only a slight one. It would take time and more treatment before they could promise me anything more than the possibility of fathering a child, and even then only with the right woman; one possessed of the kindly-disposed-to-my-sperm cervical mucus which would help achieve fertilisation.' At her expression he said: 'I told you it would get clinical.'

Tessa nodded. 'Go on,' she urged, not in the least put off by his frankness, rather fascinated by what he was saying but, even more, thrilled by the fact that he was actually saying it, was adult enough – no, *man* enough – to say it. Had it been Harry, nobody – but NOBODY – would ever have known.

She brought her attention back to him. '. . . so they made no promises.' Nicholas paused again, then said: 'I had not long been back from Switzerland when I ran into you for the second time at the Maragon wedding and knew I wanted to see more of you. Only at that time you did not wish to see more of me. Fate, however – did I tell you that I am a great believer in Fate? – would not be gainsaid. When we met for a third time I knew I was meant to do something about you. So I did.' His eyes held hers hypnotically. 'My instincts were right. When I left you that morning I had also decided that whatever it took to achieve fertility, I was prepared to do it, absolutely no holds barred . . .'

His eyes still held hers as his face came nearer. Tessa returned his kiss ardently, unable to prevent her wholehearted response; that of a woman for whom her own miracle was in progress.

Lifting his head he said softly: 'I have been remembering. Have you?'

'Constantly.'

'I fought it, it was so sudden. Did you?'

'Yes.'

'Neither of us expected it to happen, did we?'

Tessa released a long, shaky breath. 'No,' she admitted, happy to do so at last.

'But it did, didn't it?'

'Oh, yes . . .'

He kissed her again, lingeringly, sweetly, before resuming his story, his voice and body totally relaxed now, sure not only of himself but her.

'So I made Zurich my base – the Bank has a branch there – in order to undergo an intensive course of daily treatments. At the end of it they did further tests and whereas they had said there was a possibility, the improvement was now such that they were prepared to go as far as a probability, but only with the right woman, as I have already explained. That is why, when your mother told me you had had a miscarriage, I automatically assumed the child was your husband's. I had been warned, you see, that all I had was a probability; it never occurred to me that I had already met the right woman the doctors talked about; that the miracle had taken place and that you were already carrying *my* child!' His voice and face were exultant. 'The proof that you had indeed come into my life for a purpose.'

'My father always said that nobody – no matter how devout – had the remotest idea just how mysterious were God's ways.'

'I am not devout but I will say Amen to that.' Raising her hands he put his mouth to each palm in turn. 'Forgive me for being such a brutally doubting Thomas, but you see, I had already wrongly interpreted that note of yours to mean that you were returning to your husband with the intention of trying again; but you weren't, were you? You were going to leave him?'

'Yes.' For a moment Tessa almost confessed her own sin – that of deliberately using him – but instead she asked: 'Why didn't you get in touch with me on your return, when you learned about Harry's death?'

'I did not know he was dead until my mother told me ten days ago. I went straight to Richmond but you had already come down here, so I decided you had enough to contend with and instead went back home and read and re-read your note, finally deciding I had let my own "probability blues" colour my interpretation of it. For which I am most heartily sorry.'

'Well . . . I have my own sin to confess. I was going to tell Harry I had committed adultery so as to make him divorce me . . .'

Nicholas sat back as enlightenment dawned. 'So that was why you accepted my invitation? I knew there was something . . . you gave me such a cool, calculating look across the luncheon table.'

'Don't tell me you weren't making your own calculations! Anyway, when I accepted, all I had decided to do was spend the weekend with you; that would have been enough for Harry, who would automatically have assumed the worst anyway . . .'

'The worst?'

Tessa shook her head. 'Only in his eyes. He would never have believed me if I had told him it was the best. In any case, events overtook me and I never got to tell him anything. That's why I turned you down. I didn't dare take the risk of involving you in something that was none of your concern and might have got messy.'

'That was very honourable of you, but I have to tell you that I did not particularly care what your motives were. All I was conscious of were my own . . .'

Their eyes met, held, then Tessa closed her eyes as he kissed her again.

'So . . .' she said eventually, luxuriating in the satisfactory resolution of it all 'You were furious because you thought it was Harry's child I'd lost?'

'Yes. Quite simply I was consumed by blind, jealous rage. A new experience for me. When your mother dropped her bombshell I told myself I had been right in the first place; that your weekend with me had been a cold-blooded experiment on your part to weigh me against your husband, and that having done so you had found me wanting.' Bleakly but honestly he added: 'I was also jealous because I desperately wanted it to have been *my* child. Not only proof of probability and potency, but because it would also have been yours. *Our child*. I had come to believe that you were in my life for a purpose, but it took this to reveal what that purpose was'. He held her eyes again. 'Which brings us to a beginning or an ending. Which do you want it to be?'

'Do you need to ask?'

'I need to be sure. You've seen what a doubting Thomas I can be. This is something new for me.'

'What is?'

'Love.'

Tessa drew in a sharp breath. 'Is it?'

'For me, yes.'

Tessa said simply, gladly: 'Yes, for me too.'

'How did you know?'

'I wanted your child.'

They smiled bemusedly at each other.

'Now I think we need time in which to find ourselves,' Nicholas said contentedly. 'Love can not only *be* blind, it *can* blind. I want us both to see clearly and still be sure. These past weeks I have thought a great deal about you, me and a possible future together. I don't want to go on the way I have been; separating the physical act from its emotional counterpart. With you I want to become – *involved* – in all the ways a man can become involved in and with a woman.'

Tessa was thrilled to the core of her being. No one had ever spoken to her like this before. Harry had not been able to, and she had blamed him for it. Which had been wrong. She was the one who had expected more than he was capable of giving. Not so with this man. With Nicholas Ould, there were depths and heights and breadths she had not even begun to define. The very thought dizzied her. Wanting him to know this, to start off without any hangovers, she said: 'I think you are right. I want to discover you too.' Her face shadowed. 'Perhaps, if Harry and I had ever taken the time to look beyond the sex . . .'

'Did it hurt when he died?'

Tessa shook her head. 'Not really. I had long ceased to feel anything for him. I don't think he loved me any longer either. Had he done so he could not have betrayed me to casually with so many other women.'

'So it died a long time before he did?'

'Yes. We don't have to take our pasts into our future.'

'But we are our pasts.'

'I want different things now.'

'So do I, but it is past experience that has showed us what they are.' She loved the way he cut through her doubts. 'What do you want?' he asked.

'You.'

'How much?'

'Very much.'

'Enough to take the chance?'

He knew. Of course he knew. With his experience of women how could he not?

'Yes.'

'One more thing. Who was the man who was here when I came?'

Tessa drew in an appalled breath. 'Oh, my God . . . Ian!' He had totally slipped her mind.

'Who is Ian?'

'My best friend in the job, also my mentor . . .'

'I don't mind you having male friends. I have lots of female ones.'

'I don't think Ian is capable of such – magnanimity.' Tessa hesitated briefly. 'Since Harry's death he has wanted more than friendship. I could not give it. Not to him. I was going to tell him, but I don't think that will be necessary now. He will be hurt, and I'm sorry, but we cannot love to order. Who was it who said: "The agony of loving is only equalled by the tedium of being loved"?'

'I don't know, but whoever he was he was right.'

Tessa continued, as she was determined to go on. 'There is something else. You ought to know that I have – well, will have once I'm well again – a Board coming up soon. That's a panel of senior police officers who meet to consider candidates for promotion. This one is for Chief Inspectors.'

'Good for you.'

'You wouldn't mind?'

'Why should I? I have a full-time job which takes me away a lot.' Straight-faced, he went on: 'At least I would know how you were spending your time without me. These are things we have to work out between us. Your job, my job, our pasts, our future, a life together. You'll have to bear with me. I've never lived with anyone except my parents. But I'm adaptable. And I learn fast. I think what we need is a good long while to live together, get to know each other, find out the things we like and those we don't like, reach the stage of being able to complain or quibble or just plain argue, all problems aired and limits defined. You need a rest from marriage. And I need you.' A glimmer of a smile underlay the sudden seriousness of his expression. 'Where women were – please notice I say were – concerned, after taking, I could always leave them. Want I could understand; need seemed beyond me. That's how I knew I was done for that morning, when I found the last thing I wanted to do was leave you . . .'

'Where did you go when you had to go abroad again after

you called at Richmond?' Tessa asked, after a while, reminded by what he had said about leaving.

'Hong Kong. There was a minor crisis which needed my attention. Some misplaced funds.'

Tessa smiled at him lovingly but all of a sudden tiredness swept over here and she yawned. 'And did you put it right?'

'Yes. I told you, remember, that I always finish what I start. Well, by the time I left Hong Kong I had finished what somebody else had started.' With satisfaction he declared: 'I had also finished him.' His voice sharpened when he went on to ask: 'What is it?' because her eyes had closed. 'Are you all right?'

'Tired . . .' Tessa murmured. 'Too much excitement for one day.'

'Then rest. I want you fit and well enough to take to *Aguas Frescas*. I'll be back tomorrow and every day until I can. In the meantime I'll go and find your tactful mother and tell her that her little strategem worked.'

Tessa yawned again. 'My mother is used to running everything and everyone,' she warned sleepily.

Nicholas bent to kiss her a lingering goodbye. 'Ah,' he said, his voice filled with a sudden, gleeful relish, 'but she has yet to have her first run-in with mine!'